The Chron

Caylen-Tor

by

Byron A. Roberts

Cover art by Martin Hanford

Illustrations by Martin Hanford

and Samuel Santos

ISBN 978-0-9909900-6-2

CONTENTS

BOOK I: THE SEIGE OF GUL-AZLAAN

BOOK II: THE BATTLE OF BLACKHELM VALE

BOOK III: THE KING BENEATH THE MOUNTAIN OF FIRE

Book I: The Siege of Gul-Azlaan

The war between the Imperium and the Vyrgothian Kingdoms had raged for decades without cessation. Years of bitter struggle and a myriad epic battles had resulted in the great armies of the Southern Expanse becoming locked in a gruelling, perpetual stalemate. However, shortly before the Second Cataclysm reshaped the face of the antediluvian world, the balance of power shifted significantly. The tide of war duly began to turn with series of decisive imperial victories, including the fall of the great Vyrgothian fortress-city Gul-Nomedes. The breaching of that ancient bastion's mighty walls shook the Vyrgothian Alliance to its core. The remaining fortresses of Gul-Azlaan, Gul-Tryarch and Gul-Kothoth yet remained inviolate, but the war-weary Over-King swiftly issued a decree that they be reinforced for imminent attack, enlisting sell-swords and mercenary companies from far and wide to bolster the citadels against the resurgent imperial war-machine. And so it was that the vast armies of the Emperor Koord, emboldened by their momentous victory, pressed inexorably onward into the heartland of their ancestral foe to besiege the hoary, time-worn bulwarks of Gul-Azlaan…

Chapter I
The Imperium Ascendant

Beneath a glowering and pitiless sun, two men traversed the arid desert. The younger of the pair was clad in a chainmail hauberk, leather breeches and buckskin boots. Studded leather vambraces bound his forearms and a notched broadsword was scabbarded at his waist. He was hard-muscled and his blond hair was gathered into a ponytail, while a flaxen beard adorned his weathered face. The older man was garbed in leather lamellar armour and wore a white hooded cloak edged with gold braid. His black hair and pointed beard were streaked with grey and he carried an ornate scimitar with a hilt of polished ivory.

The blond man wiped sweat from his eyes and glanced skyward, noting a trio of circling vultures whose stark forms seemed to cut a black swath through the endless vista of azure. "Gods!" he rasped. "This is a blighted place. Fit for neither man nor beast!"

A smile creased the older man's deeply lined, sun-bronzed face. "You northern folk are ill-suited to desert life, Caylen," he said, his voice deep and thickly accented. "But for those born into the unforgiving embrace of the dunes, survival is an art swiftly learned."

Caylen grimaced, running a dry tongue over his parched lips. "Give me the forests and mountains of my homeland any day, Viseth. Wolves and bears may prowl its shadows, but at least a man won't die of thirst and have his bones bleached by the sun."

Viseth nodded grimly. "There are things beneath these shifting sands far more deadly than your wolves and bears, northlander."

Caylen's brow furrowed but he said nothing more, merely casting a wary glance at the brooding dunes which surrounded them.

For another five hundred yards the warriors strode the desolate terrain in silence, the marl and sandstone hard beneath their booted feet. At length they crested a steep rise and dropped low to the ground, edging their way to the summit of a great escarpment which overlooked a vast, gravel-strewn arroyo far below.

"Behold," growled Viseth, squinting into the shimmering heat-haze. "The Imperium!"

Caylen's grey eyes widened as he gazed down upon the colossal army. Surrounded by a vast cloud of billowing dust, the Imperial Host advanced slowly and inexorably across the arid terrain to the dolorous beat of a myriad thunderous war-drums. Sunlight glinted on the countless spears, javelins, swords and axes borne by the assembled legions, and emblazoned upon every regiment's banner was the martial sigil of the Imperium; a sable scorpion and two crossed tulwars against a field of vivid crimson.

"Quite a sight, isn't it?" hissed Viseth.

In awed silence Caylen continued to stare at the Grand Expeditionary Army of the Emperor Koord. At the force's vanguard, serried regiments of spear-men clad in scale-mail armour marched in rigid formation, followed by legions of iron-helmeted swordsmen encased in lamellar cuirasses and bearing tulwars and crescent shaped shields. Hundreds of cowled archers flanked the swordsmen, each carrying a slender black recurve bow. Some of the bowmen also carried broad pavises and scimitars, while others bore bronze-tipped javelins and serrated chakrams. The imperial cavalry and charioteers advanced with the infantry, the horsemen armed with long, iron-tipped lances, oval leather shields and clad in cured leather tunics reinforced with bronze scale-mail. Following closely behind the cavalry, cohorts of engineers escorted the army's supply caravans which were drawn by truculent camels, and at their rear the empire's great siege engines and ballistae ground the desert gravel beneath their broad wooden wheels, laboriously hauled by scores of heavily muscled beasts of burden and toil-hardened slaves.

"There!" snapped Viseth, pointing suddenly towards the centre of the great imperial host. "Can you see him? It's the emperor himself!"

Caylen peered into the dust-choked distance and descried a figure mounted atop a chaffroned grey steed, resplendent in elaborate armour of cerulean steel. The rider's helmet boasted two shining silver wings and a great crest of blackened mammoth hair, and he wore a voluminous cloak of panther skin edged with gleaming argent braid.

"Koord!" breathed Caylen. "The old goat himself has come to see this battle. We are honoured, it would seem."

Viseth smiled mirthlessly. "Aye, and he's surrounded by his thrice-cursed Iron Phalanx. Fanatics, every damned one of them! Who else can you spy down there?"

Caylen shielded his eyes from the sun and gazed once more upon the great army. At the emperor's side rode a warrior clad in golden plate armour and a billowing cloak of sable. The man's pauldrons were fashioned in the form of twin tigers' heads and his gleaming, open-faced helm was crowned with a plume of snow-pale horsehair.

"That must be Baalthus Vane," growled Caylen.

"None other," Viseth replied. "The Imperium's greatest general. Never have the emperor's forces met defeat under his command. And as always, the Legion of the Ebon Tiger marches with him."

Caylen scowled as he beheld a legion of black-garbed warriors emerge from the swirling dust. They were clad in sable robes and hauberks of golden scale-mail, their faces hidden behind full-face bronze helms. Each legionary bore a curved tulwar, a short-hafted spear and a hardened leather shield with a bronze rim. The lead warrior carried a standard which bore the legion's far-famed sigil, a black tiger's head snarling against a coruscant field of gold.

"Even amongst my clansmen, tales of the Ebon Tiger are told," muttered Caylen.

Viseth nodded. “They are the renowned Emperor’s Lance. Elite of the Imperium. They have wrought red ruin from the satrapies of the east to the beast-haunted jungles of the far south. They are unmatched.”

Caylen grinned wolfishly. “They are just men, Viseth. And they’ll die like any other men when they get a yard of cold steel in their guts.”

“Confidence can be a boon, northlander,” Viseth sighed. “Be mindful it does not turn to arrogance, for that serves no man well.”

Caylen shook his head. “How has the Over-King endured for so long against such a foe?”

“Heed me, my friend,” Viseth replied. “Unity has been the salvation of the Vyrgothians. Only when the Great Houses united in common cause against the Imperium did they ensure their survival. The alliance of kingdoms is powerful. In unity, there is strength.”

“But against these damnable hordes?” Caylen muttered. “The renegade kings Kalides and Actaeon refuse to even commit to the alliance. It’s only a matter of time before the Imperium prevails.”

“Perhaps,” said Viseth wearily. “But the whims of the war-gods are ever changing, and the walls of the Vyrgothian fortresses are high.” With that, he unfastened a goatskin gourd from his belt and took a swig of tepid water. Then he handed the gourd to Caylen, who drank deeply.

“Let us return to Gul-Azlaan!” enounced Viseth. “We have scouted the foe as General Kleitos instructed. Now we must inform him that the hounds of the Imperium shall be baying at his gate come the dawn!”

And the two men scrambled back down the rocky slope into the calescent embrace of the desert.

Chapter II
Ruminations Before the Storm

In the shadow cast by the walls of the great fortress, Caylen and Viseth patiently awaited the opening of the western gate's reinforced wicket door.

"No matter how many times I see this place, it still awes me," Caylen whispered, gazing up at the towering limestone and granite edifice.

Viseth nodded. "Aye, she's an impressive old thing, to be sure. But if you think Gul-Azlaan is a marvel, you should see Gul-Kothoth."

"I've heard the tales. It's even bigger, or so I'm told."

"The largest of the Vyrgothian fortress-cities," Viseth replied. "Walls so high they're wreathed in clouds. Some say it wasn't built by men, but by giants or titans."

"Indeed," smirked Caylen. "And I suppose dryads and dendans guard its gates?"

"We mere mortals can but wonder," said Viseth with a grin.

Caylen surveyed the colossal fortress, noting the distant crenelated battlements atop the structure's mighty walls. Machicolated parapets studded the weathered stone and countless cruciform arrow loops had been hewn into its surface. The walls of Gul-Azlaan were eighty-five feet high and twenty feet thick, and no army could hope to tunnel beneath them due to the rocky substratum which underpinned the fortification; to the east and west of the citadel stretched an expanse of rugged foothills which eventually rose to become the craggy peaks of a distant mountain range. The fortress had been built with a stout granite keep at its centre, and the labyrinth of civilian structures which once sat within the walls of the hoary stronghold had long since been demolished or converted into an array of storehouses, stables, armouries and barracks. And atop the four lofty watchtowers which flanked Gul-Azlaan's cyclopean ramparts flew the banner of the Vyrgothian Alliance, a white griffin emblazoned upon a field of azure.

Finally, the sturdy wooden door yawned noisily open and the two men were swiftly ushered inside by the bastion's gatekeepers. A sallow-faced guard clad in battered leather armour strode from the shadows to meet them.

"General Kleitos awaits you in the keep," the man barked.

Viseth scowled. "May we not wash the dust from our bodies and wet our parched throats first?"

"Later!" the guard snapped. "Be swift, for the war-council has convened!"

Caylen and Viseth were duly escorted to the fortified keep wherein the defenders of the fortress had gathered to contrive a strategy for the impending siege. As he entered the sparsely furnished circular chamber, Caylen regarded those who had assembled therein. At the room's centre, behind a broad oaken rostrum strewn with scrolls and parchments, stood General Kleitos, the veteran Vyrgothian officer charged with the defence of Gul-Azlaan. He was clad in battle-worn plate armour and a cerulean cloak, and his ashen, rugose face wore a deeply harrowed expression. The general was flanked by a retinue of staff officers who gazed impassively at the two men as they joined the solemn gathering. To the right of the Vyrgothians stood a black-haired, olive-skinned warrior encased in a red leather hauberk. Caylen knew this man to be Captain Aegidius, master of the Company of the Crimson Falcon, the largest mercenary band stationed at the fortress. Many regarded the Crimson Falcon as little more than brigands and pirates, but their renown as deadly warriors was well deserved. In the shadows behind Aegidius lurked the hooded, black-clad warrior known as Mazares, Lord of the Shadow Hand. The inscrutable Mazares and his small company of searingly efficient hired killers had swiftly risen to martial prominence during the War of the Satrapies some years ago. It was said that to face the Shadow Hand in battle was to face certain death. Across the room, leaning against a trestle table with a flagon of ale in his grasp, was the towering, chainmail-armoured northman Haakon the Grey. Caylen was well acquainted with this reaver, having spent many an evening drinking and dicing with him in the barracks. Haakon grinned as Caylen entered the room, his plaited grey beard flecked with beer-froth. Beside him was his long-hafted and double-headed axe, the notched blades shaped like the beaks of twin birds of prey. Seated upon a rough-hewn chair to Haakon's right was a diminutive, raven-haired woman clad in a leather lamellar cuirass. Her dark, almond shaped eyes regarded Caylen intently, and the lacquered black scabbards of her two slender short-swords gleamed in the light from the chamber's many torches and braziers. Caylen knew this woman only as Chiyome, but she had borne many other names during her adventures in the distant lands of the eastern feudal lords.

General Kleitos glared disdainfully at the two men and motioned for them to hold position by the doorway. "Scouts. What of the foe?"

Viseth met the general's gaze evenly. "Come the dawn, the emperor himself shall be at your gate. And he has not come to parlay. He brings his full might to bear against you, including the Ebon Tiger."

Kleitos sighed wearily. "So be it, the die is cast. The Over-King has ordered that we hold this fortress, and we shall obey."

Captain Aegidius frowned and folded his arms. "When will the reinforcements arrive?"

"They will not," Kleitos rumbled. "I have today received a dispatch informing me that the defence of Gul-Azlaan falls to us alone."

Haakon drained his flagon and slammed it noisily down upon the trestle table. "Ha! As I suspected. If they could spare any more troops, they wouldn't be hiring private armies to man their walls!"

"The Over-King has full confidence in our ability to withstand the imperial assault," snapped Kleitos.

"I'm sure he does," Aegidius muttered. "But this does not bode well for the outcome."

A young Vyrgothian officer to the right of General Kleitos stepped forward. "I expected as much from your kind, sell-sword rabble! You'll abandon us the first chance you get, I'll wager!"

Aegidius smiled coldly. "Not before I'm paid, you soft-bellied pup."

The young officer's face turned ashen and his hand brushed the hilt of his sabre.

"As you were, Captain Tymon," Kleitos rumbled.

Heedless of his general's command, Tymon's thin mouth curled in a sneer. "Curse the royal mandate that enlisted mercenary scum into this army! We don't need you perfidious dogs to hold these walls. You are bereft of honour!"

Chiyome laughed suddenly, the sound like ice. "Honour? There is no honour in war. Only blood and death."

"Begone then, woman!" Tymon seethed. "All the more glory for us. When the sagas are told of this battle, only the deeds of the brave shall be enshrined in legendry!"

"There will be no tales sung of you, stripling," hissed Chiyome. "The bards do not recall the names of the men who fall in the fray, only the names of the tyrants who order them to their doom."

"Enough!" boomed General Kleitos. "Tymon, one more word and you'll be in irons, regardless of whether or not your father holds a position in the war ministry!"

Tymon grudgingly fell silent, but his amber eyes continued to shine brightly with anger.

Kleitos then turned to address a burly, black-bearded officer to his left. "Quartermaster Demetrius, what is your appraisal?"

"This fortress is well provisioned," Demetrius declared. "We have supplies and fresh water in abundance. We can endure for weeks, if need be."

"The siege will not last long," whispered Chiyome.

"She is right," Aegidius snapped. "The gates of Gul-Nomedes were breached too easily. That debacle was a display of hubris I thought you Vyrgothians would not repeat. Mayhap I was wrong."

"Nomedes was undermanned and ill prepared," countered Demetrius. "A strategic error which will not be committed again. The remaining Gul fortresses are now fully garrisoned. Rest assured, we are ready."

Aegidius laughed mordantly. "Unopposed, the imperial army passed through the gate at the Wall of Lithios and razed the spires of the trade cities to the ground. Unopposed, the imperial navy sailed five hundred triremes up the Kandakis River to besiege Gul-Nomedes. And unopposed, the emperor has now marched his legions to this very fortress. The Crown has been woefully slow to react and the aegis of the Over-King will ultimately count for naught. I pray it is not too late to save the Vyrgothian realm."

"Thank you, Captain Aegidius," said Kleitos quietly. "I shall be sure to relay your critique of the war council's stratagems directly to His Majesty when next I visit the royal court."

Aegidius sighed and said no more.

"At any rate, I have also prepared certain other defensive measures," Kleitos said, his gaze sweeping the assembly. "Measures against which steel and siegecraft will scarce avail the foe."

"Enough prattle!" growled Haakon. "What of our pay? We have yet to settle up for the full amount."

"All covenants will be honoured by the treasury," sighed Quartermaster Demetrius wearily. "And there will be no discussion of wages at this, the eleventh hour!"

Caylen leaned close to Viseth. "Let's just hope we survive to spend our coin," he whispered.

Viseth nodded solemnly and made the sign of the protective scarab. "Gods of the Twelve Temples be merciful!"

"My Vyrgothian regulars will serve as our main line of defence," Kleitos enounced. "They are steadfast men. Most are veterans of the border wars and they are no strangers to siege and skirmish. These walls will not be easily breached."

Suddenly, Mazares stepped forth from the chamber's shadows and spoke, his words uttered in the guttural dialect of the eastern satrapies.

Quartermaster Demetrius scowled. "Does anyone here speak the Anatak tongues?"

Viseth smiled as he translated the warrior's words. "He said that he hopes your men have made peace with whatever gods they pray to, for they shall be meeting them ere long."

Suddenly, General Kleitos hammered his gauntleted fist down upon the rostrum before him. "Silence! I will tolerate no sedition within these walls! The scaffold awaits any man whose words adversely affect the morale of this fortress. Mark me on this, for it is my solemn oath!"

No one in the room deigned to reply.

"Now, I suggest you all get some rest," glowered Kleitos. "Tomorrow will be a very long day." With that, he strode from the chamber followed by his retinue of Vyrgothian officers.

Haakon watched the men depart, then sighed heavily and picked up his empty flagon from the table. "Well then," he grinned. "Who's going to join me for a drink?"

Chiyome fixed the northman with a withering glare. "Fool. How can you drink yourself into a stupor on the eve of battle?"

"Ah, my delightful little harpy," Haakon replied, smiling broadly at the woman. "The real question is, how can you not?"

Chapter III
A Benighted Lament

Beneath a waning crescent moon, Caylen prowled the battlements of Gul-Azlaan. Slumber had not come easily to him, so he had slipped silently from the barracks to walk the great walls and ponder the impending battle. Never before had he faced an army such as that which now marched upon the ancient fortress. Since leaving his tribal homelands nearly ten years ago, he had lived the perilous but rousing life of an adventurer, eventually earning considerable renown as a sword-for-hire amongst the warring nations beyond the southern frontier. Serving in the warbands and private armies of ambitious barons and ructious satraps had ultimately led him to the unceasing war between the Imperium and the Vyrgothian Alliance, during which his martial skills had swiftly won him a tidy sum in gold and silver. When word came that the Over-King was recruiting mercenaries to garrison the remaining Vyrgothian fortresses, Caylen had enlisted in the defensive battalion of Gul-Azlaan like so many other sell-swords and roving warhirds. The lustrous lure of southern silver had been beguiling, but as he gazed out at the benighted desert and considered the colossal host which now closed inexorably upon him, Caylen could not help but wonder whether a purse full of foreign coin was truly worth a bloody and ignominious death upon a desolate, sand-scored rampart.

"So, you cannot sleep, either?" came a sudden voice from the darkness.

Caylen spun to see Viseth lithely ascending the narrow stone steps from the lower levels. He held an ornate pipe carved from a mastodon tusk from which a tendril of pale smoke rose lazily into the night air.

"That's a big army out there, Viseth," replied Caylen sullenly.

"That I grant you," Viseth said, drawing at his pipe and exhaling a plume of exotically scented smoke. "But the size of the army does not always decide the outcome of a battle."

"Then you think the fortress can hold?"

Viseth smiled. "I'm no prophet or seer. What the Fates have decreed for this place, I do not pretend to know. But nothing is ever certain, my young friend."

"Nothing save for death," Caylen muttered. "If these walls are breached, we die."

"There is truth in that," assented Viseth. "By and large, the Imperium takes no prisoners. The non-commissioned officers and the regular troops will be massacred or conscripted. The higher ranks may be ransomed or slain, depending on the emperor's mood. As for any captured mercenaries, well... I dare not speculate."

Caylen gazed up at the lambent moon, his hand closing around the hammer-shaped amulet which he wore about his neck. "This will be the biggest battle I've seen. It will be a fine test of my fortitude. May the gods ensure that my steel never misses its mark in the fray."

"Get yourself a good curved sword, my friend," Viseth said, tapping the hilt of his scimitar. "They are far superior to your northern blades."

Caylen slowly drew his broadsword from its leather scabbard, the moonlight glinting upon its chalybeous, rune-etched steel. The weapon's hilt was bound in leather and its lobed, wedge-shaped pommel was inlaid with bright copper. Engraved knotwork bands adorned the sword's stout crossguard and its blade tapered to a fearsome, needle-sharp point.

"I favour the straight sword," Caylen said. "It's much better for thrusting and parrying. And it's far more effective against chain-mail armour than your fancy eastern meat-cleavers."

Viseth grinned. "Ah, but the curved blade can be drawn faster, and it has more of a cutting area than your northlander steel. And of course, a scimitar's angle of attack is far superior."

Caylen scowled and rammed his blade back into its scabbard. "I'll not debate bladecraft with you, Viseth. And if it's all the same to you, I'll stick with Wolf's Tooth."

Viseth nodded. "As you wish. And that is a good name for a sword, I grant you."

"And what do you call yours?" asked Caylen.

"Yasmina. After a woman I knew when I was younger. She was beautiful and elegant, but she could cut a man to the quick. It seemed appropriate."

"I've known a fair few wenches like that."

"What man has not?" muttered Viseth.

Caylen sighed heavily. "I fear these walls cannot be long defended. When I ponder the outcome of this siege, I foresee only ruin."

"The solution is deceptively simple," Viseth replied, a gleam in his eye. "Don't be here at the end."

"Retreat?" whispered Caylen. "That smacks of nithingswerk."

"A well-timed withdrawal can often represent the wisest of strategies."

"You have extensive experience of this?" asked Caylen.

Viseth grinned. "How do you think I've survived this long, boy?"

"I simply assumed you were blessed by the gods."

Laughter suddenly welled in Viseth's throat, but there was scant little humour in the sound. "My friend, back home in Numadai I have one insufferable wife and twelve children. I was never a wealthy man, so I was forced to ponder what I could do to support such a splendid brood. I considered becoming a spice merchant like my brother, but I decided that the boredom would probably kill me within a year. As it happens, I have always had something of a gift for fighting, so after careful deliberation I chose the life of a sell-sword. Not surprisingly, I found that I was rather good at bladecraft and butchery. At any rate, over the years I have amassed enough gold and jewels to provide a very comfortable life for my family. And yet I have not returned home. Not once. In truth, the longer I spend away from them, the more I realize how much I prefer being out here at the frontier between life and death, roving and slaying, living every day as if it were my last and savouring the heady thrill of the battlefield. Such is my burden, not my blessing. Such is my secret shame."

For a long moment, neither man spoke. Then, Caylen turned to Viseth. "Twelve children?"

Viseth smiled wryly, refilling his pipe with the russet flakes of a redolent herb. "As far as I can recall."

"No wonder you left."

"Indeed," Viseth sighed. "Now lad, what else vexes you this night?"

Caylen's brow furrowed and he turned once more to gaze out at the night-clad dunes. "I was thinking about what you said yesterday. About unity and strength. My clans are constantly at war with one another, perpetuating undying conflicts which date back many generations; battling over ancestral names, tribal borders and blood-oaths sworn so long ago that no man recalls why the damned vow was even made in the first place. What if one day an army such as the Imperium marches against my homeland? How could we hope to defeat such a foe if we are too busy fighting amongst ourselves? Perhaps it is time my people were united. Perhaps it is time one king ruled the clans."

Viseth nodded. "There speaks wisdom, young Caylen. Mayhap your destiny calls you."

"If I survive this siege, I will go north," Caylen declared solemnly.

A sudden movement in the tenebrous half-light caught the attention of both men and they spun, hands on their sword-hilts.

Poised atop a parapet to their left was a tall man clad in voluminous sable robes. A deep cowl concealed his features and he grasped a gnarled wooden staff encarved with glyphs and arcane symbols.

"Where did you spring from?" barked Viseth.

The hooded man stared intently into the night, his gaze sweeping the aphotic expanse of the desert. "The Circlet of Night… its resting place has been discovered," he hissed.

Viseth frowned. "What did you say?"

The man slowly turned to regard them. His gaunt face held a deathly pallor and his sapphirean eyes seemed to glow faintly in the darkness. "The Obsidian Crown has been found."

"What does that mean?" Caylen asked.

The black-clad man turned back to study the desert. "To you, nothing. To the kings and emperors who play this grim game of war… it will represent the difference between supremacy and damnation."

Viseth sighed wearily. "A wizard. They always speak in riddles. Veiled meanings and cryptic nonsense. Pay him no heed, Caylen."

The robed man spun to address Viseth. "The truth in my words is clear to those with the wit to descry it, outlander."

"Well, unless you're a battle-mage, I care naught for you," snapped Viseth. "Of what use will you be during the siege, wizard? Will you summon a djinn to rain fire down upon the foe?"

The man laughed coldly. "Such a vulgar display of arcane power is beneath me, sirrah. You know nothing of the subtleties of my art. At any rate, I favour the more… *earthly* rites."

Viseth scowled. "Aye. I thought as much."

Suddenly the cowled man began to descend the stone stairway to the courtyard, his black cloak billowing behind him. "We all must pay tribute to the gods of war," he rasped as he disappeared into the gloom. "But for some of us, the sacrifice demanded will be greater. Now take heed, for the foe is upon you."

Caylen and Viseth turned to stare out at the dunes just as a score of plangent Vyrgothian war-horns sounded the alarm across the lofty ramparts. In the distance, the glow of thousands of torches could be seen illuminating the darkness. Slowly, the horizon began to blaze with an undulating radiance which rivalled the rising of a midsummer sun. The legions of the Imperium had arrived at Gul-Azlaan.

Chapter IV
The Secret of the Shifting Sands

Caylen stood upon the battlements with Viseth and Haakon, gazing down at the assembled might of the imperial host. As the dawn had broken, the legions had erected many thousands of tents and picketed their hundreds of horses and camels. The enemy's camp was astir with activity as the regiments busied themselves with the myriad preparations for the impending clash. The army's colossal siege engines, vast three-tiered scaffolds perched on iron axles and great wheels of solid cedar, had been moved laboriously into position and now stood adjacent to an array of large mangonels, onagers and battering rams.

"There certainly are a lot of them," growled Haakon, adjusting his knotwork-etched iron helmet.

Caylen sighed. "Indeed, there are."

"Caylen, did I ever tell you that my no-good, wayward half-brother Wulfgar fights as a sell-sword for the Imperium, bringing dishonour to the Egilsson family name?"

"You did not, my friend. What will you do if you meet him in the fray?"

A wide grin spread across the northman's bearded face. "Gut the little bastard, of course!"

Caylen and Viseth smiled as Haakon hefted his axe and began to descend the wooden ladder to the lower levels.

"Where are you going?" Caylen called after him.

"For a drink," Haakon shouted back. "They won't attack for a while."

"He's right," muttered Viseth. "They will make us wait. First, we must endure the formalities."

As if on cue, a trio of riders began cantering from the imperial camp. At length, they reined in their mounts before the wall and waited silently. Moments later, the great western gate yawned clangorously open to allow two Vyrgothian horsemen through.

"And so, the terms are duly offered," Viseth said, watching as the riders exchanged words far below.

"What do you think they're saying?" Caylen asked.

"Oh, the usual wearisome speeches between heralds," Viseth muttered. "His supreme majesty the divine Emperor Koord demands that you open these gates and surrender this fortress. The lives of your men shall be spared, and all that nonsense. And of course, the standard response is being given."

"To hell with your cursed emperor?" grinned Caylen.

"Words to that effect, no doubt."

Below, the imperial riders wheeled their mounts and began to gallop back to their army's camp. In turn, the Vyrgothian horsemen withdrew into the fortress as the vast gate thundered balefully shut. The defenders waited silently as the sun slowly rose to its zenith in the cloudless sky. Many warriors lining the battlements hefted sturdy iron-pronged poles with which to repel siege ladders, while others filled pottery jugs with noisome concoctions of pitch, oil and resin to hurl down upon the foe.

"Ah, here comes the grand proclamation," Viseth said, gesturing to the battlements.

Caylen watched as General Kleitos stalked to the highest parapet of the western wall. The man's armour glinted in the sunlight and his cerulean cloak billowed about him as he removed his barbute helm and addressed the assembled Vyrgothian troops.

"No fancy speeches from me," the general boomed. "I'm a fighting man, not a poet. Hold this fortress! The Over-King commands it! Defend these walls with your lives!"

With that, Kleitos replaced his helmet and began his descent to the courtyard.

"Very rousing," muttered Viseth mordantly. "That's certainly filled the troops with renewed confidence."

Still tracking the general's movements, Caylen noticed him glance suddenly upward at the walls and nod almost imperceptibly. Swiftly following Kleitos' gaze, Caylen immediately spied a familiar cowled figure atop the ramparts, clutching a gnarled staff. The hooded man subtly acknowledged the general's signal and turned slowly to regard the imperial host.

"Something's afoot," Caylen whispered.

Viseth glanced at him. "Eh? Did you say something?"

The resonant clarion of a Vyrgothian war-horn abruptly split the relative silence and a defender perched atop the western watchtower bellowed the alarm. "Prepare for bombardment!"

Caylen squinted into the distance, piercing the heat-haze to witness the colossal arms of the imperial mangonels being drawn inexorably back by scores of hard-muscled troops. "So, it begins!" he hissed.

Scant seconds later, a murderous storm of jagged boulders filled the sky. The great slabs of granite spiralled languidly through the air, accompanied by a sound akin to the howling of a mournful wind. For a single, time-lost moment the world suddenly seemed to fall deathly silent and still, then the ruinous rain of stones struck the walls of Gul-Azlaan with a thunderous, ear-splitting cacophony, shaking the ancient battlements and sending up vast clouds of viscid dust and debris. Men were dashed to red pulp by the impact and a great section of the upper wall shuddered and cracked as huge chunks of the ramparts crumbled away to fall slowly to the sand far below.

And yet the hoary walls held firm.

Brushing fragments of stone from his hair, Caylen clambered to his feet and gazed out at the imperial army. Already the mangonel crews were preparing their vast engines of destruction for another pitiless, cataclysmic volley.

"We won't stand much more of this," spat Viseth, ashen-faced.

Suddenly, a sound became apparent to the defenders of the fortress. It was a fell sound vaguely akin to words, but voiced in a baleful tongue which no man present could scarce fathom. Beginning as a sibilant whisper and rising swiftly to a sonorous, magniloquent pitch, the ireful incantation crested the clamorous wave of the battlefield and rang out across the blighted vista like a storm-borne thunderclap.

All eyes were drawn instantly to the hooded man atop the battlements, his sable cloak awhirl like a dancing shadow, his twisted staff held high to the abyssal heavens. The sorcerer was etched blackly against the virgin azure sky, proclaiming his darksome conjuration in a time-lost dialect which no human had uttered since the primeval seas had risen to devour the first bastions of the ancient god-kings countless millennia past.

"By the Twelve Temples!" exclaimed Viseth. "He is a battle-mage after all!"

Caylen turned to stare out at the imperial host. "But what manner of war-spell does he recite?"

Viseth shook his head. "The gods alone know!"

As Caylen watched in rapt silence, the ground beneath the distant imperial mangonels slowly began to shake. The movement was subtle at first; an almost imperceptible shifting of the dolent sand dunes which flanked the great army. Then, a latticework of deep furrows abruptly appeared in the arid surface of the vast gravel-strewn arroyo upon which the legions were assembled, and a baleful, augural rumbling sound not unlike distant thunder became audible to the men of both armies. Within seconds the noise had burgeoned to an ear-splitting din and the earth proceeded to seethe and undulate like the churning surface of a sun-seared sea.

Then, from the riven sand erupted a titan born of fever-dreams and primeval legendry. The great worm exceeded one hundred and fifty feet in length and was twice as broad as a tundra-mammoth. Its colossal spiked head sported a gaping triangular maw studded with hundreds of curved dagger-like teeth and its vast, segmented body was encased in chitinous armour plating. Amidst a billowing storm of sand and stone the creature bore down upon the imperial war machines, its mighty bulk smashing the nearest mangonel to shards of wood and twisted metal. A score of men and beasts were crushed instantly to red ruin by the thrashing of the monstrous sand-worm, and keening chaos enveloped the imperial host. The creature drove its mighty head into another ballista, utterly obliterating the machine and the troops which flanked it. A single volley of imperial arrows was desperately loosed against the fiend, but the shafts merely rebounded harmlessly from its mottled, adamantine hide. Again, the titanic beast struck pitilessly against the imperium's engines of war, its abyssal mouth closing murderously upon a fully laden onager. The machine was instantly ground to mangled wreckage by those glistening scimitar-fangs and the sundered remnants were rapidly ejected in a viscid torrent of noxious slime. A trebuchet was abruptly reduced to detritus by the worm's next arc of destruction, the broken bodies of many legionaries crashing to the sand with the remains of the shattered construction. A heartbeat later, two of the imperial host's lofty siege engines were ravaged, their scaffolds rent to jagged splinters and their great iron axles irrevocably cloven.

Caylen watched enthralled as the spectacle of carnage continued, following the movements of the direful monster with grim fascination. Then, he glanced back at the watchtower upon which the sorcerer stood, still bellowing his baleful incantation to his colossal, chthonic vassal. The clansman's brow furrowed as he witnessed the gaunt wizard suddenly drop to his knees, his ensorcelled staff tumbling from his grasp. The arcane recitation abruptly ceased and a scant second later the cowled man completely collapsed, the flesh of his face and hands seemingly aglow with a strange, rutilant incandescence. As Caylen watched, the sorcerer's body rapidly transmogrified into a lifeless, cinereous husk which then promptly crumbled to pulverulent ash, leaving only his empty sable cloak billowing forlornly upon the stone parapet.

Instantly, the sand-worm's rampage ceased, its great head rearing languorously backward. The behemoth loomed silent and motionless for a single moment, then its vast jaws snapped shut and it plunged abruptly into the massing dunes. The ravaged earth shook with its departure and as the dust settled, the imperial army began to reckon with the devastation which the titanic beast had left in its calamitous wake.

"By the gods!" Caylen exclaimed. "What a fiend!"

"The big ones are said to prowl only the deepest desert," said Viseth. "No man has seen a monster like that for more than a hundred years!"

Caylen sighed heavily. "We've lost our battle-mage. That spell evidently exacted a heavy toll."

"Well, that wizard proved his worth, without a doubt," Viseth replied. "Conjuring that blessed worm may have just increased our chances of survival tenfold!"

Chapter V
Red Steel on the Ramparts

For two days following the sand-worm's attack, the imperial forces launched no assault against the fortress. The pensive Vyrgothian troops observed from the ramparts as the legions proceeded slowly and methodically with their preparations for the siege. The emperor's great sable pavilion had been erected towards the rear of the imperial host, its vibrant scorpion-sigil banner rippling idly in the gentle breeze. The empire's sole remaining siege tower stood ready and the colossal iron-headed battering ram known by the legions as "The Bringer of Woe" had been hauled into position behind the assembled ranks. And so, the soldiers of both armies waited, sharpening their swords, checking the buckles on their cuirasses and waxing their bowstrings.

Finally, at dawn on the third day, an imperial clarion thundered three baleful notes and the legions surged into action. Ranks of archers bent their deadly bows of horn and wood and unleashed a storm of shafts against Gul-Azlaan which all but obscured the light of the rising sun. Scores of men fell before the black hail of slender arrows and the Vyrgothian archers duly loosed volley after volley in response. For many minutes, death rained pitilessly from the sky above the battlefield, the stone and sand swiftly becoming a red charnel-field of gruesomely transfixed flesh.

At length, the volleys ceased. The baleful beat of countless goatskin nakers then resounded across the desert and the imperial siege tower slowly began its advance. The great construct lurched ponderously across the arid ground toward the looming walls of the fortress, grinding the sand beneath its iron axles and broad wooden wheels. The vast scaffold was armoured with planks of oak upon which had been affixed stiff leather hides, and from its wide base protruded long poles at which strained dozens of heavily muscled slaves who woefully pushed the engine onward, compelled by the cruel whips of their captors. Scores of troops accompanied the tower, bearing broad shields and pavises with which to protect the labourers from shafts and stones. As the siege engine drew closer to the walls, the imperial archers unleashed another withering volley of shafts just as the defenders began to target the juddering tower with canisters of pitch and oil. Ceramic jugs shattered against the armoured timbers of the tower, spattering a viscid, flammable ichor upon the reeling construct. Instantly, a wave of flaming arrows howled from the battlements and the upper platform of the siege-engine became enveloped by a sheet of searing flame. Thick black smoke billowed from the burning wooden planks and the tower's broad beams swiftly began to smoulder. Volleys of suppressing arrows and sporadic springald bolts continued to lance forth from the imperial ranks as the tower trundled and clattered its way ever closer to the base of the western wall. From the ramparts, the defenders hurled great razor-edged stones down upon the beleaguered imperial troops, along with crude containers of burning sulphur and quicklime. Huge casks of boiling oil were tipped onerously over the battlements, the blistering liquid spattering against armour, shields and flesh. Finally, the swaying, smouldering tower reached the western wall of the fortress and its wheels ground to a juddering halt. The thick hempen ropes supporting the great drawbridge at the tower's face were slashed and the wide breaching platform crashed swiftly down upon the battlements. A score of swordsmen clambered desperately up the wide ladders in the construct's interior and with a guttural battle-cry on their lips, the first imperial troops surged forth from the tower and gained the walls of Gul-Azlaan.

Caylen parried a furious strike from an imperial swordsman and riposted, driving his broad blade deep into the throat of his foe. He dragged the reddened sword free as the man crumpled to the ramparts and spun to face another warrior who was vaulting over the battlements. Before the man could attack, Caylen brought his blade down hard across his outstretched sword-arm, shearing through armour, sinew and bone. The warrior howled in pain and Caylen booted him squarely in the chest to send him flailing back over the wall.

Another swordsman loomed suddenly before Caylen and aimed a vicious thrust at his midriff. Caylen desperately knocked the blow aside and drove his steel through the man's lamellar armour, sundering leather and cleaving the flesh and muscle beneath. The man toppled screaming from the stone ledge to plummet to the courtyard far below. Bellowing a guttural war-cry, Caylen then engaged an imperial warrior who had just pulled his sword free of a Vyrgothian defender's belly. The man raised his tulwar too late to block the blow, and Caylen's steel bit deep, slicing into his opponent's jugular and sending a vibrant spray of arterial blood arcing across the ramparts.

A scarred swordsman suddenly leaped to the attack and Caylen barely parried his vicious thrust before delivering a devastating counterstrike which clove the legionary's crescent-shaped wicker shield and all but severed the man's arm at the bicep. Screaming in pain, the swordsman lost his footing upon the reddened stone and plunged to the gore-churned sand.

Wiping blood from his eyes, Caylen hefted his sword and surveyed the battle which was raging upon the walls of Gul-Azlaan. Imperial troops were still swarming from the smouldering siege tower, but were paying a calamitous price. The defenders had met the foe with steel and fury and thus far the legionaries had failed to make any significant headway upon the bloodied ramparts.

Caylen glanced towards the eastern watchtower where the fray was raging and saw the northman Haakon in the midst of the carnage, his great axe clotted with brains and crimson gore. As he watched, two imperial swordsmen fell to a single pitiless blow of that murderous axe, their cloven bodies pitching from the battlements like butchered meat.

Suddenly, a great crackling and groaning din crested the clamour of the battle and Caylen turned to see the imperial siege-tower finally began to buckle, its beams and stanchions at last yielding to the fire which had inexorably exacted its ruinous toll. The great construct began to topple gracefully, listing like a great ship lashed upon a tumultuous storm-wracked sea. But before the tower crashed to charred and smouldering shards upon the sand, one last imperial warrior leaped across the ravaged breaching platform and onto the wall of the fortress. The man was a giant, standing nearly seven feet tall. He was clad in blackened scale-mail armour and a full-faced, spiked iron helm, and he wielded a great curved tulwar with a notched and glyph-scored blade. Three Vyrgothian warriors fell instantly before that vast sword, their armour rent and sundered.

Caylen watched enthralled as Haakon suddenly spied the towering swordsman and strode resolutely to meet him, his mighty blood-kissed axe dripping red. Like two titans born of legend the men met, rutilant sparks erupting from the resounding clash of their steel. Locked in a gruelling battle of untrammelled might, neither warrior yielded an inch, their colossal weapons grinding and shrieking in a cacophony of pattern-welded death. Suddenly, the giant swordsman drove an armoured knee into Haakon's groin and the northman bellowed in pain and rage, his axe faltering momentarily. Seizing the advantage, the huge imperial warrior drew back his blade for a devastating strike, but Haakon instantly hammered a mighty fist into his foe's mail-clad ribs. The sound of cracking bones was audible even over the battle's tumult and the swordsman reeled backwards, his curved blade dropping for a single fleeting instant. In a flash of crimson and silver, Haakon's ensanguined axe struck, cleaving through armour, flesh and bone to sweep the swordsman's head cleanly from his body. A great fountain of blood erupted from the cloven neck stump and the giant's corpse pitched over the battlements to crash down upon the war-churned sands.

Cheers arose amongst the defenders as Haakon gathered up the swordsman's head and hurled it as far as he could from the ramparts and back towards the imperial army. The battle raged balefully on for many gruelling minutes before the last of the imperial troops who had gained the wall were finally slain. The defenders unceremoniously hauled the dead over the battlements as the first engagement of the siege drew to a close, the ramparts slick and slippery with blood beneath their feet.

Viseth suddenly vaulted lithely to the parapet upon which Caylen stood, his once pristine cloak and cowl now stained bright crimson.

"You look like a butcher," observed Caylen.

Viseth smiled. "As do you, my friend. Thankfully, none of this blood is mine."

"Their tower is finished. When will they attack again?"

A sustained, funereal note from an imperial war-horn suddenly sounded in the distance.

"At once!" Viseth hissed, hefting his imbrued scimitar.

A vast cloud of imperial arrows once again darkened the sky as Caylen and Viseth leaped for cover behind the battlements. Caylen gathered up a fallen soldier's wicker shield scant seconds before the volley struck, the shafts raining down like a baneful torrent of havoc. Countless hundreds of iron-tipped arrows tore into flesh or rebounded from the stone walls, the screams of the wounded and dying echoing throughout the fortress. Four more volleys followed and many dozens of defenders fell, their bodies transfixed by the barbed shafts of the foe.

Caylen dislodged three black-feathered arrows from his shield and guardedly peered over the battlements. Hundreds of imperial troops were rushing towards the wall, many bearing scaling ladders, ropes and grappling irons. The Vyrgothian archers proceeded to loose volley after volley into the approaching horde, felling scores of the attackers, but the teeming throng persisted, vaulting and trampling over the bodies of their slain comrades until they inexorably reached the base of the western wall. Scaling ladders clattered against the stone and grappling irons clawed the battlements as the imperial troops pressed their attack. The defenders maintained a withering hail of shafts as the legionaries began their ascent, slaying scores of men as they desperately climbed the great ladders and knotted hempen ropes. Casks of boiling pitch and hot sand were tipped over the wall to lash the ascending warriors, sending dozens of men to a searing, blistering doom. The Vyrgothian troops waited impassively until the broad ladders were fully laden with attackers before they hooked their ridged, iron-tipped poles around them and pushed the climbers from the wall, watching with grim fascination as the ladders and legionaries plummeted to the sand below. By stark weight of numbers, a contingent of imperial troops finally gained the battlements and forced a wedge through the defenders' line, enabling countless more warriors to successfully scale their ladders and ropes to clamber onto the embattled walls. As the glowering sun ascended the cloudless sky above Gul-Azlaan, the clamour of combat once again resounded throughout the bastion and the bitter, pitiless battle continued apace.

Parrying a lateral strike from an imperial soldier, Caylen dropped deftly to one knee and drove his blade up into his assailant's abdomen. The man screamed and Caylen pulled his sword free in time to block a brutal blow from a second warrior whose gaunt face had been blistered by the touch of hot oil. Caylen hammered his boot into his foe's knee and swept his sword out in a strike which opened a great gaping furrow in the man's neck. A glancing blow from a tulwar struck Caylen's midriff and he spun to parry a second strike from the attacker before bringing his broadsword down in a pitiless arc which hewed through leather and bone to hack the man's hand off at the wrist.

The stone ramparts were slick with blood as Caylen engaged another imperial warrior, driving the crossguard of his sword into the man's face before grasping him by his cuirass and hauling him over the wall. Roaring an oath, Caylen vaulted back into the fray and dealt a terrible blow to an attacking legionary which tore through the man's lacquered breastplate to shatter his clavicle and sternum. A tulwar suddenly bit deep into Caylen's vambrace and he whirled to the counter-attack, his blade rending leather and flesh to open a yawning fissure in his foe's abdomen. The legionary's entrails spilled forth to land wetly at his feet in a steaming, pulsating mass. Another warrior struck a glancing blow against Caylen's shoulder and instantly lunged low in an attempt to drive his blade into the clansman's gut. Caylen knocked the sword aside and riposted with a grievous strike which punched through the face-guard of the man's helmet and out through the base of his skull.

"Your fighting style is little more than crude butchery," came a sombre voice at Caylen's back.

He spun to see Chiyome crouched behind him in a defensive stance, her twin short-swords slick with blood.

"Mayhap," growled Caylen. "But it gets the job done."

Chiyome laughed mirthlessly. "In the past two minutes alone, I've saved you from three blades in the back. It's a wonder you've lived this long."

Caylen wiped blood from his eyes and lips. "Perhaps you prefer the style of the Shadow Hand," he said, pointing towards a section of the ramparts where Mazares and his black-cowled cohorts were engaging the attackers. The blades of the darkling assassins wove a swift and scintillant web of death about their foes as they leaped and spun in a sublimely graceful but searingly deadly dance of murder. Mazares dispatched two imperial troops with a single blow of his slender blade and before the second had fallen he was already engaging his next adversary. Vaulting lithely over the head of the legionary, he landed silent and cat-like at his foe's back and severed the man's quadriceps tendon with one cruel stroke. Spinning in a coruscant pirouette, Mazares then sheared through the jugular of another attacker and leaped over the collapsing body to open the femoral artery of the man behind him. And all who bore witness to that elegant and beauteous carnage knew that the ramparts of Gul-Azlaan ran red wherever the pitiless blades of the Shadow Hand sang their sombre song of death.

"Feh!" spat Chiyome derisively. "Such an overly flamboyant technique. A dire waste of energy."

Caylen's full-throated laughter rang out across the battlements. "By the gods, nothing pleases you does it, woman?"

"Surviving this debacle would please me," replied Chiyome. "This fortress has no strategic value. It is merely a lonely outpost in the middle of a blighted desert. This emperor is mad to expend so many men to take it."

"True enough," Caylen said. "And he'll sacrifice his entire army to do it, if he must. I now realize that every single man bleeding and dying on these walls is nothing but grist to be ground in the mill of regal ambition."

Chiyome nodded. "Heavy is the burden of sovereignty, for it robs a man of compassion and replaces it with hubris."

"With tyranny but a small step from there," muttered Caylen.

Chiyome flashed a rare smile at the clansman as she prepared to leap back into the fray. "Such wisdom from your lips, northlander? Perhaps you are not as ignorant as I thought."

And the battle raged on.

Chapter VI
A Fortress Besieged

The forces of the Imperium launched two further escalade assaults during the hours of daylight and one more under cover of darkness three hours before the dawn. All three attacks were beaten back by the defenders of Gul-Azlaan, but at great cost; the soldiers manning the walls suffered increasingly withering losses and as the sun climbed slowly over the horizon on the fifth day of the siege, it became woefully clear that the outnumbered Vyrgothian army would be hard pressed to repel another full imperial assault. A great black throng of vultures circled lazily over the reeking charnel-mounds piled at the base of the bastion's western wall as the Imperium readied its troops for another attack, this time preparing the colossal battering ram which had reduced the gates of so many fortresses to naught but splinters and kindling during a myriad previous campaigns. The Bringer of Woe's iron tip had been fashioned in the form of a giant spiked gauntlet, and it swung noisily upon its great chains as the troops hauled it laboriously into position. The depleted ranks of archers maintained a steady hail of arrows from the ramparts, most of which clattered upon shields or embedded themselves in the scorching sand. And the great battering ram moved inexorably closer, hauled by forty steel-thewed men and shielded by a massive scaffold of timber planks and water-soaked hides of goatskin, its iron-reinforced wheels crushing and grinding the bodies of the slain to masses of putrefying pulp upon the arid earth.

Wiping his freshly oiled and honed blade, Caylen watched General Kleitos ascend to the highest parapet of the fortress and gaze grimly down upon the approaching foe. After several moments, the general turned sullenly to regard the defenders who still manned the battlements.

"The end has come," Kleitos thundered, his voice clear and resonant. "Soon, the empire will breach that gate and gain entry to Gul-Azlaan. All of you have fought valiantly, and for that I thank you on behalf of the Over-King. My Vyrgothians will battle to the last man, giving no quarter and asking none. Such is their solemn vow, such is their sacred duty. But the sell-swords and mercenary companies enlisted by the Crown may depart, with full pay as per our covenant. Decide now, and choose your fate." With that, the general climbed down from the ramparts and returned briskly to the keep, accompanied by his retinue of staff officers.

Caylen scabbarded his sword as Viseth and Haakon moved to stand beside him.

"Are you two worthless brigands staying on?" Haakon growled.

Viseth smiled. "Not a chance, my friend. I shall be off before the first timbers of that gate have yielded. And you?"

A great wolfish grin creased the northman's weathered face. "I always stay for the close of a battle! The best fighting is always at the end!"

Chiyome leaped lithely from a narrow parapet above and stood before the three men, regarding them dispassionately. "I take my leave. I found it interesting to fight alongside so many oafs and dullards." Then, she fixed Caylen with her sparkling gaze. "I believe you were my favourite." And without another word, she turned and swiftly descended to the courtyard.

"Enlighten me," muttered Viseth as he watched the woman depart. "Which one of us feels the most insulted by that?"

"Good riddance!" Haakon spat. "Her tongue was sharper than her swords."

"To be sure!" laughed Viseth.

"And what of you, clansman?" Haakon said, turning to Caylen. "Fight on, or slink off like a gutter rat?"

"I have yet to decide," rumbled Caylen.

“Well, best not ponder for too long,” Viseth said, peering over the blood-stained battlements. “The enemy have once again come knocking on our door.”

Caylen gazed down to see that the imperial horde had reached the base of the western wall. The Vyrgothian defenders grimly commenced their bombardment of the troops, hurling slabs of granite and canisters of quicklime down upon the foe. A volley of fire-arrows was loosed against the armoured battering ram, but the sodden goatskin hides affixed to the construct’s timbers prevented the flames from taking hold sufficiently. Scaling ladders and grappling irons once more assailed the walls and the thunderous din of the ram’s metal-sheathed head striking the mighty iron-reinforced gate rose portentously above the cacophony of battle.

“The gate won’t stand much of that hammering,” Caylen muttered.

“And that’s not all we have to worry about,” whispered Viseth, staring at the distant horizon. “The desert’s fury has been awoken!”

Caylen followed Viseth’s gaze to see a vast billowing maelstrom of sand seething in the far distance. The colossal, nebulous tumult grew wider with each passing second, seemingly devouring the desert vista until its titanic mass appeared to encompass the entirety of the horizon. Higher and higher the searing tempest rose as its caliginous bulk swiftly began to obscure the azure sky.

“How long before that storm hits us?” Caylen whispered, transfixed by the sight of the roiling vortex of dust and sand.

“Mere minutes!” hissed Viseth.

“Bah! It’s just a bit of sand!” bellowed Haakon, bounding across the ramparts to where a grappling iron had clamped onto the crenelated stone. “It won’t spoil the battle!”

Viseth nodded to Caylen. “The Devil of the Sands will make no distinction between armies! Mayhap there is time for just one more skirmish before I depart!”

Caylen hefted his sword. “Heading home at last, old man?”

A crooked smile crossed Viseth's rugose face. "Why not? I think it is finally time to visit my wife and children. I grow weary of these games of war, played out by vainglorious kings and emperors. Mayhap my adventuring days are over. We shall see."

Caylen grinned. "I'd wish you luck, but I still think you are blessed by the gods!"

"Nonsense, my friend!" exclaimed Viseth. "The gods are quite indifferent to me, I assure you. I am merely sharp of mind and fleet of foot!" And with that, he loped across the ramparts to join Haakon in the fray.

Caylen was poised to follow when a gauntleted hand suddenly grasped his shoulder. He spun to see Quartermaster Demetrius, his face haggard and drawn.

"To the keep, clansman!" Demetrius barked. "General Kleitos would speak with thee!"

Caylen's brow arched quizzically. "Concerning what, pray tell?"

Demetrius scowled. "That is for him to divulge. Now come, time is of the essence!"

The Vyrgothian banners perched atop the watchtowers had begun to billow ever more violently in the rising wind as Caylen clambered down the stairways and ladders to the courtyard, following hard on Demetrius' heels.

The discordant clamour of the imperial battering ram swinging on its iron chains and crashing pitilessly against the main gate was all but deafening as Caylen vaulted to the dusty flagstones and began to run towards the keep. He winced as a foul stench suddenly assailed his nostrils and turned to see scores of wounded and dying men littering the blood-sodden floor of the surgeon's pavilion which sat in the shadow of the southern wall. Caylen felt a cold chill run through his frame as he grimly noted the many wicker baskets laden with amputated limbs and the masses of black, bloated flies which swarmed and crawled upon the twisted piles of rotting and gangrenous flesh.

“The true face of war,” rasped Demetrius. “In all its red and ruinous glory.”

Turning away from the disquieting sight, Caylen saw that a line of Vyrgothian soldiers had assumed formation before the citadel’s beleaguered gateway, their faces deeply etched with solemn expressions. Above them, a group of archers crouched pensively upon the broad parapet overlooking the main gate, their bodkin-tipped arrows nocked. Caylen and Demetrius halted as they spied Captain Aegidius and the remaining warriors of the Company of the Crimson Falcon standing with the defenders, their swords and spears at the ready.

“It seems that not all the sell-swords are so eager to abandon the fortress,” Demetrius observed.

Caylen strode briskly to the captain’s side as the gate shuddered once again with the merciless impact of the colossal battering ram, fragments of stone falling ominously from the massive, rough-hewn lintel. “There’s a sandstorm bearing down on us, Aegidius. A big one.”

“My thanks, clansman,” Aegidius replied. “That will be a boon as much as a hindrance during the final battle.”

“You’re seeing this through, then?”

A weary smile creased the captain’s sweat-streaked face. “Aye, too bloody right I am! I’ve lost good men on these walls, and the Crimson Falcon will make those imperial bastards suffer for each one of our fallen brothers. The debt of steel will be paid!”

The young officer Captain Tymon strode suddenly from the Vyrgothian ranks to face Aegidius. “I was wrong about you, Aegidius,” he said. “You are a man of honour. I will stand beside you, if you’ll allow it.”

Aegidius sighed wearily. “Lad, you can stand wherever you damn well like, as long as you give me room enough to swing my steel!”

Tymon smiled thinly and both men turned to face the fortified arch. A vast crack had appeared in the centre of the timbers, running the length of the metal-studded gate behind the iron bands which reinforced the sturdy oaken panels.

"Northlander!" snapped Demetrius. "Do not keep the general waiting!"

Quickening his pace, Caylen followed the Quartermaster up the keep's stone stairway and through the reinforced doorway. Within the fortified citadel, General Kleitos was engaged in a heated discussion with a group of his lieutenants. Caylen glanced about the circular chamber and noted the mercenary swordsman Mazares standing before a low trestle table. He watched as the black-cowled warrior silently accepted a small hessian pouch from a sallow-faced officer who was intently studying an array of scrolls and parchments.

Suddenly, the voice of General Kleitos rose resonantly above the prate. "Quartermaster Demetrius, escort that assassin and his men to the eastern tunnels."

Demetrius nodded and stepped back to the keep's wide door, motioning for Mazares to follow.

The hooded swordsman strode swiftly to the archway and turned, his darkling gaze sweeping the men in the room. Then he spoke, his words precisely uttered and heavily accented. "The Shadow Hand bids farewell to those who stay, for only death waits them." With that, Mazares stalked from the keep, his cloak billowing behind him.

Kleitos sighed as he dismissed his aides and beckoned Caylen to his side. The two men swiftly ascended a narrow, rough-hewn spiral stairway to emerge into a sparsely illuminated chamber piled high with wooden casks and hessian sacks. There, the general fixed Caylen with a bone-weary glare.

"In a few moments, I shall be venturing forth to lead my troops in the final defence of Gul-Azlaan," said Kleitos somberly. "The

Over-King bade me hold this fortress. It is clear that I cannot now carry out that order or fulfil my duty to the Crown. And yet, I shall leave the foe nothing. This bastion will fall, but by the gods, it shall fall hard!"

Caylen nodded. "You will fight to the last man. You have vowed as much."

"More than you know," Kleitos breathed. "Hearken, outlander, for what I am about to tell you may seem passing strange. Gul-Azlaan is not the first fortification to have been built upon this site. One of the six legendary Onyx Pyramids once stood here, and ancient cults and hoary religions have long held this place sacred. Aye, the ground beneath our feet was sanctified to an array of elder gods thousands of years before the first stones of this fortress were ever laid. I tell you now that certain remnants of those old faiths yet persist, deep within the black catacombs below these walls."

Caylen's brow furrowed as he listened to the general's words.

Kleitos rubbed at his red-rimmed eyes as he continued. "The priests of the Vyrgothian realm invariably shun such places, deeming them blasphemous and unholy. But certain shamans and sorcerers have delved deeply into the malign lore which surrounds those old cults and the dark avatars which they venerated. At any rate, know that in the caverns beneath Gul-Azlaan may well exist the means to destroy the imperial army!"

Caylen's eyes widened. "A sorcerous weapon? An artefact to smite the Imperium?"

"In a manner of speaking," Kleitos said. "In truth, I suspect it embodies a solution so chillingly final that I am loath to even consider it. But our fall is imminent, and such a time of desperation demands a measure equally desperate."

"I'm not sure I like the sound of this," growled Caylen.

"And yet you will heed me, regardless!" Kleitos snapped. "Before his demise, my sorcerer explored the caverns beneath this fortress. He spoke of a black altar before which the ancient ophidian cultists once bowed in obeisance, blindly worshipping some malefic, long dead abomination… conducting foul arcane rites and uttering oblations to the vile things which crawled and slithered in the abyss. He translated the glyphs etched into that altar and fathomed their meaning."

"And what did he glean from them?" Caylen asked guardedly.

"That altar holds some manner of great destructive power, mayhap the means to bring this fortress down upon the heads of our enemy! Last night I sent three men into the catacombs to scout the site. They have yet to return. I want you to descend into those caverns and discover the secret of that damnable shrine!"

Caylen's eyes narrowed. "Why me? And why alone?"

"This is my last throw of the die, and I can spare no more troops," Kleitos breathed. "Moreover, I've witnessed your prowess in battle. You're one of the finest warriors here, and if I'm to send any man into that abyss, it'll damn well be one who has the wits and the might to deal with what may await him!"

"What else?" hissed Caylen. "What will you offer me to undertake this perilous task?"

"Gold, clansman!" Kleitos exclaimed. "Tenfold more wealth than you would have earned defending this blighted bastion! Enough to live like a prince for a time, or indulge your every whim in the lotus-tinged fleshpots of the Seven Wicked Cities!"

"I have friends on those walls," Caylen said quietly. "Good men, fighting for you and your vaunted king. If I should succeed, you must assure their safety."

Kleitos nodded. "I shall give the order to abandon the fortress, should it become apparent that you have prevailed. You have my word as an officer of the Vyrgothian Alliance."

"Grist for the mill of regal ambition," muttered Caylen.

"What was that?"

"Nothing, general. At any rate, I'm no stranger to delving into the black depths of dungeons and catacombs in search of plunder."

"Well? What say you?" snapped Kleitos. "Demetrius can escort you to the undercroft which leads to the lower reaches."

"What say I?" growled Caylen, turning briskly to the stone stairway. "I say just make sure you pay me that bloody gold in advance!"

Chapter VII
That Which Dwells Below

The arid, scouring wind had intensified as Caylen and Demetrius raced from the keep and bounded across the courtyard to the northern wall. Stinging clouds of sand had begun to billow about the fortress and the sky had assumed a gloomy, crepuscular hue as the storm inexorably tightened its grip upon the desert. Peering through the haze, Caylen saw that scores of imperial troops were surging over the battlements to be met desperately by the defiant steel of the outnumbered defenders. The main gate had been all but breached, its great iron-sheathed draw-bar perilously close to being sundered by the pitiless impact of the imperial battering ram. Many Vyrgothian soldiers were abandoning the engagements upon the ramparts and racing to the courtyard in anticipation of the inevitable yielding of the bastion's gateway. Glancing back over his shoulder, Caylen saw General Kleitos stride from the keep and take position with the defenders, his burnished barbute helmet upon his head and a cerulean longsword in his grasp.

Shielding his eyes from the swirling sand, Demetrius halted before a narrow, arched doorway set into the northern wall.

"Follow," he barked, hauling the door open and loping across the threshold.

The two men emerged into a dank chamber which boasted a crudely hewn stone stairway leading down into deep shadow.

Demetrius swiftly gathered up a burning brand from a bracket on the wall and began to descend the cracked and crumbling steps.

"What do you think of the general's plan?" Caylen asked as he followed the Quartermaster into the depths.

"Utter madness," Demetrius said tersely. "But of course, this entire war is madness and the men who fight it have long since been rendered bereft of reason."

"What will I find down there, by your reckoning?"

Demetrius sighed. "Death, most likely. But you have your gold to make this fool's errand worth the risk, at least."

Caylen grinned and patted a slender leather pouch filled with golden coins which swung from his belt. "Its luster does have a way of bolstering one's resolve."

At length, both men found themselves within a wide chamber strewn with fragments of ancient statuary and the cracked remnants of hoary stone tablets.

Demetrius gestured to the eastern wall of the chamber where a jagged archway brooded in the shadows.

"There!" he said, handing Caylen his burning brand. "Go, and may the gods protect you!" With that, he turned and hastened back up the narrow staircase.

Securing his sword in its scabbard, Caylen slowly approached the graven arch. A set of dusty stone steps wound downward into the moldering darkness which roiled beyond the light of the guttering flame.

"Looks like a blasted tomb," muttered Caylen as he steadfastly began his descent into the black.

Caylen shivered at the almost preternatural cold which swiftly enveloped him as he strode further into the chthonic depths, and for many minutes only the glow from his burning brand served to illumine his path. Finally, after what seemed an eternity traversing the gloomy tunnel, a gently undulating viridian light began to fill the narrow passageway and he emerged into a colossal, atramentous cavern. Gazing about the vast subterranean grotto, Caylen saw that a latticework of luminescent green veins had been incised into its smooth black walls in a pattern akin to an eldritch spider's web. Whether the lucent filaments were a natural feature of the cave or the work of long dead artisans, Caylen could scarce fathom, but the slender furrows cast an eerily lambent glow throughout the darkling subterrane.

Glancing downward, Caylen instantly descried the faded and cracked remnants of a vast mosaic which adorned the chamber's riven floor. Suppressing a shudder, he noted that a series of patterns vaguely reminiscent of black wings and tentacles were partially visible upon the shattered tesserae tiles. "Best not to tarry here," the clansman whispered to himself.

Brandishing his torch, Caylen moved warily into the depths of the gloomy cavern. He had walked for no more than fifty yards before the partially obfuscated outline of a large structure loomed suddenly from the shadows before him. As he drew closer to the object, Caylen swiftly discerned that it was a mold-mottled shrine of ancient black stone. Jagged fragments of cloven walls and sundered pilasters jutted from the ruin's foundations like the broken teeth of some primeval behemoth. Quickening his pace, Caylen swiftly closed the distance to the hoary edifice and at length found himself standing before a crumbling corbel arch flanked by the aphotic remnants of a great moss-encrusted wall. A deeply cracked lintel engraved with strange sigils crowned a yawning aperture in the ravaged structure, and Caylen crept closer to the rough-hewn doorway to peer beyond its tenebrous threshold.

Gazing into the temple's ruined interior, he saw that the majority of its roof had evidently long since collapsed, leaving a chaotic mass of basaltic rubble and granite shards strewn about a dank and mucid antechamber. Fragmented rays of viridescent light vied for dominance with the amorphous shadows which writhed blackly within the silent vault. In the centre of the room brooded a stygian aperture reminiscent of the maw of a large well, its slime-flecked perimeter delineated by countless cracked marble tiles. Beyond the gaping pit, Caylen instantly spied the altar of which General Kleitos had spoken. It was hewn from black stone, standing some seven feet in height, and its surface shimmered in the half-light as if covered by a coating of viscid slime. An array of intricate glyphs had been etched into the base of the altar, and a carving of some grotesque, squatting creature adorned a wide plinth at its pinnacle. As Caylen stepped closer, he discerned that the effigy boasted a disquieting amalgamation of both human and reptilian features, its body covered in graven scales and its gnarled hands sporting curved talons. The distended face of the carving was frozen in a toothsome rictus grin, and its black ophidian eyes glimmered balefully in mute malevolence. At the altar's centre, set just below the vile statue's clawed feet, was a small pedestal crowned by a single wedge-shaped jewel which glowed faintly with a wan, emerald light.

With a start, Caylen suddenly became aware of a disquieting stench which hung heavy in the shrine's foetid air; a noisome mixture of putrescence and mold-riddled decay. He took a tentative step forward and his foot struck something upon the blackened stone floor. Lowering his brand, Caylen saw that a twisted array of human remains lay scattered at his feet. The remnants of several ravaged arms littered the cavern, their mutilated tips rent and ragged as if torn or bitten from their torsos. A partially devoured leg sprawled close to the perimeter of the pit, its shattered bone jutting dreadfully from its lacerated and blood-encrusted flesh.

"Looks like I've discovered the fate of your men, General," muttered Caylen, his fingers slowly curling around the hilt of his sword.

From the depths of the stygian pit there suddenly came a thunderous sound like the rushing of a great torrent, accompanied by a vile fetor as of rotting meat. Caylen stepped back swiftly and dragged his blade free of its scabbard.

He then stood transfixed and mesmerized as a waking nightmare rose languidly from the miasmic well. The creature was bloated and amorphous, its pallid flesh translucent and glistening with muculent slime. It sported a score of undulating tentacles and in the centre of what passed for the beast's membranous head, a slavering maw studded with countless hooked fangs pulsated obscenely.

"By the gods!" Caylen hissed, casting down his brand and hefting his sword. "What an abomination!"

The pit-fiend arced its tumescent head toward Caylen and a torrent of yellow ichor suddenly vomited forth from its loathsome mouth. The viscous, venomous liquid spattered Caylen's blade, hissing and bubbling upon the surface of the coruscant steel. Instantly, Caylen drove his sword into the beast's vile flesh and the honed edge bit deep into its quivering, excrescential bulk. A blossom of putrid, greenish blood erupted from its riven hide and the abhorrent thing shrieked in sibilant agony.

"Ha!" roared Caylen triumphantly. "You bleed, devil! And if you bleed, you can die!"

With a speed belying its great size the creature struck, clamping its hooked fangs into Caylen's mail-clad arm. The withering stench of the fiend's acrid breath assailed Caylen and white-hot pain lanced through his body. The beast's great scimitar fangs sank deeper into his limb as its pallid, sinuous tentacles began to encoil the clansman in a vice-like grip.

"No!" Caylen thundered. "I'll not be fodder for you, demon!"

With righteous rage, Caylen thrust his sword into the creature's glistening skin, twisting the blade viciously. Plumes of smoke instantly began to billow from the behemoth's head and it abruptly released its death-hold, its miry tentacles flailing furiously. Caylen immediately drove his sword upward into the beast's gaping orifice, the blade piercing its gelatinous flesh to the hilt. With a resonant crack and a gout of noxious liquid, the sword's point emerged slick and steaming from the top of the monster's malformed, globose head. A great tremor ran through the thing's feculent body and Caylen onerously dragged his befouled blade free of the glutinous mass. The fiend's great bulk crashed against the perimeter of the well and Caylen swiftly leaped forward, sword poised. Summoning all his might, he savagely hacked three of the aberration's sinewy tendrils from its mucilaginous body. Hot, viscid liquid gushed forth from the monster's twitching bulk in bubbling torrents and the cloven tentacles tumbled gruesomely to the stone floor of the chamber, still writhing and threshing wildly. With a final horrisonant, ululating roar, the beast sank slowly back beyond the aphotic threshold of the well and disappeared into the abyssal depths.

Drawing breath in ragged gasps, Caylen stumbled back from the edge of the pit and wiped flecks of slime from his eyes. Blood trickled freely from his arm where the creature's teeth had sundered his chainmail, but he paid the wound no heed and stalked resolutely around the perimeter of the well until he stood before the black altar. The green jewel pulsed steadily with a lambent glow and Caylen slowly extended his hand, intending to lay hold of the gently glimmering crystal. Suddenly, the viridescent gem flared brightly, its multifaceted depths burning with a searing emerald luminescence. Simultaneously, the veins of green energy etched deep into the cavern's black walls blazed dazzlingly, illuminating the vast chamber with a fulgid radiance. Caylen retracted his hand and took a tentative step backward, hefting his slime-befouled blade. Then, to his astonishment, a fell voice abruptly emanated from the altar. The sound was a sibilant whisper akin to the slither of a serpent's scales against flesh, and its eldritch rasp bore an edge of palpable malevolence.

"Who dares stand before the serpent-stone of the Z'xulth? Who aspires to awaken the Ophidian Oracle?"

Caylen lowered his blade and sighed exasperatedly. "So, you demand introductions, do you, spirit? So be it. I am Caylen of Clan Wolf, son of Culain-Ulvur, grandson of Black Vargr, the Iron Butcher of the Tundra. I am bleeding, covered in gore and damn well pressed for time, so let's get on with it, shall we?"

A moment of silence ensued, then the ghostly voice spoke again. "Ah, the scion of wolves, child of the northern moon! But what is this other scent which I detect about you? The blood of something else flows within your veins… something ancient and arcane, born of the sylvan realm and the primeval verdure of the ageless Forest King!"

"I did not venture into this verminous tomb to maunder on about my ancestry," said Caylen with a scowl. "I've divulged quite enough to you already, spectre!"

"So be it," hissed the spirit of the black altar, its timbre darkening with vexation. "Why do you disturb this sentinel's slumber, O wolf-kin of the desolate heathland?"

"To destroy my enemies," growled Caylen. "No more, no less."

The tone of the rasping voice abruptly became deeper, its volume markedly increasing. "Long have we watched the ascent of your kind, bearing witness as you crawled from the primordial ooze and scrabbled desperately for survival upon this blighted sphere. Mewling spawn of the sea! Flaccid, fleshy aberrations subject to the cruel whims of the Star-Gods, slowly evolving to become the implacable foes of the ancient Serpent Kings! And now you stand as descendants of the First Ones, they who survived the Great Cataclysm and duly returned to the cold embrace of the abyssal oceans, or fled to their hoary vaults deep beneath the labyrinthine earth, there to be warmed by the ersatz light of their great Vril-sun! And ever you remain oblivious to the insidious threat of the Z'xulth, those baleful avatars who lurk and seethe beyond the threshold; the darksome overlords who ceaselessly seek to sunder the tenebrous shackles which bind them so that they may surge forth from the infernal outer-darkness to reclaim their rightful thrones throughout the cosmos!"

"As I said, I'm pressed for time," gnarred Caylen. "And now my patience wears thin. Pray get to the point."

"Man of the north, descendant of the ancient Ice-Kings, we see your destiny played out upon the empyreal tapestry of fate. Behold, the thrice-crowned king, wielder of the three-tongued serpent, breaker of armies, scourge of emperors, bane of the chaosphere and ruler of men! All hail Caylen-Tor, the Wolf of the North, enthroned not by birthright, but by blood and steel! Many foes shall be ranged against thee, wolf-king. Beware the dread demon who wears the skin of a prince! Beware the king of serpents who broods upon his black atoll! Beware the scion of the white witch who shall wreak vengeance against your progeny! Beware the immortal chaos-liege who slumbers in his tomb of ice!"

"An enlightening prophecy indeed," rumbled Caylen. "But will you do as I ask? The battle rages even now!"

"Yes," the voice hissed. "The power of this ophidian shrine shall smite those who strive and die for the fortress above. Your wars and the men who wage them are merely fleeting echoes in the abyssal void. Kings die and empires fall, their legacy fading beyond memory until only dust remains to be swept away by the heedless winds of time. Kingdoms of shadow, ruled only by ghosts."

"Mayhap you are right on that score, spirit!" thundered Caylen, raising his blade. "But I yet live, and as long as blood courses through my veins, ever shall I fight on!" And with that, Caylen brought his sword down upon the green crystal, shattering it into a thousand incandescent shards. Instantly, the viridescent veins within the walls of the cavern flickered and dimmed, their light guttering like a candle flame buffeted by the wind. Suddenly, the black tiles beneath Caylen's feet commenced to tremble and small fragments of rock began to fall from the shadows above. A colossal grinding din then echoed throughout the chamber and Caylen heard the ominous sound of crumbling stone booming from the distant reaches beyond the shrine. "I have outstayed my welcome here," he muttered, moving swiftly around the perimeter of the pit to gather up his still burning brand from the cave floor. Hefting the torch, Caylen sprinted from the ruined vault and back across the darkling grotto, jagged fragments of black rock crashing down all about him as he ran. And from the depths of the shrine, audible even above the tumult, the sound of malign, ethereal laughter followed him.

Chapter VIII
The Fall of Gul-Azlaan

Caylen emerged from the arched doorway and surged headlong into the furious, flaying embrace of the sandstorm. Shielding his eyes against the maelstrom of stinging sand and dust, he cast down his brand and scrambled across the corpse-strewn courtyard. The fortress was in the grip of abject chaos. Vyrgothian and Imperial troops alike stumbled and lurched through the scouring tempest, heedless of all but the desire to escape the rage of the desert storm. Strangely, the ground beneath Caylen's feet seemed to be shifting imperceptibly, akin to the surface of a placid lake disturbed by an errant breeze. Ceasing his flight momentarily, Caylen spat sand from his parched mouth and squinted painfully through the dark veil of dust. Small furrows and fissures had become visible in the courtyard's flagstones, expanding rapidly like a latticework of cracks upon the face of a smitten looking glass. To his astonishment, he suddenly descried a familiar lambent green glow emanating from the ground between the growing fractures, and above even the mournful howl of the scouring wind and the din of battle, Caylen could clearly hear the baleful and ominous rumbling which had dogged his every step from the abyssal catacombs below.

Suddenly, a hulking form loomed from the swirling sand and Caylen instantly raised his sword. A heartbeat later, he recognized the towering, dust-cloaked figure with its battered iron helm and blood-caked grey beard. "Haakon!"

"Clansman!" boomed the gore-spattered reaver, laying hold of Caylen's shoulder. "All hell has been loosed upon this fortress! The retreat has been sounded! I'm heading for the east wall!"

Without another word, the two men sprinted desperately through the storm, leaping over fallen warriors as they made for the entrance to the bastion's escape tunnels. After many harrowing moments of flight, they reached the fortified passageway. Several

Vyrgothian troops were already rushing past the open, iron-clad gate, their swords still red from battle. Hefting his axe, Haakon vaulted across the threshold and into the shadows beyond. Caylen was poised to follow when an imperial swordsman suddenly surged from the stinging dust-clouds and barrelled into him, almost knocking him from his feet. Screaming an oath, the man spun blindly and swung his tulwar in a desperate arc which Caylen barely parried. Hammering his fist into the legionary's jaw, Caylen swiftly drove his sword through the man's lamellar cuirass and deep into his gut. The warrior's legs buckled and Caylen dragged his blade free, stumbling over the fallen body. The thunderous din of rending stone suddenly resonated from above and Caylen peered anxiously through the billowing veil of sand to see a great fissure gaping upon the face of the embattled structure before him. A vast section of the eastern wall had begun to crumble and huge chunks of jagged granite were tumbling languorously earthward. With a final frantic leap, Caylen cleared the perimeter of the gate just as a colossal fragment of sundered stone crashed to calamitous ruin upon the sand, effectively sealing the entrance to the tunnel irrevocably. Gasping for breath and rubbing grains of sand from his stinging and red-rimmed eyes, Caylen stumbled into the darkness.

Haakon emerged from the gloom and struck Caylen roughly on the back. "Well played, lad," he grinned. "I thought you dead for sure."

"I'm not so easy to kill," Caylen rasped. "What happened to Viseth?"

"I lost sight of him when the storm hit us. I expect the old goat found a way out. Or died. One or the other."

A Vyrgothian officer then strode from the shadows of the tunnel, bearing a flaming torch. "Follow me, and make haste. I can't fathom why the earth trembles so, but if this passage collapses it will be our tomb!"

Caylen and Haakon followed the man down the winding passageway as small fragments of stone tumbled ominously from the tunnel's carven ceiling.

"What of General Kleitos?" Caylen asked.

"Dead," the man replied tersely. "He led the final defence of the main gate. When the damned walls began to shake, he ordered the retreat. But he would not abandon the fortress. With a group of his oath-sworn officers, he fought until the end. I saw him fall, and by the gods he took more than a few of those imperial dogs with him!"

Caylen sighed wearily. "How much farther?"

"No more than a mile," the Vyrgothian officer growled. "This passage merges with the caverns at the base of the eastern foothills. The survivors will be gathering there."

"Bloody imperials!" thundered Haakon. "They didn't even send in the Ebon Tiger. I was looking forward to crossing blades with those preening bastards!"

"As was I, to be honest," replied Caylen.

"And I never did find my brother in the fray. Mayhap he perished in the conflagration, if he was even there."

"Mayhap. If not, I'm sure your reunion will happen one day, old horse."

Haakon scowled. "The emperor must have unleashed some black sorcery to breach the walls in the end, I'll wager."

"Aye," muttered Caylen, his brow furrowing. "Black sorcery indeed."

The three men walked in silence for many long minutes, traversing the dark, narrow tunnel with trepidation. Eventually, the minacious tremors ceased, although the distant echo of crumbling stone persisted. At length, the passageway widened and they emerged into a large cavern illuminated by many burning torches. Some forty troops filled the darkling grotto and a score of wounded soldiers were sprawled upon the rocky floor, receiving the rudimentary ministrations of their comrades. Caylen recognized several mercenaries who wore the livery of the Company of the Crimson Falcon gathered close to the tunnel entrance, their haggard faces engraved as one with the same sombre countenance. He frowned as he realized that Captain Aegidius was not amongst them.

"I'm going out for some air," Haakon growled as he made for the cavern's exit. Caylen nodded and followed the northman from the grotto, shielding his eyes against the sudden glare of the desert sun as he stepped through the latticed, wrought iron gate which had been embedded into the narrow cave mouth. Mercifully, the sandstorm had passed, its elemental wrath finally exhausted. Swiftly weaving their way through several groups of sullen Vyrgothian soldiers, the two men climbed to the top of a low, rock-strewn hill and gazed out across the vast expanse of the calescent dunes.

Gul-Azlaan had fallen, its cyclopean walls reduced to sundered ruin. Only the northern watchtower and a large section of the adjoining ramparts remained intact, a strange greenish smoke rising languidly from the mass of rubble and shattered stone which once had been the indomitable fortress. Caylen's brow arched sardonically as he saw the Imperial banner being slowly hoisted atop the watchtower's solitary flagstaff.

"Pompous fools," rumbled Haakon. "They're welcome to it. Or what remains of it, at any rate."

"They paid for it in blood," Caylen sighed. "A pile of rock in the middle of the desert. Centuries from now, men may remember that a great battle was waged here. But they will not recall the names of the slain, nor what truly compelled them to strive and die for the folly of prideful kings."

* * *

As the sun sank slowly below the western horizon, Caylen stood with Haakon gazing out across the brooding desert. The setting sun bathed the dunes in a rutilant glow and the sky was streaked with great swathes of crimson. Both men carried goatskin gourds filled with water and a meagre pouch of barley groats and strips of dried meat which had been issued to them at the Vyrgothian camp. Before them lay the remnants of an ancient statue, its sundered body now all but buried by the restless sands, leaving only fragments of sun-bleached stone to stand as mute testament to whatever forgotten king or forsaken deity the ruined effigy once represented.

"Where will you go now, northman?" asked Caylen.

"I've a mind to travel east," Haakon enounced. "Following the trade routes of the spice merchants. I hear the Golden Pharaoh Khutu-Amhun has placed a hefty bounty on the heads of the Grand Vizier and the Seven Acolytes of Zul-tekh. I mean to earn some coin in the realm of the Immortals!"

"So be it," said Caylen. "Although I do not envy you your journey into those blighted lands, for I hear they are rife with dark sorcery, fiend-haunted tombs and baleful curses."

"Ha! I pray you are right!" grinned Haakon. "It's about time my steel faced a worthy test! And what of you, clansman? What road will you travel?"

Caylen's eyes narrowed. "I shall return home, to the land of my tribes. My people are in need of a king, one who will unite them and make them strong against any foe. Mayhap that task shall fall to me."

"Ambitious," said Haakon. "I like that. Keep your blade sharp, lad!"

Caylen and Haakon clasped wrists in the warrior's grip. Then, the bearded reaver hefted his axe and strode eastward into the dusk-cloaked desert.

Lost in grim contemplation, Caylen stared silently into the darkness for several moments before finally casting his gaze skyward. The crescent moon emerged slowly from behind a veil of lambent cloud, painting the desert sky with sombre sapphirean hues. The clansman sighed, securing his broadsword in its scabbard. Then, he turned swiftly toward the distant mountains and began walking north.

Although the Imperium counted the siege of Gul-Azlaan as a victory, the considerable losses which the Grand Expeditionary Army suffered during the final engagement significantly delayed the furtherance of the imperial campaign. It was some time before the legions of the Emperor Koord renewed their assault against the Vyrgothian Alliance, finally mobilizing a massively reinforced army to march against the entrenched garrisons of the Over-King a full three years to the day after the desert bastion's momentous fall. Like Gul-Nomedes and Gul-Azlaan before it, the ancient stronghold of Gul-Tryarch duly suffered the wrath of the imperial war machine, ultimately leaving only the colossal fortress of Gul-Kothoth to stand inviolate against the emperor's forces. The ensuing defeat of the renegade King Kalides at the Battle of the Plains of Kai-Vorg effectively put the Imperium's armies within striking distance of Vyrgothia's last bastion, and the decades-old war finally looked set to end with an overwhelmingly decisive imperial victory…

Meanwhile, Caylen of the Wolf Clan travelled ever northward, embarking on many adventures as he sought to return to his tribal homelands. His voyage across the pirate-thronged Middle Sea wrought a blood-swathed legend, while his journey through the dragon-haunted wastelands of Kur and the war-torn territories of Zulantia was fraught with dire and deathly peril. At length, he finally reached the rugged frontier of his ancestral realm with but one goal in mind; the prophesied unification of his people's warring chieftains under the aegis of a single, undisputed king…

Book II: The Battle of Blackhelm Vale

Turmoil has engulfed the Eastern Kingdoms. In the guise of a seductive palace courtesan, the nefarious sorceress Zyrashana has seized the ancient throne of Mytos K'unn by traitorous subterfuge and the insidious machinations of her dark spellcraft. Moving swiftly to consolidate her regal power and safeguard her newly usurped throne, Zyrashana has implemented a grand campaign of military conquest, annexing several neighboring satrapies and duly proclaiming herself the Divine Empress of Mytos K'unn. Commanded by Zyrashana's merciless warlord Talus Ebonfyre, the legions of Mytos K'unn have advanced westward across the Antediluvian Continent, pressing deep into the sovereign realm of the embattled Delanian Commonwealth…

Chapter I
Declarations of War

King Gustanhav of Delania sat astride his chanfron-clad palomino charger and surveyed the army which opposed him. Three hundred yards distant, the legions of Mytos K'unn had assembled beneath their sable and crimson banners, the pale morning sunlight gleaming upon a fathomless sea of curved swords, iron lances and broad spearheads. Each warrior was clad in the livery of the eastern empire, their lamellar cuirasses emblazoned with the personal sigil of the Empress Zyrashana herself; a blood red serpent coiled against a field of stygian black.

Turning in his saddle, the king's gaze swept the regiments of his own army which had been marshalled to meet the foe upon the field of battle. Ranks of spearmen armoured in leather brigandines stood silently at the vanguard of the force, flanked by units of light cavalry and plate-armoured knights. Columns of infantry clad in mail hauberks and bearing shortswords and reinforced kite shields stood in perfect formation behind the paladins, while at the host's rear, ranks of archers waited with their great war-bows of yew and horn.

The king was clad in shimmering scale-mail, bronze vambraces and intricately embossed and riveted gauntlets. His pauldrons were polished to relucent brilliance and a great azure cloak trimmed with ermine was draped about his armoured frame. A silvern cuirass encased his torso and his legs were girt with shining greaves. An ornately engraved helmet crowned with a crest of black horse hair completed his martial attire, and in his right hand he wielded a slender longsword of limpid blue steel.

Lifting his gaze to the heavens, Gustanhav smiled mirthlessly as he beheld a throng of expectant crows circling high above, their distant shapes etched starkly black against the cloudless sky.

"Only the eaters of the dead truly win on days such as this," the king whispered.

To Gustanhav's right, a young captain clad in the colours of the Royal Cerulean Templars raised the visor of his plumed helm.

"True enough, my liege," the man said, squinting to get a clear view of the enemy host which waited across the verdant, grassy plain. "But we'll still give these dogs a fine kicking today, I'll wager."

The king turned to the young captain, watching the banner he proudly held as it rippled idly in the gentle breeze. The royal sigil of Delania, a golden chimaera passant against a field of sapphirean blue, seemed to glow with a coruscant radiance in the morning sun.

"The tremor in your voice belies your confident words, lad," the king said. "This is your first action, is it not?"

"Aye, sire," the young man replied. "I've been waiting for this since I first enlisted in the ranks of the Templars. It's an honour to be at your side."

"Indeed," sighed Gustanhav, turning once more to study the legions of Mytos K'unn. "I suppose it is."

At the vanguard of the imperial host, the king discerned a towering warrior atop an armoured grey steed, his face hidden behind a great horned helm. A gleaming steel cuirass cocooned the man's huge frame and argent chainmail covered his arms. Studded pauldrons adorned his shoulders, over which hung a cloak of black panther skin secured by a golden chain. In the man's hand was a huge curved scimitar with a pommel wrought in the shape of a jackal's head.

"Talus Ebonfyre," the king hissed.

"Yes, my liege," said the young templar. "That one's renown precedes him. It is said that he's possessed by a demon… a fiend which bolsters his strength tenfold in battle."

The horseman to the king's left removed his bronze barbute helmet and wiped his parched lips. His hair was grey and he sported a voluminous braided beard. Armoured in engraved iron, he wore the twin golden cloak-pins of a Delanian general.

"Bah! You shouldn't believe everything you hear in the taverns, boy. He looks human enough to me!"

"But General," the young captain exclaimed. "A witch ruling Mytos K'unn and a demon leading her armies? Mayhap we should have brought a battle-mage with us."

The general fixed the younger man with a withering glare. "This battle will not be won by conjurer's tricks, nor by offering up mewling infants for divine favour. Steel will prevail here today. Steel and flesh!"

"Or perhaps even diplomacy, given the chance," said the king. "Send the herald."

The general turned in his saddle and motioned to two waiting horsemen. At his signal they slowly coaxed their mounts from the assembled ranks and out onto the plain.

The general turned again to face the king. "Sire, once again I must protest your decision to take the field. If it does come to a clash, you..."

"I will not retire, General," said Gustanhav icily. "For hundreds of years, the kings of Delania have led their forces upon the field of war. I do not intend to break with that tradition today. These arrogant dogs have dared to invade our kingdom. If they will not retreat peaceably, then I will personally see them repulsed. Such is my decision. Is that clear?"

"Yes, my liege," muttered the general, running his fingers through his sweat-matted hair before carefully replacing his helmet. The seasoned officer had seen more campaigns than he could easily count, but today he could feel a cold sweat trickling down his back beneath his woolen jerkin and mail-shirt. Today more than any other, the general felt the icy tendrils of fear close about his heart.

"Look, they've sent out a rider," the young captain said, pointing to where the Delanian herald's party had been met by a single horseman from the ranks of Mytos K'unn.

"Good," said the king. "Now we shall see whether or not we can avoid bloodshed on this fine morning."

The young captain touched a gauntlet to the ornate, jeweled sigil which secured his cerulean cloak about his shoulders. The clasp was fashioned in the form of a slender woman with two great silver wings. "Ihstara protect us," he whispered.

"Trust in your sword, lad," the general growled, "for the gods are deaf to the pleas of men these days."

High above, the carrion birds continued to circle patiently.

* * *

The Delanian herald studied the man who had ridden forth from the army of Mytos K'unn to meet him. The imperial envoy was gaunt, hook-nosed and sported a forked black beard. A jagged scar snaked from his left eye to his upper lip, creasing his swarthy face in a perpetual sneer. He wore the armour of the Iron Jackal Legion, and a cloak of black goatskin hung from his shoulders. The scarred man sat astride his horse silently, offering neither greeting nor invitation to speak. After several moments, the Delanian herald cleared his throat and began to deliver the speech which he had committed to memory.

"It saddens my great and noble king that our envoys could not find a path to peace in these turbulent times. But know this; your incursion into the sovereign lands of Delania will not be tolerated. Once again, we demand that you withdraw this army from our realm and do not again deign to cross our borders. Leave the field now, and my king may yet feel magnanimous enough to forgive this blatant and insulting act of war."

For long moments, there was no response to the herald's entreaty. Then the black-clad warrior spoke, his words guttural and heavily accented.

"I am Oghul-Tolodes, servitor of the Great Empress, and general of her armies. I speak for Talus Ebonfyre, supreme commander of Queen Zyrashana's Imperial Expeditionary Force, Overlord of the Legions of Mytos K'unn, Master of the Iron Jackal, Scourge of Numadai, Bane of the Bazalanin Host, Router of the Eighth Army of Azesham. Hearken, for these be his words. Surrender now, or not one of your warriors will be spared. Throw down your swords and allow our forces unopposed passage to your capital, or every Delanian on this field will die and we shall march on your royal palace bearing your king's head as a trophy of battle."

The Delanian herald had anticipated many potential replies to his adjuration, but such a belligerent declaration of naked hostility had not been one of them. After several seconds of speechless silence, he finally found his reply.

"How dare you? There will be no surrender!"

Tolodes merely smiled, saying nothing as he wheeled his mount.

"What will happen now?" the herald's aide asked, his face ashen as he watched the black-clad general depart.

"Now?" the herald whispered as he turned his horse back to the Delanian army. "Now the crows will feast upon the eyes of the slain."

Chapter II
At the Court of the Wolf-King

Caylen-Tor sat alone in his sparsely furnished throne room, gazing out through the stone chamber's single window as the setting sun turned the moors and crags the colour of fire. The king's great granite fortress at Ulfheim was perched atop a jagged promontory, its broad shadow falling perpetually across the tribal settlement which sprawled in the wide vale far below. Caylen frowned as he descried a single, distant eagle soaring idly upon the dusk winds, suddenly realizing that he envied the bird its freedom. Several tumultuous years had passed since his grand coronation, and with each passing day he became ever more convinced that the crown was a direful burden and the throne room was little more than a grimly gilded prison.

Is liberty the price demanded by power?

Caylen's corded forearms, etched with a latticework of battle-scars, rested upon the ornately carved arms of his great oaken throne. His fists were clenched, causing his knuckles to whiten and the veins in his hands to pulse like azure serpents. His blond hair was shaved tribal fashion from his temples to the back of the skull, the remaining ponytail braided from the crown and tied in a thick topknot which fell unfettered to his waist. A flaxen beard adorned his scarred and weathered features and three rings of gold pierced each of his ears. A great golden torc encircled his bull neck, while a hefty bronze amulet in the shape of a short-hafted warhammer hung from a braided leather thong to rest against his sternum. He wore a sleeveless shirt of gleaming silver chain mail, trimmed with leather at the neck and shoulders, dark leather trews and studded buckskin boots. A grey wolf-skin cloak was draped over his broad shoulders.

Caylen-Tor's grey eyes narrowed as he watched the crimson sun sink slowly below the distant hills.

Does the sun set also upon my reign?

A large broadsword rested against the flank of Caylen's throne, and the glimmer of its bright steel caught his eye. Grasping the weapon's rawhide-bound hilt, he freed the sword from its ornate leather scabbard and watched the reflection of the sun's dying embers dance along the notched, pattern-welded blade. The crossguard of the weapon had been fashioned into the shape of three intertwined serpents, their forked tongues ablaze with copper-inlaid fire. The pommel was a serpent's claw which clutched a huge ruby in its ophidian talons. Glyphs and runes were etched into the mirrored surface of the radiant blade. Caylen was well versed in the old tongue, and he knew that those runes proclaimed the sword to be *Caled-draca, the great Battle Dragon; the Three Tongued Serpent of the North!* Forged by master blacksmiths and artisans to stand as the symbol of the tribal alliance, this was the sword of the king... the sword of Caylen-Tor! With a weary sigh, he slid the great blade back into its scabbard.

A grand symbol for such a fragile unity!

Three raps abruptly sounded at the throne-room's great wooden doors, summoning the king from his grim reverie. An officer of the tribal guard entered the darkened room and bowed, his hauberk bearing the stylized sigil of the wolf which was the symbol of Caylen's own clan.

"Your thegns await, great Tor," the guard intoned.

Caylen nodded. The guardsman had called him *Tor,* the word for king in the old tongue. It was a practice he encouraged amongst his followers, if only to remind the more unruly clans of the alliance that he *was* the king and that his word, in theory at least, had the effect of law throughout the tribes.

"Proceed," Caylen growled.

The guard began to light the torches and braziers arrayed about the chamber, serving to illumine the encroaching darkness.

Then, two men entered the room, each making the Salute of the

Hammer as they approached the throne.

General Oughtred Bearsark was a giant of a man, standing just under seven feet tall. His red beard was forked and braided, and intricate knotwork tattoos adorned his shaven head. A black leather patch covered his left eye socket, and a huge bearskin cloak was draped over his chainmail-clad frame. In addition, he wore studded leather vambraces, trews of thick wool and high boots of cured sheepskin. By his side was a huge, long-hafted axe, its great notched head etched with battle-runes. A veteran of countless tribal wars, Oughtred was chieftain of the Raven-Saters clan, and had been swiftly appointed supreme commander of the tribal armies upon Caylen's ascension to the throne, answerable only to the king himself in all military matters.

Beside Oughtred stood the man known as Wulfric Oakenbrand. He was wiry and lean, but hard muscled. His copper coloured hair was gathered in a ponytail, and he sported a few days' worth of stubble. He stood three inches shy of six feet in height and his pale green eyes gleamed with cunning and wiliness. Wulfric wore a hooded leather jerkin, a shirt of dyed green wool edged with russet braid, leather leggings and doeskin boots. Across his chest was a broad leather baldric which housed four slender throwing knives with hilts of carved bone. Oakenbrand hailed from the forest kingdoms to the south, and had found his way into the tribal armies as a wandering outlaw during the wars against the Tundra Nomads some four years ago. Caylen had witnessed the mercenary's skill with a blade during the Battle of Hag Moor, and much to the chagrin of several elder members of the tribal council, had formally offered him the position of Chief Ranger, an appointment which the wolfshead had readily accepted.

"Welcome, friends," the king said. "What word from the frontier?"

"Our scouts have intercepted a merchant convoy from the satrapies," replied Wulfric. "Word is that the imperial legions passed into Delanian territory a fortnight ago. The royal army marched to meet them. It did not go well."

Caylen's brow furrowed. "Meaning?"

"The king is dead, his army routed. The legions have sacked the capital."

Caylen sighed heavily. "So, Delania has fallen. And now the jackals are baying at our gates."

"So it would seem, sire," said Wulfric. "There are also reports that a smaller imperial force has struck at the frontier cities of Zulantia and raided the border settlements of Turanan."

"Indeed." Caylen's icy gaze then fell upon Oughtred Bearsark. "And what of the imperial outriders that were captured near the border? Have they told you anything useful?"

"They gave us nothing," gnarred Oughtred. "Not even when we carved the moon-wheel into their backs."

"Then they are well trained indeed," mused Caylen.

"Several of them were set free, as you instructed. They were told to take your message directly to their commanders."

Caylen smiled coldly. "Let us hope my warning reaches the ears of the empire's generals."

"Our best rangers have been assigned to watch the borderlands," said Wulfric. "Nothing will escape their sight, we can be sure of that."

"How long do we have?" asked Caylen.

"Difficult to say for sure," Oughtred replied. "Two months, if the empire fully resupplies and commits to fortifying the capital. No more than that."

"Then war is upon us, it seems," the king said, turning to glance over his wolfskin-clad shoulder. "Wizard, show yourself!"

From the shadows behind the oaken throne, a black-cloaked figure emerged to stand at the king's left hand. In the dimly flickering torchlight, the diminutive man seemed somehow to be an extension of the darkness which had disgorged him. A deep cowl concealed his features, affording only a fleeting glimpse of deeply lined, leathern skin and gleaming feral eyes. In his bony hands the man gripped a staff of gnarled ash, carved with many runes and tipped at both ends with round caps of bronze.

"Drogha Tul. My shaman and sage." Caylen said, casting a wary glance at the cowled man.

"Greetings, Wolf-King," Tul rasped, his sepulchral voice like crackling parchment. "The blessings of the gods be upon thee."

"What have the runes told you, old man?"

Tul smiled mirthlessly. "They speak of blood, of fire and of death. The future holds war and strife."

"I expected nothing less," said Caylen. "Have you sent word to the Fen-Witches of the Great Mere?"

Drogha Tul scowled. "Aye. Their high priestess remembers the favour she owes you. They will do their part, should the need arise."

"So be it."

As he gazed at the shadowed figure, Caylen realized how little he truly knew about the shaman whose services the Wolf Clan had employed for so many generations. Tales of the wizard Drogha Tul had been told around the tribal hearth fires for as long as any clansman could remember, and no one, not even the tribal elders, could guess the man's true age.

"Will the empress weave spells against us?"

"Indeed, sire," said Drogha Tul, his rheumy eyes sparkling from the deeps of his cowl. "The Witch-Queen is a fey creature, dabbling in petty magicks and invoking vulgar minor demons to do her bidding."

"Witches and demons!" spat Oughtred contemptuously. "The empire is truly a charnel-pit of nithings and deceivers!"

Drogha Tul nodded. "Zyrashana's chthonic priests empower her troops with battle-spells so that all fear is driven from their hearts in the fray. Her warriors rival our own *ber-serkr* marauders in their ferocity."

"Pah! It will matter little," Oughtred rumbled. "Her hordes will still fall in the massed throng of battle, enchantments or not!"

Wulfric moved closer to the old wizard. "And what of her vassal, the one called Ebonfyre? Are the rumours true?"

"Host to a fiend born of the Z'xulth," whispered Tul. "A terrible foe he is, stalking the battlefield with his great curved sword, leaving sanguine ruin in his wake. Slaying ten to his left, ten to his right, men and beasts falling with each stroke of that cursed blade."

Caylen-Tor's eyes narrowed. "Well then, I shall meet this demonic champion in the thick of the fray, and prove that he bleeds like any other man when kissed by good northern steel."

Tul shifted his grip upon his twisted staff. "As you say, Wolf-King."

"Bah! Enough talk of witchery!" Caylen bellowed, turning to Oughtred. "Now general, what of the foe's movements?"

Oughtred moved to a nearby trestle table, removing a rolled leather map from a satchel at his belt.

"The legions have been pressing west since annexing the satrapies of Azesham and Numadai two seasons past. I believe they aspire to reach the western baronies before winter. Now that Delania has fallen, our lands constitute the swiftest route to the coast."

The general unfurled the scroll and pressed it onto the table, revealing the detailed representation of the tribal alliance's borders that had been etched into the bleached surface of the leather. Then he pointed to a location at the map's northern edge. "It will be Blackhelm Vale, the Gate to the Northlands. That valley is the only path through the mountains for such an army."

Caylen gazed into the flickering torchlight and after long moments of contemplation, he spoke. "The tribal war-council shall meet at moonrise nine days hence. Let word go forth that the Wolf of the North summons all the chieftains of the alliance to his great hall at Ulfheim. Gather the Witenagemot! Such is the king's decree!"

The officer of the guard hurried from the chamber to carry out Caylen-Tor's order.

With a sigh, Wulfric moved in to study the map and the valley which Oughtred had pinpointed.

"Blackhelm Vale, eh?" he muttered.

"Aye," said Oughtred. "There's no doubt that is where the empire shall begin their incursion into our lands."

Caylen-Tor grasped the hilt of *Caled-draca* once again, his voice scarcely more than a malevolent whisper. "Then that is where they shall fall!"

Chapter III
Woe to the Conquered

Talus Ebonfyre reclined upon the ornate jeweled throne within the Delanian palace's royal audience chamber, flanked by twin columns of intricately carved granite which towered towards the shadowed ceiling. His deeply oiled, jet-black hair had been scraped back and braided, the strands secured with onyx ringlets. He wore a shirt of black silk, leggings of blackened leather and knee-length riding boots. A dark woolen cloak edged with sable hung from his broad shoulders and at his belt was a black sheath within which rested a curved dagger with a hilt of polished ebony. Even in the golden light which the room's many braziers and cressets provided, Ebonfyre's face seemed to maintain a deathly pale pallor, his high cheekbones and grim, thin lipped mouth accentuating his cruel countenance. Torchlight flickered in Ebonfyre's eyes, seeming to gutter and fade in their abyssal depths, as he studied the captive Delanian prince who now stood before him.

"Greetings, your highness," growled Talus, his voice deep and grave-cold. "I trust your sojourn in your father's dungeon has afforded you ample time for rumination?"

The bruised and shackled young nobleman met the general's gaze defiantly, his eyes burning with hatred. He said nothing.

"Behold the carnage which surrounds you, princeling of the realm," Ebonfyre hissed. "Your walls are breached, your temples are in ruins and your splendid citadels have been razed to the ground. All because your vaunted king would not swear allegiance to the banner of Mytos K'unn."

Talus Ebonfyre's fingers slowly curled around the hilt of the dagger at his belt. "Is all this a fair price to pay for such arrogance?"

The young prince threw back his head proudly. "To the pit with you, devil! And your accursed queen of whores!"

Ebonfyre smiled icily. "Ah, such admirable defiance. A family trait, mayhap? Quite misplaced, of course."

Talus Ebonfyre's dagger suddenly hissed from its sheath and he surged from the opulent throne to drive the blade into the heart of the young prince, twisting the steel cruelly before dragging it free. Blood erupted from the wound and splashed to the marble dais as the youth collapsed lifeless to the stone floor's mosaic tesserae tiles.

Ebonfyre regarded the reddened blade in his grasp. "Steel is wondrous in its disregard for rank and birthright. It so readily spills the blood of thrall and king alike."

Resuming his seat, he motioned to the guards flanking the doorway. "Put his head on a pike to rot alongside his father's. It will be a fitting family reunion."

The sentries duly gathered up the corpse and hurried from the chamber.

Ebonfyre closed his eyes, striving to quiet the dark voice which had begun whispering to him the moment his steel had pierced the flesh of the prince. He tightened his grip on the dagger, feeling again the restless stirring of the fiend which dwelled within him. Focusing his mind, he strengthened the tenebrous reins which for the most part kept the beast fettered in its incorporeal prison. Sensing the displeasure of the entity, Ebonfyre smiled. *Not yet.* The beast would be unleashed soon enough, then it would once again drink its fill of carnage and be replete before returning to that lightless corner of his mind where it seethed and slumbered.

Such a malefic and insidious entity of untrammeled carnage!

The ruinous aftermath of the energumen beast's unshackling was still vivid in Ebonfyre's mind, the red vista of its slaughterous rampage crystal clear in his memory. A hoary creature of the utter darkness, it was ageless beyond measure, and had long been summoned and conjured by the nefarious acolytes of the Z'xulth across the fathomless aeons. The darksome bargain which had been struck between Zyrashana and the tenebrous entity was a covenant of matchless evil, and Ebonfyre could ever taste the torrents of rage and malevolence which seethed and roiled within its inhuman mind.

A fitting host I am, for such a ravenous essence of black chaos, cast crudely in the form of a man! Nothing more than a means to an end... but what a sublimely villainous web is woven!

Peering deep into the benighted abyss of his psyche, Ebonfyre beheld once more the closing moments of the confrontation with the Delanian army, and felt anew the opiate bliss of battle as the martial memory unfolded vividly before his mind's eye...

Countless Delanian corpses littered the grassy plain, their silvern armour battered and riven by the blades of the imperial host. The sturdy steeds of the king's knights lay butchered atop their broken riders, and the bodies of templars and spearmen were strewn twisted and cloven amidst the crimson mire. Talus Ebonfyre vaulted from the saddle of his grey charger and surged headlong into the fray, his black cloak billowing like a shadow, his great curved blade whirling like a coruscant vortex of pattern-welded death. Three paladins raced to meet him, and he swept the head of the first man from his armoured body in a gruesome shower of blood and bone. His scimitar hacked off the sword-arm of the second knight and the man fell quivering to the earth where he swiftly received the pitiless final blessing of Ebonfyre's envenomed steel. The third paladin's strike was knocked aside with disdainful ease and Ebonfyre's sword punched through his cuirass to emerge slick and sanguineous from the man's shattered back. Dragging his scimitar clear, Ebonfyre stalked toward an embattled young templar whose mount had been hacked from under him and arced a brutal blow at the man's visored helm. The azure-cloaked knight boldly threw his longsword up for the parry, but its canescent steel was instantly shattered to silver shards by the force of Ebonfyre's pitiless blow. The great curved blade hammered down unchecked and clove through the young knight's pauldron and breastplate, leaving a terrible ragged wound which gaped redly from neck to sternum. Gouts of hot blood erupted from the fallen templar's corpse and Ebonfyre instantly spun to face an older warrior whose barbute helmet had been dashed from his bloodied head. The man's braided grey beard was flecked with gore and a mad fervor shone in his eyes as he drove his notched broadsword in for the attack. Ebonfyre parried the strike amidst a blossom of red sparks and delivered a lightning riposte which bit deep into the man's gardbrace, unbalancing him for a fleeting moment. Pressing the advantage, Ebonfyre hammered his sword two-handed directly into the warrior's cuirass, transfixing him with the ruinous yard of searing steel. Pulling his blade free, Ebonfyre turned and saw the mounted form of King Gustanhav and his two remaining royal guards desperately fending off an attack by three black-clad marauders of the Iron Jackal Legion. Leaping over the bodies of the slain, Ebonfyre spun his great sword and lanced it downwards in a devastating arc which all but hewed off the chanfron and crinet-clad head of the king's steed. Crashing to the bloodied earth with the body of his ravaged mount pinning him in place, Gustanhav gazed up at the hulking form looming over him and raised his ornate longsword defiantly.

"Vile revenant!" the king spat furiously. "I shall not yield! You shall yet fall, heretical devil!"

"Your kingdom is mine, Gustanhav!" growled Ebonfyre, a rutilant glow burning behind the eye-slit of his great horned helm. "And not kind shall my rule be!" With that, he swept the king's head from his body with a single blow of his gore-kissed blade.

Gathering up the grisly trophy by the crest of its helm, Ebonfyre lifted it to the crow-glutted sky and bellowed his inhuman rage to the heedless heavens...

Abruptly, Ebonfyre's eyes snapped open and he let the bloodied dagger fall to the tesserae tiles, swiftly clearing his mind of the battle's tumultuous memory. Before him, a scarred, black-garbed man was bowing silently at the dais of the marble throne.

Ebonfyre sighed wearily. "What is it, General Tolodes?"

"My lord," the general said, "a scout has returned from the wilderness to the west. He requests an audience."

"Scouts report their findings to their staff officers, not to me."

Tolodes swallowed hard before speaking again. "With respect, my lord, he says he bears news for you alone."

Ebonfyre leaned forward. "Indeed? Then we shall hear this news."

Tolodes motioned towards the chamber's door and the scout warily approached the throne. Kneeling, the man pressed his forehead to the floor.

"Speak!" thundered Ebonfyre.

"Dead, my lord," the man rasped, his voice hoarse with fear. "All but myself! Like ghosts from the shadows they were! We did not see them until they were upon us!"

"What are you babbling about?" Ebonfyre barked at the supine man. "Who assailed you?"

The scout lifted his head from the tiles, but did not dare meet his dark overlord's gaze. "Savages, my lord, painted savages! The warriors of the tribal king, he who is called the Wolf of the North!"

Ebonfyre's eyes widened and he partially rose from the throne. "Caylen-Tor? The barbarian chieftain? He has dared spill the blood of the empire's agents? What else? Out with it, dog!"

The scout's words welled in his fear-tightened throat. "The tribesmen who spared me, my lord. They bade me return here with a message for you. A message from Caylen-Tor himself."

Talus Ebonfyre reached down and grasped the scout's tunic, dragging the man roughly to his feet so that their faces were mere inches apart. "What is this message?" he hissed.

The scout's voice was no more than a guttural rasp. "If... if the dogs of Mytos K'unn dare set foot within the boundaries of the tribal alliance, they shall be soundly whipped and driven howling back into the east!"

Ebonfyre surged fully to his feet, hurling the terrified scout to the floor. "Madness!" he thundered, striding from the marble dais. "Does this king of savages truly think he can stand against the empire? Does this blue-daubed barbarian actually believe he can challenge the might of these legions?"

The guards within the royal chamber gripped their spear-hafts silently, eyes downcast, not daring to gaze upon their lord's rage.

Like a great ireful panther, Ebonfyre strode towards the arched doorway of the throne room. At the threshold, he spun to face Tolodes. "Summon Ulagchi the Night Seer. I wish to make contact with the queen!"

"At once, my lord," General Tolodes said, hastening from the opulent chamber.

Talus Ebonfyre gripped the carven frame of the doorway, an insistent and malefic voice whispering within his mind. Silencing the sibilant tones with great effort, he stalked furiously from the throne room.

"So, the painted savage wishes to test me," he snarled. "Good! The Iron Jackal shall hunt once more and devour its prey! By all the black gods of chaos, I vow that the rule of this barbarian king shall end in carnage and red ruin! Caylen-Tor must die!"

Chapter IV
The Gathering of the Nine

"Hail the One King!"

Caylen-Tor acknowledged the salute of the tribal chieftains who had gathered within his great long-hall, raising a ceremonial ale horn and draining its contents in a single swallow. Wiping the froth from his beard, he reclined in his ornate oaken chair at the great circular Table of the Sun as a retinue of skalds and bards took position before the chamber's blazing hearth. The saga-spinners readied their reed pipes, bone flutes and lyres and duly began to recount a fanciful tale of the Wolf-King's myriad adventures. With a weary sigh, Caylen folded his mighty arms across his broad chest and feigned interest as the bard's saga unfolded.

Steel agleam in the rising sun,
The war-hird's blades were honed;
A host of foes atop the crags,
The Wolf-King now enthroned!
Blood-clad men from 'cross the vale,
Their spears and swords aflame;
An army raised to heed the call
And meet the clansmen's bane!
Witch-fire burning with the dawn,
Blades clashing on the heath;
To rend their flesh and crack their bones
Betwixt the wolf pack's teeth!
Blood-worms bloat and sup their fill,
Crows gorging on the slain;
Swords resonant in thunder-song,
Shields cloven now in twain!
A legion hewn to riven ruin

Beneath the Wolf-King's sword,
All gore-flecked meat to glut the grave;
Death-fraught, this bronze-girt horde!
The kiss of steel is never sweet,
Its oath a blood-sworn vow;
The judgment of the axe is passed,
Red seas and serpent-prow!
Corpse-mounds piled to touch the sky,
All hail the gods of war!
Doom-fated they who dare incur
The wrath of Caylen-Tor!

The clamour of countless tankards and goblets striking the wooden trestles arose at the conclusion of the tale and Caylen wearily dismissed the skalds with a wave of his hand. Then, a frown darkening his scarred features, he studied the clan chieftains who had assembled around the great oaken table.

Oughtred Bearsark of the Raven-Saters clan sat scowling, his powerful arms folded across his mail-clad chest.

Grimm Ironhand of the Long Spears, his once blond hair and beard now the colour of snow, gazed impassively at his fellow rulers.

Brodir Finn of the Peak Dwellers, raven locks held in place by a bronze circlet, drummed his fingers impatiently upon the carven table.

Conal of the Moon Hunters gripped an earthenware goblet of mead, his blue eyes gleaming beneath his furrowed brow.

Chieftain Uarraig of the Bloodwing, his craggy face heavily weathered, stared unflinchingly at the king.

The shield-maiden Red Cairenn of the Tree Folk clan, woad spirals etched upon her aquiline countenance, idly twirled her long crimson braids and whispered an ancient oath.

The chieftains of the Walkers-in-Shadow clan and the savage tribe of the Flesh Renders had not heeded the call for assembly, and their chairs were vacant.

At the very centre of the table, the great sword *Caled-draca* was displayed proudly upon a carven plinth, torchlight glimmering upon its chalybeous blade. Around the perimeter of the table, runic sigils had been etched into the wood representing each of the nine clans. A series of elaborate knot-work carvings also adorned each section of the oak, all eventually becoming one with the great spiral sun-wheel which ringed the mighty *Caled-draca*.

Behind Caylen's ornate chair stood Wulfric Oakenbrand, silently drawing at a carved bone pipe and exhaling tendrils of pale smoke. The shaman Drogha Tul waited in the shadows at his back. The various attendants and thanes of the other chieftains were similarly positioned behind their tribal overlords.

Finally, Caylen-Tor spoke.

"I give you my hail, brothers of the great Alliance, honoured emissaries of the Nine. What I have to say to you this night will be blunt, for as you know I did not become king by the grace of a poetic tongue."

"Nor by birthright," Uarraig quipped, a sneer creasing his features. Caylen ignored the remark, although his eyes shone balefully as he glared at the Bloodwing chieftain. Uarraig could not long meet that lupine gaze, and looked away.

"A great foe shall soon march against us," Caylen continued. "They seek to drive their banner of occupation deep into the sacred earth where our ancestors lie buried, the earth upon which our forefathers bled and died. It is my intention to engage the legions of Mytos K'unn in battle, and repel them."

Murmurs arose around the table. The voice of the Moon Hunter chief Conal then rose clearly above the mutterings.

"Repel them? The army of Mytos K'unn is undefeated and hardened by war. If the massed army of Delania couldn't halt them, what chance do we stand?"

Caylen's voice thundered out to suppress the ensuing prate.

"Yes, the Delanian army has fallen," he said. "But know this... they had not fought a major campaign since the Zulantian border wars nearly a decade past. Years of peace caused them to grow idle and weak. They paid the price."

Grimm Ironhand nodded. "There is truth in that."

"But I do not intend to engage the foe in pitched battle," continued Caylen. "I seek to strike at them in the old way... the way our people have taught since before the ancestral sagas were first carved into the great rune-stones!"

Grimm Ironhand's snowy brow arched. "You mean the *wyrd-seaxcraeft*?"

Caylen's eyes blazed with passion. "Aye! We will strike from the shadows of the trees, attack the foe from the depths of the moon-mist, rise up from the heather in the dead of night! Our peoples are as one with the land we fight to protect. The spirits of our ancestors shall bleed the sacred earth red with us!"

"Fie!" roared Uarraig. "Do you truly believe the vast legions of Mytos K'unn shall succumb to such tactics? It will take more than ghosts and fog to overcome that horde, I tell you!"

Oughtred laughed derisively. "And when did you become an expert on warcraft, Uarraig? Not once have you led the Bloodwing in battle."

Uarraig's knuckles whitened and he shot Oughtred a murderous glance. "I am not deaf to the rumours from the east!" he hissed. "First the empire crushed the Eighth Army of the Satrap of Azesham. Then they wiped out the massed ranks of the lancers and infantry of Numadai. Following their victory over Delania, they have raided the bastions of the Zulantian Protectorate and burned frontier settlements in Turanan. Would you aspire to stand in the way of the tempest and try to alter its path? They cannot be stopped!"

"They *will* be stopped here!" thundered Caylen-Tor. "I'll see that accursed witch dethroned, I swear it!"

"The imperial legions are as the scythe in the summer field!" Uarraig shouted. "Resisting them would be a useless gesture!"

The murmurs escalated to shouts, curses, and oaths. Some decried the naysaying of Uarraig, others concurred with him. At a subtle gesture from Caylen, Wulfric moved forward to address the assembly, his voice cresting the wave of clamour.

"The armies of the empress are veterans of pitched battles; great forces clashing upon the field of war. The strategy of which the king speaks will be alien to them. If we were to bring them to battle at the place of our choosing, we would have the advantage."

"Folly!" bellowed Uarraig. "The Wolf-King would see us dead! He seeks to rule a kingdom of corpses!"

Oughtred Bearsark then bellowed above the din, his face crimson with rage. "What nithing-speak do I hear around this great table? Caylen-Tor has seen a hundred campaigns, from the siege of hoary Gul-Azlaan to the red heathland of Hag Moor! He is the Wolf of the North! None of you should dare say him nay!"

"I dare!" Uarraig barked. "Is this an alliance, or the court of a tyrant? I will be heard!"

"Speak, then." Oughtred rumbled. "Let us hear your serpent tongue."

A moment of silence followed as Uarraig directed a baneful stare at Oughtred. In response, Oughtred calmly stroked his great beard, his single green eye sparkling expectantly.

At length, Uarraig continued, his tone measured. "The legions will not be as easily repelled as the Tundra Nomads. The queen's army seeks only the tin mines and treasuries of the western kingdoms. Our realm is woodland and wilderness, heather and crag. I maintain that if we do not oppose the empire, they will simply march peaceably through our territory, and not a single clansman's life need be lost."

Oughtred surged to his feet. "And while we're at it, why don't we bend over and let the whoresons bugger us to boot? Your words smack of cowardice, wormcast! If you had a spine, I would leap over there and wrench it from your quivering body!"

Uarraig rose, his hand on the hilt of his shortsword, his attendants reaching for their weapons. "Raven-Sater filth! I should gut you like a swine for such an insult!"

Oughtred smiled, his hand slowly curling around the haft of his great notched axe. "You may try, sirrah."

"Enough!" bellowed Caylen, his voice like thunder. "No blood will be spilled in this hall. No blades shall be bared between the brothers of this alliance. Now, sit!"

At the king's command, Oughtred and Uarraig grudgingly resumed their seats.

The shaman Drogha Tul then moved from the shadows behind Caylen to stand at the perimeter of the oaken table.

"Heed me, men of the north. There will be no peaceful march through your lands. The legions will rape and ravage, pillage and burn. They will put your people to the sword and claim this realm without mercy, exacting tributes to their foul empress and demanding that you swear fealty to her agents. Such is their way. You must expect no less."

For long moments, an unbroken silence greeted the shaman's words. Then, Caylen-Tor sighed and rose to his feet, his face a mask of dour determination.

"I have heard you this night, brothers and sisters, now you will hear me. When the golden torc of the One King was placed about my neck, I swore to the gods that I would defend this land and its people from all those who would take up arms against us. The alliance was forged to unite the tribes into a single force during such perilous days as these."

The eyes of Uarraig narrowed to feral slits as Caylen continued.

"For countless generations, we have warred amongst ourselves, and foreign foes have raided and looted our steadings, being allowed free reign to slaughter and plunder because only individual clans stood against them. But now, for the first time, we are united and the time for petty squabbling and rivalries is past. Our enemy marches against us and we cannot afford to stand idle with blades sheathed and bows unstrung."

Oughtred hammered the table with his fist. "Aye!"

"In unity there is strength!" Caylen boomed. "Until we are truly united, we are vulnerable. Only when all the clans speak and act as one will this truly be a tribal alliance!"

"Well said!" shouted Grimm Ironhand.

"It is time," Caylen said. "The vote must be taken. The Wolf Tribe will fight. Alone if need be. Which clans will join us?"

Oughtred rose to his feet. "The Raven-Saters are with thee, Wolf-King! My *ber-serkr* horde will revel in red slaughter! Let the dogs of the empire dare to befoul our land, and by the gods I'll notch a few more widows to my axe haft!"

Grimm stood, leaning upon a gnarled cane of carved elderwood. "Aye, *anwealda*. You are the son of Culain-Ulvur, and the grandson of Black Vargr, both of whom were my sword-brothers. You will have the aid of the Long Spears."

Uarraig remained seated. "The Bloodwing will not stand with thee, Caylen-Tor. You have heard my words this night."

Red Cairenn folded her arms. "The Tree Folk will fight only if our own sovereign territory is directly threatened. Until that time, our swords will remain unslaked. You will have the aid of my Fen-Witches as their oath demands, but that is all I can offer."

Conal did not rise. "Nay. Engaging the army of Mytos K'unn is folly. Their numbers are too great to oppose. The Moon Hunters will not commit to this ill-conceived campaign."

Brodir Finn rose slowly. "Your argument has swayed me, Caylen-Tor. At any rate, the legions shall attempt to pass through Blackhelm Vale, and that ancient site is sacred to my people. Aye, the Peak Dwellers are with you!"

Uarraig spoke again, gesturing to the two empty chairs around the circular table. "And I'd venture that as Tolwyn of the Walkers-in-Shadow and Beathach of the Flesh Renders haven't even bothered to grace this meeting with their presence, we can hazard a guess as to their answers, eh?"

Caylen nodded, his gaze sweeping every chieftain present in the chamber. "So be it. Thus ends this conclave. Go in peace, my brothers and sisters. May the gods be with thee."

The long-hall slowly began to empty as the Emissaries of the Nine departed into the night. Wulfric and Oughtred moved pensively to Caylen's side.

"Politics," seethed Caylen. "Give me the honesty of a battlefield over this pit of vipers any day!"

Drogha Tul nodded. "A lesson well learned, Wolf-King. The perilous art of statecraft is often every bit as dangerous to a king as the threats he may face upon the field of war. A wise and mindful ruler would be well served to have effective strategies in place for both such disparate theatres of conflict."

"You're a veritable oracle of sage wisdom, old man," growled Caylen mordantly.

Wulfric began refilling his pipe, a sombre expression upon his face. "Four out of the Nine. Can we win with so few?"

Caylen shrugged. "I don't know. But I'll tell you this; whatever happens, we'll write a legend in bloodshed the likes of which no man will soon forget."

"Ha ha!" roared Oughtred, taking up a clay goblet of mead from the oaken table. "I'll drink to that!"

Chapter V
The Witch-Queen's Decree

Talus Ebonfyre strode into the gloomy antechamber wherein Ulagchi the Night Seer waited, closing and bolting the heavy oaken door behind him. He then turned to regard the hunched, black-cloaked figure standing silently in the centre of the room. The acolyte's vulpine features were partially concealed by a dark cowl and his ankylosed hands were encased in sable gloves. Ebonfyre had made no effort to conceal the fact that he held the perfidious Shadow Cultists in deep contempt, but Zyrashana had decreed that they should march with the army and he knew they served their nefarious purpose all too well.

The sinuous, diminutive figure silently motioned to a great mirror which had been placed near the far wall of the chamber, its polished surface encased within a frame of intricately wrought obsidian. Two carved ebony serpents supported the mirror, their scaly black bodies coiled upon the stone floor. Ebonfyre nodded and moved swiftly to the silvered glass, gazing at the panoply of hues which roiled within its coruscant depths. "Summon the empress," he growled.

Raising his gloved hand, Ulagchi hissed a sibilant incantation in an eldritch tongue before shuffling back from the mirror to melt into the shadows of the chamber.

The lambent vortex writhing within the nebulous depths of the crystal burned momentarily brighter before rapidly transmogrifying into the lissome silhouette of a woman clad in diaphanous robes of opalescent silk. Scant seconds later, at the heart of that vespertine vista, Talus Ebonfyre found himself gazing upon the arresting image of Zyrashana, Divine Empress of Mytos K'unn. The queen's countenance was cruelly beauteous. Her skin was the colour of alabaster and her long, lustrous tresses were snow-pale, though her elfin features showed not a single line or crease suggesting any trace of advanced age. Her eyes sparkled like twin emeralds, and as the fell eidolon's gaze focused on Ebonfyre, her fulsome ruby lips pouted in a maddeningly sensual manner. Ebonfyre inhaled sharply and the image of a viper nestling in a bed of blossoms briefly flashed before his mind's eye. Averting his gaze, he bowed before the darkly compelling visage.

"General Ebonfyre." The queen's voice was husky, akin to the purring of a great pantheress. "What word do you bring me from the theatre of war?"

"Delania has fallen, my queen," said Ebonfyre. "The realm has paid the price for scorning your gracious demand for servitude. The serpent banner now flies above the Sapphirean Spire. Your empire expands."

"This I know," the image of Zyrashana whispered. "What more?"

"The border settlements of Turanan have been sacked, and the Zulantian frontier outposts are even now aflame. Resistance is scant. The road west lies open."

"And yet something vexes thee, my general. Tell me."

Ebonfyre glanced up at the image shimmering within the glass. "Great Empress, the barbarian chieftain Caylen-Tor will stand against us. He has declared his intention to oppose our march through the wilderness over which he holds sway."

The Witch-Queen's viridescent eyes narrowed malevolently. "Such foolish pride," she hissed. "His painted primitives cannot hope to match our legions. The blood of the divine queen Tanit Vyperia courses through my veins! I will not be thwarted by a base-born savage!"

"He is audacious, my empress. Without fear, by all accounts. The saga of his life as a sell-sword and a reaver is well known to the folk of the northlands."

Zyrashana's lip curled in a sneer. "I care nothing for tales sung by bards and poets! We must reach the western coast by autumn's end. This king of heathens must not delay us!"

"The land is treacherous, my queen," Ebonfyre said, his muscles tensing. "Mountain and vale, not given to easy traversal. Caylen-Tor's clansmen claim the lands from the snow-bound steppes to the frontiers of Darkenhold. A patchwork alliance of tribes at best, but the woad-men of the north are tenacious warriors."

Zyrashana's tone darkened. "I mean to engage the rebellious satrapies by the spring. Seizing the coffers of the western fiefdoms and controlling the spice routes are integral to that campaign. Ultimately, the lands beyond our frontiers shall fall. I shall rule unopposed. Do you not wish this to be so, my loyal servitor?"

Ebonfyre's pallid brow furrowed. "I do, my empress."

"Then reach the Atlantean Sea before the first frosts of winter. Cut a swath through the lands of Caylen-Tor and teach this barbarian king an unforgettable lesson in warcraft. Let the world see what happens when a savage who sports the pelt of a wolf across his brawny back dares to oppose me." A toothsome smile then illumined Zyrashana's beguilingly beautiful face. "Succeed, and all that I have promised you will at last come to pass. You wish to rule the world by my side, do you not?"

Ebonfyre gazed into the queen's emerald eyes, seeing the faint trace of mockery which sparkled there. He set his chiseled jaw as he strove to conceal his true thoughts from those searching eyes and the cunning mind unceasingly at work behind them. "I wish to rule, my queen."

"Then set to your task, Talus Ebonfyre. The black spirit of Xul will ensure your success."

"And the rite of exorcism?" said Talus tersely. "You will keep your vow, once your desires are fulfilled?"

"All in good time, my dog of war," Zyrashana whispered seductively. "First you must do my bidding. Then we will speak of spells and rituals. Now, carry out my orders. I await news of your glorious victory."

The contours of the queen's eburnean image began to fade, the details rapidly blurring until nothing but an amorphous, undulating spectrum of hues remained. At length, the colours within the glass dissipated until only the piceous darkness of the antechamber was reflected within the obsidian frame.

Ebonfyre relaxed his muscles, exhaling slowly. Then he turned to Ulagchi, who was still lurking silently in the shadows.

"Get out!"

The dark figure glided swiftly to the door, unlocking it and disappearing into the black corridor beyond.

Alone, the general moved to a low trestle table opposite the doorway, upon which stood an amphora of wine and three bronze goblets. He filled one of the vessels and drained its contents in a single swallow. As he refilled the goblet, he caught sight of his own reflection within the great mirror, seeing his eyes glinting in the guttering torchlight. For a brief moment, he glimpsed something staring back at him, something alien and iniquitous which gazed at him through his own eyes, something... *else.* Whispers of treachery and deceit filled his ears, sibilant and insidious promises of power and dominion. Ebonfyre closed his eyes, quieting the voice, quelling the darkly insistent entreaties which coursed through his mind. Then, his eyes snapped open and he strode to the mirror, glaring irefully at his fuliginous reflection. Abruptly, Ebonfyre drove his fist into the glass, shattering it into countless jagged shards. Sighing heavily, he drained the goblet and moved back to the trestle table.

"Yes, we shall march for Blackhelm Vale," whispered Talus, filling his vessel once more with Delanian red wine. Several crimson drops spilled to the table to merge with the beads of blood which were steadily issuing from his riven, shard-studded knuckles. "Caylen-Tor shall pay dearly for deigning to oppose me. I shall make an example of this barbarian king and his ramshackle warband of painted savages. *And we shall yet see who ultimately rules from the throne of Mytos K'unn!"*

Chapter VI
The Serpent in the Dreamscape

Caylen reclined in his oaken bed, staring grimly at the chamber's ornate ceiling timbers. Carven images of totemic tribal animals gazed solemnly down upon him from the broad rafters; wolves, bears, ravens, eagles, boars and stags, all appearing to sit in baleful and silent judgement upon the harrowed Wolf-King. Plumes of pale smoke rose languorously from the guttering flames of the room's wide hearth, slowly disappearing into the depths of the darkling shadows. With a weary sigh, Caylen glanced at the beauteous form of his wife who lay slumbering beside him. He had become handfasted to Astrid Grimmsdottir shortly after his coronation ceremony and the union had been welcomed by most of the tribal elders, particularly by Astrid's father, the chieftain Grimm Ironhand. During the three years since the marriage, Caylen had sired two children; a bright-eyed and winsome daughter and a bold and roguish son. Now, as Caylen somberly pondered his progeny's uncertain future, a great fire of resolve burned anew within his soul. "I'll not have my heirs growing up in an outpost of a foreign empire!" he whispered angrily to the darkness.

Astrid stirred fitfully at his side. "Caylen?" she breathed.

"I've awoken you, lass. Such was not my intent."

"What troubles you?" she asked, fixing Caylen with an anxious gaze.

"The looming war," growled Caylen, brushing a lock of Astrid's golden hair from before her ice-blue eyes. "But I will not burden you with such matters."

Astrid frowned. "I worry for my father," she whispered. "He will fight alongside you, although his strength has waned with the passing of the years."

"Do not fret about old Ironhand!" grinned Caylen. "He's still a better warrior than most of the clansmen half his age! At any rate, I shall watch over him in the fray."

Astrid's pale brow furrowed. "Why have you thwarted my ambition to join the battle? It vexes me."

Caylen sighed. "You are a mighty shield-maiden, Astrid. But know that I will not imperil you. If I am slain, it will fall to you to rule in my stead and raise our children."

"You shall not perish!" hissed Astrid fervently. "You will endure and see our children grow. Every day they ask that you train them in the art of the blade and the bow."

"And so I will," enounced Caylen. "When this battle is won, I shall make doughty warriors of them, that I vow!"

"Drogha Tul seems to think they are destined for greatness. He believes they will one day fulfil some ancient tribal prophecy."

Caylen scowled. "That old wizard is constantly casting the runes or peering into the scrying pools. He's obsessed with his damned omens and auguries."

"You know, old Hertha says our daughter should not be taught the craft of war," said Astrid. "She reckons it's a man's game."

"Tell her she's wrong."

Astrid sighed. "I have, but she does not listen to me."

"Well she damn well should," said Caylen, grasping Astrid's eburnean shoulders and drawing her close. "You are the Wolf-Queen, the daughter of Ironhand! You're more than a match for any man in the fray!"

"I certainly overcame your defences," replied Astrid with a seductive smile.

Caylen grinned and planted a lusty kiss upon his wife's fulsome lips. And only many hours later, when his passion was fully spent, did he finally succumb to a fitful slumber.

Caylen-Tor stood upon a barren, rocky plain, surrounded by black trilithons which jutted from the desolate ground like jagged, broken teeth. Above him, a vast cerulean moon gleamed balefully, its edges limned with a ring of rutilant flame. Around his forearm coiled a great viridescent serpent, its sinuous body tightly encircling his muscles. From the serpent's toothsome maw, three blood red tongues flickered forth, and the creature's azure eyes gleamed with a fearful malefic light. Gazing into the distance, Caylen beheld several dark shapes moving within the desolate vista; slithering shades almost imperceptible against the stygian tapestry of the night. As he watched, the fell shapes multiplied, growing in number until the darkling horizon was a black unbroken sea of undulating shadow. The brooding sky darkened further and the shapes shimmered and writhed as they approached, seeming now to be as one with the massing dark, their amorphous bodies becoming an extension of the blackness as if they were composed of the very oppressive, sweltering darkness itself. Inexorably, the tenebrous shapes slithered and shambled toward him until they were so close that he could smell their hot foetid breath, a stench akin to the bloated bodies of slain warriors which had split to spill their mold-mottled contents to the hungry earth. Suddenly, the serpent encoiled about his sword-arm shrieked in primal ophidian rage and ruinous arcs of cerulean lightning lanced forth from between its envenomed jaws. The jagged tendrils of energy clove into the dark eidolons, dealing coruscating ruin and destruction. The black shadows withered and dissipated at the touch of the purifying radiance, their aphotic countenances fading like smoke dispersed by the wind. Time and again the crackling azure lightning issued forth pitilessly from the three-tongued serpent, until the great sea of black fiends was no more and only a supine darkling mist remained to creep away across the piceous plain. Slowly, a looming shape became evident within the sinuous remnants of the fog. It was a slime-flecked altar hewn from black stone, crowned by a leering serpentine effigy which boasted a distended, fang-studded maw and baleful ophidian eyes. With a shudder, Caylen realized he had seen the vile carving before, in the atramentous, primeval caverns deep beneath a desolate desert fortress. Long ago, it had spoken cryptic words of prophecy in a sibilant, inhuman tongue. Shifting his gaze from the squatting aberration, Caylen glanced skyward. High above, the sanguineous disc enshrouding the moon dissolved abruptly and the benighted vista became bathed in cool, lambent light. The mournful howl of a solitary wolf echoed in the far distance and Caylen slowly raised his sword-arm. The serpent was gone.

Caylen awoke with a start, a sheen of sweat glistening upon his brow, his breathing ragged. He glanced quickly about his bed-chamber to see the dying embers of the hearth-fire glowing faintly in the darkness. Astrid slumbered soundly beside him, her lissome, somnolent form bathed by the pale moonlight which filtered through the room's narrow window. Sighing heavily, he raised his hand to wipe his brow, and froze. Etched deeply upon the flesh of his forearm, clearly visible in the moon-gleam, was the deep imprint of a serpent's scaly hide. An uneasy smile crossed Caylen's face and he looked to the corner of the room where his armour and weapons were arrayed upon their pedestals. His bronze scale-mail cuirass and his intricately engraved iron helmet with its chainmail aventail were displayed proudly upon an oaken frame, while the tribal sword *Caled-draca* stood upright on its wooden plinth, flanked by his broadsword Wolf's Tooth and his fearsome, rune-etched war axe. Moonlight danced faintly upon the great sword's serpent carvings, the bejeweled ophidian eyes glimmering balefully.

The dragon! The Three Tongued Serpent has awoken!

Beside him, Astrid awoke suddenly from her slumber. "My lord?" she whispered. "What is wrong?"

"Nothing," Caylen said, gently stroking her spun-gold tresses. "A dream. A good omen. Go back to sleep."

He slowly covered his wife's alabastrine shoulders with the fur blankets and settled down once more in his oaken bed, staring silently into the darkness which was rapidly retreating before the onset of the dawn.

Chapter VII
Blood and Steel in the Verdure

The Imperial Expeditionary Army of Queen Zyrashana moved slowly westwards, like a great black serpent winding its way across the landscape. Talus Ebonfyre rode at the head of the Iron Jackal Legion, his subordinates flanking him.

General Tolodes eyed the terrain disdainfully. "Miles of cursed marshland behind us, the crags and woods of the barbaricum ahead," he spat. "We should have embarked from the Zulantian coastal garrisons, approaching the western kingdoms via the trade routes from the south."

"You do not approve of these tactics, Tolodes?" rumbled Ebonfyre ominously.

The general tightened his grip upon his rawhide reins. "I live only to serve the Empire, my lord. I merely point out an alternative. These damned lands are near impassable."

"The southern route would have extended our journey by hundreds of leagues, adding months to our campaign," Ebonfyre said. "There is no other route through the mountains and we cannot yet risk facing the Zulantian army. Black pirates prowl the Middle Sea, preying even upon the triremes of Koord's navy. Mark me, this is the only road open to us, such as it is."

"Of course, my lord," breathed Tolodes. "The empress shall prevail."

"Indeed," growled Ebonfyre, adjusting his black cloak about his shoulders. "But do not expect a swift end to this expedition. This continent has known conflict without end for more generations than the chroniclers can easily reckon. The jarldoms of the north are riven by civil war. The satrapies of the east are ceaselessly embroiled in revolt and rebellion. In the south, the once mighty fortresses of the Vyrgothian kings lie in ruins. Only Gul-Kothoth now stands defiant against the Emperor Koord's armies. And yet even that proud bastion must ultimately fall. The world is in a state of constant war."

Tolodes frowned. "Our legions shall prevail, my lord. The foes of the empress shall crumble before us, as did the Delanian host."

"Delania!" spat Ebonfyre derisively. "Gustanhav's army was concerned more with ostentation and pageantry than prowess in battle. It was scarcely a test of our mettle."

"It matters not," said Tolodes guardedly. "The king is dead and his army is crushed. The kingdom now belongs to the empress."

"For as long as we can hold it in her name," snapped Talus.

A black-garbed outrider reined his mount to canter alongside Ebonfyre's steed. "My lord. Two hundred yards ahead. There is something you should see."

Ebonfyre and Tolodes coaxed their mounts out of formation and galloped ahead with the outrider. Slowly, almost imperceptibly at first, the forest had begun to thicken, encroaching subtly upon the army of intruders. Behind the tangle of the brooding verdure, dark grey crags loomed on either side of the advancing legions like a retinue of dolent sentinels, and in the dim distance, beyond the rock-strewn hills, a vast expanse of shadowed moorland stretched to the dim horizon.

So, we enter the lands of the barbarians at last, Ebonfyre thought.

The outrider reined his mount to a halt before a pair of towering yew trees at the perimeter of the darkling woods. From their gnarled boughs, two imperial scouts had been hung, their bodies mottled with decay and acrawl with pale, bloated maggots. A black cloud of flies swarmed about the corpses, and from the branches of the tallest yew, a large crow, its sharp beak red with gore, watched impassively.

"Scouts from the Sixth Viper Legion," exclaimed Tolodes. "A warning to us from the savages." His pensive gaze swept the surrounding trees and crags. "Gods, these woods are thick with ghosts!

There are countless eyes upon us even now, I can feel it!"

Ebonfyre gazed grimly up at the rotting bodies. Shards of gleaming bone were visible through countless ragged gashes in the ruined flesh. In a sudden flurry of black, the lone crow swept from its perch to peck out the single remaining eye of the nearest corpse.

"We should cut them down," coughed Tolodes, watching as the orb was torn free of its socket. "Burn them. They are our men, after all."

Ebonfyre grimaced as he stared into the tenebrous depths of the forest before them. Vast boughs and boles extended as far as the eye could see, ultimately disappearing into impenetrable, sylvan shadow.

"We cannot pass through this wood." he said at last. "My Jackal scouts say the terrain is passable some leagues beyond those crags, where the land opens to a wide valley. Outrider, scout ahead. Find our path!"

The outrider thundered off to the west of the great forest, cresting a steep rise beyond which a sparsely wooded glen lay shadowed by the foothills of a distant mountain range.

"And these poor wretches?" rasped Tolodes, squinting up at the carious bodies swinging gruesomely above.

Ebonfyre was already wheeling his steed back towards the advancing army. "Leave them where they hang," he said.

* * *

Wulfric Oakenbrand knelt in the underbrush, silent and unmoving, scanning the dense forest which stretched before him. He wore a hooded jerkin over which was buckled his baldric of slender double-edged throwing knives and his face was streaked with woad and ochre. Shafts of sunlight filtered through the dense canopy of branches to cast a fragmented glow upon the forest floor.

I see you, thought Wulfric, staring at a group of towering oak trees some fifty paces to his left. He slowly slipped a blade from its sheath.

From behind the oaks, a figure suddenly broke cover and began to sprint deeper into the shadows of the wood. In an instant, Wulfric's bone-hilted knife had hissed from the undergrowth and hammered into the back of the target, embedding itself firmly between the fleeing man's shoulder blades. The figure fell without a sound and lay still. After several seconds, Wulfric rose from the underbrush and bounded over to the fallen warrior. He was quickly joined by a grey-bearded man, clad in green and carrying a yew shortbow and a notched scramasax.

"Well thrown, wolfshead," the man said.

Wulfric pulled the knife clear of the corpse and wiped the blade clean of blood before returning it to its sheath. He then rolled the dead man over on to his back, noting the red serpent embroidered on his black jerkin. A stylized jackal motif was visible below the serpent blazon.

"Look at that sigil, Eirik. This is an Iron Jackal scout. The empire has crossed our frontier!"

"Fie!" spat Eirik contemptuously. "If these thrall-bred whoresons think they can..."

Wulfric suddenly gripped the older man's shoulder, hurling him roughly to the ground. With preternatural speed, the ranger unsheathed and loosed another of his slender blades. A heartbeat later, an arrow with black feather flights punched into the gnarled bole of an oak tree mere inches from Eirik's head. Forty paces distant, a black-clad archer sprawled dead to the forest floor, still clutching his recurve bow, Wulfric's knife jutting from his throat.

Eirik scrambled to his feet. "Gods! Your eyes are sharper than a hawk's! That's another one I owe you!"

Oakenbrand swiftly surveyed the surrounding trees, then turned to Eirik and grinned. "I thought you'd given up counting by now, old man."

Eirik fixed the ranger with a grim gaze. "Why do you stay, outlander? This isn't your fight. Why do you not return to the forest kingdoms?"

Wulfric's grin widened. "You think I'd slink off in the dead of night, on the eve of battle? Gods forbid! Besides, there's still a hefty bounty on my head back home. A death-mark valid from the southern coast all the way to the borders of the Enga-Lands. So, I think I'll take my chances here, if it's all the same to you."

"Ah, of course," said Eirik with a wry smile. "I sometimes forget the perils of being branded an outlaw. Your exploits are becoming quite notorious throughout the clans. You know, if this legendary price on your head gets any bigger, I may just turn you in myself!"

"That I can believe, old man," said Wulfric as he strode into the dense verdure. "Come, we must report to Caylen-Tor!"

Chapter VIII
Moon-mist and War-fog

Atop a jagged promontory, Caylen and Wulfric stood gazing at the dark expanse of Blackhelm Vale far below them. The torches and campfires of the imperial army stretched into the distance, illumining the dusk and bathing the valley in an undulating golden glow.

"Behold, ranger," growled Caylen. "The dread host of Mytos K'unn. A battle-hardened infantry, bolstered by the infamous Iron Jackal Legion. A cavalry of lancers, charioteers and horse-archers, as well as five cohorts of auxiliaries and conscripts. That is what the Witch-Queen has sent against us."

"I was rather hoping they wouldn't come," sighed Wulfric mordantly.

"Then you'd have nothing to tell your grandchildren about," replied Caylen, a gleam in his eye.

The Wolf-King wore a golden scale-mail cuirass fashioned by the grim forge-masters of the wind-whipped Snow Jarldoms. His wolfskin cloak was draped about his shoulders and stiffened leather vambraces carved with knotwork dragons adorned his forearms. A wide leather belt encircled his waist, secured by a large bronze buckle crafted in the form of a wolf's head. He wore leather breeches, toughened buckskin boots and bronze greaves. Lines of woad and ochre covered his face. He sported no helmet so that he would remain an instantly recognizable figure to his warriors in the thick of the fray, bolstering their confidence and providing a rallying point in the midst of the battle's throng. At his left side hung the mighty *Caled-draca*, and at his right was scabbarded the well-worn blade Wolf's Tooth. The king's trusty broadsword had been in his possession for many years, its notched edge unceasingly keen and its wedge-shaped pommel and stout crossguard etched with intricate knotwork patterns.

Wulfric Oakenbrand carried an ornate yew longbow, horn-tipped and carved with knotwork and battle-runes. A number of arrows with eagle-feather flights were secured in a quiver slung over his shoulder, some of them bearing broadhead tips, others sporting slender bodkin points crafted to punch through armour and shields. His twin shortswords hung from his belt and his throwing-daggers rested in their baldric sheaths.

Oughtred Bearsark moved to stand with the two men atop the crags. The general wore a gleaming chainmail cuirass and a cloak of dark brown bearskin. An ornate bronze helmet etched with the motif of a charging boar covered his head, and his great, double-headed axe glimmered in the half-light. "They won't risk the valley at night," he rumbled. "They'll move out at dawn."

"Then let us strive to thwart their aspirations," said Caylen. "We attack as planned."

The war council had held their final meeting the night before, refining the battle plans and deciding upon stratagems until the light of dawn had streaked the sky.

"Some of the men are uneasy," said Oughtred. "None have seen a battle of this scale, not even the veterans."

"I will speak to them," Caylen said, turning and striding back to the clansmen's camp.

"The skalds had best get my name right when they sing the tale of this battle," muttered Wulfric, his gaze remaining fixed on the vast host below.

* * *

The small tribal army had set up a fireless camp atop the great rise which flanked the valley's western side. Beyond the encampment, sparse woodland ultimately gave way to the rocky foothills of the vast mountain range which separated Caylen-Tor's kingdom from that of Delania and Turanan. And beyond that, lost in impenetrable shadow, the distant snow-capped peaks at the frontiers of the Jarldoms loomed.

Caylen moved to where Drogha Tul sat beneath a young ash tree, studying his runestones intently. The shaman did not look at the king as he crouched beside him.

"What do the runes say, wizard?" asked Caylen.

"The outcome is wreathed in shadow," the aged man whispered. "The *Nornir* withhold their warp and weft. This night, a man shapes his own destiny."

"So be it," Caylen said. "Do the Fen-Witches know their role in this? Will they summon the fog at the appointed time?"

"The sisterhood will do their part," Drogha Tul replied. "Yet there is a great dark power hovering about the foe. Its origin is elusive, its source far away. It will seek to devour thee before this battle is done."

"Can you counter this threat?" hissed Caylen, gripping the hilt of *Caled-draca*. "Or must I rely solely on steel?"

The sorcerer closed his eyes and sighed. "Spells of protection are woven, Wolf-King. But there are some things against which even the finest steel will not avail thee."

Caylen smiled mirthlessly and rose. "Then your magics had best work, hadn't they, old man?"

The waxing moon slipped from behind a lambent veil of cloud, casting a ghostly light upon the camp. Shamans and clan-witches moved amongst the warriors, chanting battle-spells and invoking the tribal war-gods. Caylen made his way through the ranks, surveying the army as it prepared for battle. The banners of the tribal war-hirds were arrayed amidst the clansmen, the colourful sigils depicting totemic beasts and ancestral gods.

One of Oughtred Bearsark's towering *ber-serkr* reavers suddenly loomed before Caylen, his great warhammer glinting in the moonlight.

"Hail, Wolfclan," the man growled, holding out his hand. Within his huge palm were several bright blue mushrooms. "Will you chew the Shaman's Cap with me?"

"Not this night, Beorn," said Caylen. "I dare not succumb fully to the *hamrammr* rage. I must keep my wits about me in the fray."

The man nodded, a cruel grin creasing his scarred face. "So be it, then. I'll wager the power of your Ulfhednar battle-magicks will still protect you. But my tally of slaughter will be greater than yours!"

Caylen laughed and clasped the warrior's huge shoulder. "I'm sure it will be, brother!"

A goatskin war-drum briefly sounded three muffled beats and the clansmen ceased their preparations and watched Caylen-Tor as he moved to the centre of the camp and vaulted to the top of a flat, moss-encrusted boulder. The Wolf-King stood tall, a malefic shadow surveying his grim army. There were young and old in the ranks, men and women, veterans and raw recruits together; warriors clad in the skins of bears and wolves, some crudely armoured in leather or bronze, a few sporting mail-shirts of chain or scale. They carried hand-axes and spears with hafts of ash, some bearing langesaxes and swords of iron or steel. Many were armed with yew longbows, their quivers packed full of slender shafts. A great number of warriors carried circular rawhide-rimmed shields crafted of elder and lindenwood with iron bosses at the centre, and knotwork patterns, bind-runes and stylized animal totems were emblazoned upon their butted and chamfered boards. Many clansmen sported iron helmets, some with gilt bronze faceguards and mail aventails. Most of those assembled wore blue woad or red ochre upon their faces and bodies; sigils of power and esoteric potency.

"My brothers, my sisters," Caylen said, his voice clear and resonant. "My people! The time has come. In yonder valley, the hordes of the east have massed. They seek to despoil our land, to defile our sacred places. They will come dealing slaughter, pillage and rape. They will burn and loot our steadings. They will seek to drive their outlander banners into our soil and claim our realm for their odious empire."

Murmurs arose within the ranks, and oaths were spat.

"This land was given to us by the gods," continued Caylen. "It is the land of our ancestors, the honoured tribal forefathers who fought and died for it. I ask you now, can we do any less?"

A great cheer erupted from the assembled warriors. Swords, spears and axes were lifted to the night sky. Caylen's voice rose over the clamour. "The imperial dogs think we will let them pass through without a fight! I say they are wrong. What say you?"

The cheers escalated to a tumultuous roar, and weapons were beaten against shields and armour in a rhythmic tattoo.

Caylen dragged *Caled-draca* free of its scabbard and held the sword aloft. Moonlight glinted balefully from its oiled and polished blade. "This night, a legend shall be written! A legend which our kinfolk shall remember for a thousand years! And those who are not with us shall curse the Fates evermore for their ill judgement! I am the Wolf of the North, and by all the gods, I am proud to stand with thee!"

The cacophony was deafening and Caylen gazed skyward, the blade of *Caled-draca* pointing directly at the moon. "O grim gods of battle, empower us this night. Anoint us with the crimson rain. Feed our steel with slaughter. Let every blow be a killing blow. Grant us victory... or a warrior's death!"

The assembled clansmen began to repeat Caylen's name exultantly in a primal chant. The martial paean echoed throughout the night; an empowering clarion, a tribal invocation of war and savage pride. In the deepening gloom, the Wolf-King turned his ferine gaze upon the army, his name a word of power on their lips.

The bloodying was at hand!

* * *

General Tolodes stood before the entrance to Talus Ebonfyre's great black pavilion, staring intently into the night. Around him, the army of Mytos K'unn stretched like a fulgent sea. Thousands of tents were arrayed before the entrance to the tenebrous valley. Countless cook fires were burning, their rutilant flames dancing amidst the blackness. Many of the officers' mounts were tethered near the tents, while hundreds more horses were picketed near the camp perimeter. The army's supply wagons were drawn up near the centre of the formation, and everywhere the sable banners of Mytos K'unn had been driven deep into the earth.

A black-cloaked officer strode up to Tolodes and saluted briskly. "Sir, all sentries are in position and the watch has been doubled, as you commanded. Scouts have been deployed beyond the valley and into the surrounding crags. The field officers have assembled in your tent for the briefing regarding tomorrow's deployment."

Tolodes abruptly waved the man to silence. "Do you hear that, Captain Jungsai?" he whispered.

The captain's brow furrowed. "Sir?"

Tolodes stalked to the perimeter of the camp, motioning for Jungsai to follow. Moving past the sentries, the two men studied the mouth of the benighted valley before them. Tolodes was silent for some moments, then shook his head wearily. "Nothing. Mayhap just the wind in the vale."

"As you say, sir."

"Very well, captain. We will adopt the standard Jamukha strategy for moving through this valley at dawn. The possibility of an ambush is remote, but nevertheless..." Tolodes suddenly fell silent as he descried a glowing tendril of mist begin to writhe from the deep shadows of the vale, clinging to the darkling earth like a tenebrous serpent. The undulating, incorporeal ribbon of fog was swiftly joined by another, then a third, until at length they fused and became one, transforming into a vast unbroken tide of lambent mist which advanced inexorably across the valley floor toward the mouth of the pass.

"I've never before seen such a miasma," whispered Jungsai fearfully. "Truly, this is a land of infidels and unclean spirits!" Grasping the hilt of his sabre, he took several steps backwards as the ghostly wall of mist breached the mouth of the vale and continued toward the camp.

"Wretch!" spat Tolodes. "Do you fear a fog? Can you show no mettle save that which the queen's battle-spells give you? Inform the officers that I shall..."

An arrow with eagle-feather fletching abruptly hammered into the general's throat and dark blood bubbled noisily from his lips. Instantly, he collapsed to the earth, his fingers scrabbling desperately at the slender shaft. A heartbeat later, he was silent and deathly still. Jungsai turned briskly on his heel and began running back to the camp, bellowing the alarm. Behind him, the supine mist had already enveloped the body of General Tolodes.

* * *

Talus Ebonfyre strode from his pavilion to find the imperial encampment in the grip of ravening chaos. A thick glowing mist enshrouded the entirety of the tent-city and the discordant sounds of battle resounded from all sides. Donning his great horned helm and drawing his curved blade, he surged furiously into the lucent maelstrom, immediately discerning scores of fallen legionaries underfoot whose bodies were riddled with feather-fletched arrows. Many imperial horses had also fallen, evidently cut down in their corrals by a hail of shafts. Countless tents were aflame and the rutilant glow of fire-arrows could be seen arcing from the darkness in repeated volleys. A terrible rage suddenly swelled within Ebonfyre and the malefic spirit to which he was host began to roil and seethe in darksome fury.

"Soon, black dog of the Z'xulth... soon."

Talus gripped the shoulder of a blood-spattered legionary who was stumbling desperately through the mist. "What the hell happened, soldier? Speak!"

"This cursed fog descended upon us, my lord," the man stuttered. "And with it came arrows and spears from the left and right flanks! The enemy assails us from the hills! We know not how many!"

Ebonfyre released the legionary and stalked balefully to the centre of the embattled camp. "Cohorts assemble!" he roared, his voice cutting through the cacophonous screams of men and beasts. "Defensive pattern Khaguran!"

For many harrowing minutes the attack continued, until the ceaseless howl of the fire-arrows was replaced by the intermittent clash of steel on steel. The mist had slowly begun to disperse, and everywhere the ground was littered with fallen imperial troops. Many of the tents continued to blaze, while others had already been reduced to embers and ash. Ebonfyre moved to a group of legionaries who had adopted a defensive foulkon formation. "Follow those sounds of battle!" he thundered. "Find the savages! Kill them all!"

* * *

At length, the wall of mist diminished to little more than wisps of pale vapour and the clangour of combat ceased. Innumerable corpses littered the earth, all of them legionaries. Many of the fallen imperial troops were transfixed by arrows, while others bore wounds evidently dealt by swords, axes or spears. Grimly surveying the extent of the carnage which had been wrought, Talus Ebonfyre scabbarded his unbloodied blade and located the surviving officers and quartermasters of the imperial army. His ireful gaze slowly swept the assembly of fraught and harrowed soldiers. "Situation!"

"After the volleys cut into our flanks, we were attacked by an unknown number of primitives from all sides," a breathless captain reported. "The engagement was brief. They pressed the assault only until the mist began to disperse, then retreated."

"General Tolodes is dead, sir, and the Sixth Viper Legion has suffered ruinous casualties," rasped another officer. "I can also confirm that the Fourth Cobra Legion has been reduced to half strength. Auxiliaries are reporting moderate losses. Body counts indicate that the majority of the conscripts have been killed or wounded, and the remainder are believed to have fled into the night. Three-quarters of our supply wagons are still burning."

Ebonfyre cursed, then addressed a tall officer who sported a forked black beard. "Quartermaster Kuchar! What is the status of the cavalry?"

"The horse archers are all but lost, and the captains report that two thirds of the cavalry's mounts have either been slain or driven off. It will be impossible to send out scouting parties to recover the beasts until first light."

"Did the Shadow Cultists survive?"

Kuchar's body tensed. "No, my lord. I fear every Night Priest has been slain."

Ebonfyre's lip curled, his eyes ablaze with an unfathomed rage. "And what of the Jackal?" he seethed.

"The Iron Jackal is intact, my lord," replied Kuchar. "No losses reported."

"They could attack again at any time," an ashen-faced lieutenant exclaimed. "We must move the army away from this cursed valley!"

"No!" roared Ebonfyre. "We will not retreat! This is his doing! Caylen-Tor! He taunts me! We shall attack!"

"But my lord," the officer stammered, "advancing by night into that valley could risk the entire..."

Ebonfyre's gauntlet lashed out to strike the officer with such force that the man spun a half circle before collapsing unconscious to the ground. The surrounding troops stared uneasily at their commander, saying nothing.

"We will advance!" Ebonfyre snarled. "Marshall the troops. Give the order! I want these accursed clansmen hunted down and destroyed! Spare not one! They all shall suffer!"

Swiftly and silently, the officers moved off to prepare the army for deployment.

Ebonfyre stumbled to the shadows at the perimeter of the ravaged camp, his breathing ragged, a sheen of cold sweat upon his pallid brow. The sibilant whispers of the malefic spirit within him grew ever louder and more insistent, akin to a pitiless black tide encroaching upon a darkling shore. Vivid images streaked through his mind with disorienting speed; hideous scenes exhumed from some abyssal charnel pit of suppressed memory. Coalescing before his mind's eye, he beheld the image of a noisome antechamber, illumined only by the guttering glow of countless black candles. A myriad writhing, undraped bodies were swaying obscenely to the opiate beat of some great, unseen drum. At the centre of the chamber, Ebonfyre saw a shrouded form shackled to an aphotic bloodstained altar, struggling madly against its unyielding bonds. Looming before the captive, hypnotically beautiful in the flickering candlelight, was a lissome woman, naked but for a cloak of sable, a gnarled dagger glinting in her slender ivory hands.

Zyrashana! The Witch-Queen of Mytos K'unn!

Gazing spellbound into the rutilant vista, Ebonfyre glimpsed the flicker of a serpent's tongue as it scored the perfect and fulsome lips of his malefic empress. He descried the sheen of viridescent scales glistening in the crimson fire-glow, slick upon her flawless eburnean flesh. And for a fleeting moment, he was certain that he beheld the black slit-pupils of ophidian eyes glimmering beneath Zyrashana's cruel, alabastrine brow.

"The covenant of Maalech Xul!" he roared in primal fury.

The panoply of images abruptly disappeared. A caliginous veil of shadow hung like a pall before his eyes, and Talus Ebonfyre at last surrendered his grip on those tenebrous fetters which held the energumen beast in check.

"It is time!" hissed Ebonfyre, as if hearing his own voice from afar. "The Wolf-King's soul shall glut the maw of Chaos! Red ruin and black fury upon the accursed head of Caylen-Tor!"

Chapter IX
The Battle of Blackhelm Vale

"Form the line!" bellowed Caylen-Tor as he scrambled down the rocky slope to the nighted heather of Blackhelm Vale, his *wolfhird* hard behind him.

"The empire comes!" roared Oughtred Bearsark, his notched axe gleaming. "We've stung the beast to action. They'll risk the valley after all!"

The great tribal ram's horn clarion thundered the call to battle and the army massed around Caylen, swiftly forming a steel-toothed line which spanned the pass at its narrowest extent.

"Scildweall!" boomed Caylen, hefting the mighty sword *Caled-draca*. In the moonlight, the great blade seemed to glimmer with a cerulean luminescence. The foremost rank of warriors instantly locked shields, their spears and short thrusting blades at the ready.

"Nothing gets through!" shouted Caylen. "Hear me, Gylfir?"

At the centre of the line, a stout warrior with a braided blond beard adjusted his helmet and turned to Caylen. "Aye! Nowt's getting by us, Wolf-King! This gate's shut tight!"

Caylen nodded and took position within the front rank, brandishing *Caled-draca*. The warriors on either side of the king adjusted position to give him ample room to wield his steel.

Oughtred grinned at the ranks of archers who had assembled some distance behind the shield wall. "Masterful work, lads!" he said jubilantly. "We've given them a night they won't forget!"

"I've only a few arrows left," stammered a young bowman, his eyes wide with fear.

"Don't worry, boy, they'll soon give us some of theirs!" shouted Caylen in response. "Archers! When I give the order, keep up the volleys. Oakenbrand! Where the devil are you, man?"

Wulfric strode from the ranks of a second group of archers who bore the sigil of the Raven-Saters clan upon their jerkins. "We are ready, Wolf-King."

"Take your bowmen and get back into the foothills. Wait for Oughtred's signal for the fire-shafts. After that, when the enemy's close enough, loose at will. Rain pitiless death upon their flanks! When you run out of arrows, get back down here and join the throng!"

"Gods be with us!" Wulfric shouted, leading the bowmen towards the shadowed, gorse-covered slopes.

Caylen shifted to allow a number of swordsmen into the foremost rank. "You'll have precious little swinging room," he called to those around him. "When it comes to it, favour the thrust. Shield-bearers, be ready for volleys."

Oughtred's frenzied sleuth of *ber-serkr* warriors howled their bestial defiance behind the front rank and the surrounding clansmen shuffled swiftly away to give the fearsome reavers ample space to hack and hew.

"You hold those bear-shirts in check until the lines meet," Caylen called to the red bearded giant.

"Don't you worry about that," Oughtred replied. "Best they don't make us wait too long, though!"

Caylen grinned. "They won't."

"Why did you leave your axe at home?" scowled Oughtred, nodding at Caylen's ornate sword. "That fancy pig-sticker's no match for a good long-hafted skull cleaver!"

"Tonight, the serpent must sing its war-song, old friend," replied Caylen. "See you in the thick of the fray!"

"Aye!" said Oughtred as he joined the line some twenty paces from the king.

Brodir Finn took position in the ranks beside Caylen, staring out across the valley to where the imperial army was advancing towards the mouth of the pass. "I didn't think it would come to a pitched battle," he said ruefully, donning his battered bronze-rimmed helmet. "But I suppose it was a fool's hope to think the mist would have been enough."

"It's done its job," Caylen said, hefting *Caled-draca*. "And there are a few surprises yet in store for the foe. Faith, brother! The gods are with us this night!"

Brodir nodded pensively. "I pray you are right, Wolf-King."

"And so, we come to it at last," whispered Caylen. "The night of red steel is upon us!"

The moon emerged once more from behind a wisp of bright cloud.

"Warriors of the north!" bellowed Caylen exultantly. "May your swords sing a deadly song in your grasp! The gods have envenomed our blades with the death-kiss of a thousand serpents! Unfetter the dread war-wolves within your hearts! May their claws rend! May their jaws be reddened!"

A roar of defiant rage arose from the ranks. Swords and spears were beaten fervently against shields in a resonant thunder-song of battle-lust.

In response to the war-cries of the clansmen, the sound of a single, baleful drum rolled across the vale, beating its rhythmic tattoo from the deep shadow.

"The foe closes!" shouted a russet-bearded swordsman in the front line as he beheld the imperial legions breach the mouth of the pass and enter Blackhelm Vale.

"I see them, Guthlac!" thundered Caylen-Tor. "Let them come! We'll carve the moon-wheel in their accursed hides!"

* * *

From the rocky foothills flanking the vale, Wulfric and the Raven-Saters bowmen watched the army of Mytos K'unn move slowly across the threshold of the caliginous ravine. Shifting his gaze quickly to the clansmen's ranks, Oakenbrand instantly discerned the hulking figure of Oughtred Bearsark behind the shield wall, his great frame etched harshly in the light of the army's myriad burning brands.

"Torchbearer, stand ready," said Wulfric.

A ranger bearing a guttering torch moved swiftly to the forefront of the line of archers. The bodkin-tipped shafts of the tribal bowmen were nocked and their calloused fingers were poised upon the great bowstrings of sinew and hemp.

"Light them up!" growled Wulfric.

The torchbearer swiftly ignited the resin-soaked tows which had been tied behind the archers' arrowheads.

A scant second later, Wulfric saw the signal from Oughtred.

"Loose!" he hissed.

The volley of flaming shafts arced down toward the valley floor, followed almost immediately by a second wave from the distant opposite slope. Many of the arrows struck imperial troops, but the majority hammered home into their intended target; the pitch and oil-sodden earth where fire-trenches had been dug and concealed across the breadth of the vale.

"That's done it!" said Wulfric as he watched thick flames leap up and rapidly engulf the vanguard of the imperial force. Countless men were enveloped by the pitiless wall of fire with sickening speed. The ground upon which stood the foremost rank of the legion was transformed instantly into a raging mass of searing flame. Many troops desperately attempted to vault clear of the inferno, while others raced blindly back through the stricken lines. Officers to the rear of the immolated column desperately barked orders, attempting to control the chaos which had inundated the advancing army.

"Nock," barked Wulfric as the torchbearer moved amongst the group of archers once again, igniting a second volley.

"Loose!"

The second fire-trench was ignited and another devastating torrent of fire sprang from the earth to consume the front lines of the imperial army. The ranks behind were fleeing panic-stricken from the site of the flame pits, opening a gaping fissure in the imperial formation. From the opposite slope, concealed by impenetrable shadow, the second unit of tribal archers then began to harry the imperial army with shafts.

"Loose at will," said Wulfric tersely. "Concentrate on their archers."

The Raven-Saters bowmen loosed from their lofty vantage point, their aim true. The ranks of imperial archers fell under the withering hail of arrows, scarcely managing to rally and return a meagre volley to their foe's barely perceived location.

The shafts from Wulfric's own ornate longbow were pitilessly accurate, each arrow hammering unerringly into an imperial soldier, every one an expertly placed killing shot.

At the centre of the imperial formation, Wulfric suddenly descried a giant steel-clad warrior with a great curved sword stalk resolutely toward the undulating walls of fire. For a moment the figure stood immobile, his gleaming armour reflecting the baleful glow of the flames. Then, to Wulfric's astonishment, the towering warrior promptly strode through the first blazing conflagration apparently unscathed. Standing now between the two barriers of flame, the armoured giant slowly lifted his gauntleted hand. As if caught in the grip of a great storm wind, the two flame-walls abruptly guttered and died, leaving only glowing embers upon the scorched and smouldering earth. The fearsome figure then motioned to the waiting army and the imperial force surged forward, bounding heedlessly over the charred and lifeless husks of their fallen comrades.

"Ebonfyre!" breathed Wulfric.

"We've spent our arrows, ranger!" called one of the tribal archers, drawing Wulfric's attention from the disquieting occurrence below. “Have we done enough?”

Wulfric’s gaze returned to the imperial army as it advanced on the waiting shield wall. “Mayhap. Their skirmishers have fallen. It’s in the hands of the gods now!”

The dolorous drum of the legions quickened its resonant beat and the first wave of imperial troops continued to hurtle toward the entrenched clansmen. Several sporadic volleys of shafts arced high over the shield wall, loosed by the vastly depleted ranks of imperial archers. For the most part, the arrows embedded themselves in the broad shields of the tribal army. A return volley was launched at the command of Oughtred Bearsark, accompanied by a storm of slender, ash-hafted throwing spears. Wulfric watched intently, straining to perceive the events in the gloomy half-light of the moon-swathed valley, as the missiles hammered mercilessly into the onrushing troops. The first line of imperial warriors fell and those behind them vaulted over the slain, their martial pace unhindered. From his vantage point, Wulfric could see that the imperial charge was approaching the narrowest point of the pass where the mountainous walls flanking the vale constricted to no more than fifty paces across. And behind that incapacious, lithic channel waited the steadfast tribal army of Caylen-Tor.

“Bare your steel, clansmen!” Wulfric bellowed, dragging his twin scramasax blades from their leather scabbards. “Time to join the fray!”

And with the others close behind him, he scrambled to the steep, rocky trail which wound its way back down to the embattled valley.

* * *

“Another volley inbound!” shouted Caylen-Tor as he watched the distant imperial archers bend their recurve bows once more. He swiftly gathered up the broad elderwood shield of a fallen clansman and crouched low to the heather. "Shields!"

Five score howling shafts, practically invisible in the semi-darkness, pelted down upon the clansmen like a parlous iron torrent. The bodkin-tipped arrows tore into the tribal shields and flesh with a harrowing clamour, piercing wood, earth, thews and bone.

"That was the last one, lads!" Caylen barked, throwing the shaft-studded shield aside and hefting *Caled-draca* once more. "Get the wounded clear! Prepare for steel on steel!" Slowly, he dragged Wolf's Tooth from its leather scabbard and brandished both blades reverentially, his eyes gleaming with the exultant joy of battle.

The beat of the imperial drums boomed in the darkness, their report like distant rolling thunder. Then, a war-horn sounded three strident notes and the onrushing imperial troops shrieked an ululating battle-cry.

Caylen-Tor grinned wolfishly as he watched the foe surging toward the interlocked wall of carven elder and lindenwood. "Come on, you dogs," he bellowed. "Come taste the edge of good northern steel!"

The lines met with bone-shaking ferocity. The initial wave of imperial troops was hacked down and rent to red ruin by the blades of the clansmen. In a sanguineous maelstrom of blood and iron, scores of legionaries fell like wheat before the scythe, crashing in vain against the wall of shields like a black tide against an unyielding cliff-face.

"Get back, devils!" Caylen thundered. "You'll not pass this vale! Such is the Wolf-King's vow!"

More imperial troops clambered desperately atop the corpses of their brethren only to be met by the hungry spearheads and honed blades of the clansmen. Black iron thundered against elderwood again and again, the sound of battle splitting the night like a deafening coronach of carnage. Steel rang defiantly against steel, iron bit deep into wood, bronze and flesh. Shields were sundered, bones were shattered and blades were broken as a tumult of screams and war-cries crested the clamour of battle. Hot gouts of arterial blood spattered upon shields and armour, anointing the ranks with the primal red blazon of war. Bodies that had been rent asunder shed their steaming innards to the churned earth, turning the ground beneath the front lines into a crimson mire of slime and viscid ichor.

The ravening! The red rage of battle! The black song of slaughterfall!

Caylen-Tor furiously knocked aside an imperial sword thrust with *Caled-draca*, then drove his broadsword Wolf's Tooth deep into the attacking legionary's exposed neck. With blood bubbling from his lips, the soldier crashed heavily to the earth to join the growing ranks of the sundered dead.

"Bleed for the gods of war!" howled Caylen as he arced the great tribal sword in a devastating strike, effortlessly cleaving off the helmeted head of another warrior and sending the corpse careening into the path of his comrades. Hot blood splashed onto Caylen's cold hand and he parried a desperate blow from a snarling legionary, driving the man's curved sword down and immediately thrusting Wolf's Tooth into the soldier's sternum. The impact of the blow thrummed through Caylen's forearm and he felt the blade grating against bone. Pulling his sword free of the lifeless body, he turned aside a brutal spear thrust and riposted with a harrowing strike which cleaved open the attacker's chest. Steel tore through leather, flesh, sinew and bone as Caylen dispatched the legionary and kicked the blood-drenched corpse to the earth. A black javelin thrust silently from the teeming throng of legionaries towards Caylen's throat, but Brodir Finn's rawhide-rimmed shield deflected the blow, unbalancing the legionary and causing him to stumble forward. Caylen instantly hammered *Caled-draca* down to cleave off the attacker's arm in a shower of blood and jagged shards of bone.

"My thanks, Finn!" barked Caylen.

Brodir Finn flashed a wide grin, his teeth and face streaked with blood.

Suddenly, a curved sword slid beneath Caylen's guard, its point striking his scale-mail cuirass. Roaring an oath, Caylen drove *Caled-draca* down to shatter the scimitar into a myriad fragments, then he swept Wolf's Tooth upward to bite into the abdomen of the imperial swordsman. Shrieking in pain, the legionary was hauled from his feet by the force of the blow before Caylen dragged the blade free and propelled the man backwards into the enemy ranks.

"Let not one of these bastards through the shield wall!"

Caylen glanced to his right and briefly glimpsed the great crimson whirlwind of slaughter that was Oughtred Bearsark, dealing carnage unto the foe with his vast brain-flecked axe. The general's *ber-serkr* warriors were rending the foe's ranks like the pack falling upon the herd; pitiless in their desire to slake their primal hunger, ravening red in tooth and claw. Wulfric fought several paces further down the line, a cool and emotionless executioner whose bright steel danced in an elaborate and merciless web of death. By his side was the veteran chieftain Grimm Ironhand, his white beard now clotted red, his notched and well-worn longsword once again bloody as it had been so many times before in numberless battles over the decades.

Suddenly, the unseen imperial war-horn gave vent to three strident notes.

"They're falling back!" bellowed Guthlac as the remnants of the first wave of legionaries disengaged and began to lope back into the darkness.

"Prepare for the second assault!" shouted Caylen, wiping blood and sweat from his eyes.

Scant seconds later, another wave of imperial troops emerged from the shadows, their black armour glimmering balefully in the moonlight.

"The mounds of their own dead shall bar their way!" roared Caylen-Tor, lifting the reddened *Caled-draca* high. "Heed me! Tonight we witness the harrowing of the Witch-Queen's empire!"

The second wave of legionaries hurled themselves into the fray, their charge slowed by the multitude of ravaged corpses which littered the blood-gorged heather. A slender throwing axe crashed into Brodir Finn's shield, its iron head embedding itself in the gore-kissed wood. The clansman next to Brodir was abruptly dashed to the earth, a blackened javelin transfixing his neck. The imperial warriors thundered furiously against the tribal shield wall, their own metal-rimmed shields hammering upon the clansmen like a black storm.

"Push the bastards back!" roared Oughtred Bearsark, spinning his great gore-clotted axe. "There's yet some butcher's work to be done tonight!"

With a lupine snarl, Caylen-Tor hooked the crossguard of *Caled-draca* over the rim of a crescent-shaped shield and dragged it from the legionary's grasp, simultaneously driving Wolf's Tooth into the man's midriff. The steel split the warrior's lamellar cuirass and Caylen instantly tore the blade clear to hammer it into the jugular of a second assailant, who crashed to the earth to be hacked to red ribbons by the blades of the surrounding clansmen. A spearman leaped forth from the imperial line and *Caled-draca* instantly sheared through his leg below the knee, splitting the greave, flesh and bone with preternatural ease.

"More!" howled Caylen exultantly, his eyes ablaze with the rapture of battle, his lungs filling with the raw scent of fresh-spilled blood. "More souls to feed the wolves of war!"

Caylen aimed a thunderous blow at the head of another legionary and *Caled-draca* sundered the iron helmet and the skull beneath with a clangorous crack and a jagged shower of bone and metal. A curved blade suddenly tore into Caylen's shoulder, splintering scale-mail and cutting deep into his flesh.

"That's the spirit!" Caylen hissed before his return stroke clove the legionary's shield in twain and ripped through the man's body, shattering his ribcage to ensanguined shards. Caylen met the next attacker with a primal roar, sweeping both blades laterally to hack through the swordsman's mail-coif and shear off the top of his head. A slurry of grey brain matter erupted from the sundered skull and Caylen immediately drove his broadsword into the belly of another warrior, opening a great yawning fissure in his armour and flesh. The legionary's entrails erupted forth, landing wetly at his feet in a pulsating mass akin to a nest of writhing, pallid worms.

To Caylen's right, the clansman Gylfir fell, a black javelin jutting from his throat. Three imperial troops instantly surged through the gap in the shield wall. Caylen barreled the first from his feet and drove *Caled-draca* into his back. The second legionary struck a glancing blow against Caylen's thigh before the blade of Wolf's Tooth punched through his mouth and out through the back of his fur-trimmed helmet's leather neck-guard. The slain man crashed to the earth, his fall wresting the sword from Caylen's grasp. The third attacker stumbled over the body of his comrade and Caylen's blow hacked off his head in a scintillant cascade of crimson.

Two more legionaries instantly lunged forth from the throng, their blades awhirl. Caylen drove *Caled-draca* into the belly of the first and the man fell screaming to the heather. The second legionary swept his sword at Caylen's neck and the Wolf-King dropped swiftly to one knee, thrusting *Caled-draca* forth in a pitiless blow which all but disemboweled his assailant.

Caylen rose lithely as a towering black-bearded legionary loomed suddenly from the imperial ranks brandishing a huge serrated scimitar. *Caled-draca* met the warrior's blade with a blossom of rutilant sparks and the two combatants stood locked in a grueling test of steel and raw strength, the great corded muscles of the Wolf-King's arms bulging and rippling like an indomitable titan of tribal myth. An errant javelin bit deeply into Caylen's lower thigh and his knee began to buckle, his hulking opponent still pressing mercilessly down upon him. Spitting a curse, Caylen hammered his fist brutally into the bearded legionary's cuirass, feeling the bones beneath the lamellar armour yield before his mighty bare-knuckled blow. The legionary gnarred in pain and reflexively twisted his curved blade, reeling backwards and wrenching *Caled-draca* from Caylen's grip. Hastily snatching up a fallen clansman's ash-hafted spear, Caylen drove the weapon's iron point into the staggering legionary's chest with all his might, lifting the man from his feet and momentarily holding him transfixed by the broad, leaf-shaped blade. Blood coursed down the spear's notched haft onto Caylen's hands, and snarling a guttural oath, the Wolf-King hurled the flailing man back into the midst of the foe. Swiftly recovering his blades, Caylen bellowed furiously at the imperial host.

"Come, thralls of the Witch-Queen! I am Caylen-Tor and death awaits you this night!"

The imperial war-horn thundered again, and abruptly the second assault ended. This time, many more clansmen had joined their foes upon the corpse-mounds.

"Cavalry!" called Oughtred, gazing at the distant imperial ranks where more than three score darkling steeds were slowly assuming formation.

"Plant those stakes, lads!" rasped Caylen breathlessly, hefting his red blades. "First rank, stand fast! Spears high! Second rank, keep those points low!"

"Can we withstand a cavalry charge?" barked Brodir Finn, wiping blood from his lips.

"We must," Caylen replied. "They're getting desperate. If we can weather this, we've all but broken them!"

Oughtred moved to stand beside Caylen. "If we do withstand this, they'll send in their best troops," he whispered. "The Iron Jackal Legion, Ebonfyre's own regiment."

Caylen's eyes narrowed. "That's what I'm waiting for."

Suddenly, Wulfric appeared beside the two men, his twin shortswords and leather armour darkly imbrued with blood.

"You still alive, wolfshead?" growled Caylen, a cruel smile etched upon his gore-spattered face.

"That remains to be seen," replied Wulfric mordantly, casting a sombre glance over his shoulder at the black expanse of the valley behind them.

"Hoping for the other clans to arrive and heroically turn the tide?" smirked Oughtred. "Forget it, lad. That sort of nonsense only happens in the sagas."

"Imperial cavalry advancing!" Caylen shouted. "Hold this ground! Give not a yard!"

The mournful imperial clarion rang out across the dark expanse and seventy caparisoned black horses, their riders bearing broad shields and iron-tipped lances, moved swiftly from canter to full gallop. The rumbling tattoo of hooves filled the valley, echoing from the crags like a brooding thunderstorm. The ground began to shake as the beasts closed on the shield wall, the dark riders levelling their lances as they bore inexorably down upon the assembled tribesmen.

Then, above the rumbling cacophony, Caylen heard another sound. A voice rode the night air; a darkly sepulchral voice which although seemingly little more than a whisper was yet clearly audible over the thunder of the charging cavalry. The words uttered by this voice were unknown to Caylen, for they were fell words of power hissed in an aeons-dead tongue long since fallen beyond time and the fleeting memories of men. The Wolf-King looked to the eastern crags and beheld the figure of Drogha Tul etched black against the gibbous moon, his gnarled, ensorcelled staff held high, his stygian silhouette darker than night or shadow.

The cavalry charge abruptly faltered, the horses slewing and clattering to a chaotic halt. The steeds began to scream and snort in terror, rearing, twisting, heedless of the commands and the whips of their harried riders. Horsemen were thrown to the earth, some dashed and hammered by black hooves, others scrambling clear of the frenzied mass of equine carnage. Those not unsaddled found that they had no control over the beasts, struggling in vain to master their fear-fraught mounts. The cavalry turned in disarray and began thundering back towards the imperial line, the steeds driving headlong in a desperate charge to be free of the valley and the eldritch terror that had gripped them. The empire's infantry scrambled to avoid the onrushing beasts, parting frantically to allow the lathered mounts to surge through the ranks and careen into the shadows beyond the valley's threshold.

A deafening cheer arose from the clansmen's shield wall.

Oughtred turned to Caylen. "Now I see why you keep that old conjurer around!"

"They're undone!" Caylen bellowed to the tribal army. "They're all but beaten!"

"Aye, but they don't know it yet!" said Wulfric, peering through the gloom at the imperial host. "Something else stirs in the shadow."

A deep, malign war-horn then thundered its baleful report from the darkness of the valley.

"The Iron Jackal Legion!" rasped Oughtred. "At last, they send their best!"

Caylen-Tor stared into the black expanse that separated the two forces, surveying the foe beyond. Visible within the flickering pools of torchlight which illumined the imperial army's ranks, a column of black-armoured warriors silently slipped from the ragged throng and began to advance slowly across the valley. A banner emblazoned with the sigil of a sable jackal's head against a field of deep crimson was borne aloft at their centre.

"Can you see him?" spat Wulfric anxiously. "Is Ebonfyre amongst them?"

“He’d damn well better be,” growled Caylen.

From the shadows at the rear of the legion, a towering figure slowly manifested, striding through the serried line to march at the forefront of the formation. A huge horned helm adorned the warrior’s head and a fearsomely curved sword with a pommel fashioned in the form of a jackal’s head swung at his side. A dark and nebulous aura seemed to surround the sinistrous giant; a tenebrous eidolon which appeared to writhe and undulate blackly as the troops advanced.

Caylen raised *Caled-draca*, its chalybeous steel awash with viscid rivulets of blood. He levelled the great blade at the approaching figure and spoke, his voice no more than a whisper. “I’ve been waiting for you, demon. You will go no farther this night.”

Oughtred Bearsark moved amongst the depleted ranks of the clansmen. “This is it, lads!” he growled. “See these bastards off, and we’ve won! They’ll flee back to the east like whipped curs! One last time ‘ere the sun comes up!”

The silent line of black-armoured titans slipped from the gloom fifty paces from the shield wall, their aphotic steel naked in the moonlight. Talus Ebonfyre stalked at their centre, and for the first time Caylen could see a faint rutilant luminescence, akin to the glow of twin embers, gleaming behind the eye slit of his great horned helm.

“It *is* witchery, then,” he seethed.

“By the gods!” hissed Brodir Finn. “The empire sends pit-fiends against us!”

“Faith, my brothers!” Caylen-Tor bellowed. “They are but men, and they will bleed like men when they meet our blades!”

The great tribal ram’s horn clarion boomed in the darkness, and with a hundred war-cries on their lips, the army of Caylen-Tor met the Iron Jackal Legion of Mytos K’unn.

Chaos reigned and shrieking carnage cast its sable shroud upon the battlefield. Wood splintered, steel shattered, flesh and bone were sundered. Time seemed to stand still, grinding to a juddering halt; the sanguineous red river of battle had seemingly ceased to flow, its harrowing course no longer linear, now distorted and devoid of any semblance of form or substance. In the midst of the eldritch throng, Caylen-Tor was dimly aware of screaming, ravening shapes rearing up before him, massing like flies upon the bloated corpses of the slain, scores of stygian spectres clawing at his flesh with envenomed talons. The mighty Three Tongued Serpent in his grasp clove ruinously through the wraiths, dealing death and carnage left and right, hewing through aphotic flesh, lancing into darkling, muculent faces. Abruptly, the familiar howl of a wolf reached Caylen's ears and the maelstrom of keening chaos fell instantly silent, its chittering cacophony at once reduced to acquiescent obeisance by that imperious, lupine decree. And then, Caylen was alone, the roil and tumult of battle which had raged and seethed all about him suddenly naught but a distant and incorporeal vagary. From the black miasma which hung before his eyes stepped an image born of fevered nightmare; a vast towering horror, horned, fanged, red eyes gleaming with ceaseless malice and pitiless hatred, a curved black sword clutched within its chitinous, taloned hand. Then, with a voice like the crashing of a stygian sea upon a benighted shore, the arch-fiend spoke.

"Caylen-Tor!"

Abruptly, Caylen awoke as if from a lotus-dream. His swords were red and a mound of ravaged legionaries lay twisted and butchered at his feet. All about him the battle raged furiously. The shield wall was broken, the armies were embroiled in pitiless combat, carnage seethed untrammeled. And before him loomed Talus Ebonfyre.

"I have sought you," Ebonfyre rasped, his voice a black malediction. "And at last, I have found you. Now, it is time for you to die."

Caylen hefted his gore-flecked blades defiantly. "I've been looking forward to this," he spat. "These are my lands, and you are not welcome here. I'm going to send your head back to your empress. Tonight, the crows pick your bones clean!"

Then, the two combatants met in the midst of the sanguineous slaughter which raged upon the battlefield. Caylen arced a thundering blow toward Ebonfyre's head, but the twisted sword of the giant was there to meet it, a shower of rutilant sparks erupting from the clash of blades. Driving his spiked gauntlet brutally into Caylen's jaw, Ebonfyre hammered his sword down against his momentarily unbalanced opponent, cleaving the Wolf-King's scale-mail cuirass. Grunting in pain and spitting bright blood, Caylen immediately drove a great lateral strike at his foe with *Caled-draca*, the powerful blow only partially parried by the giant's curved sword. With blinding speed, Caylen's second blade struck, meeting its mark with no obstruction. The honed edge of Wolf's Tooth bit deep into the section of Ebonfyre's armour where the pauldron met the gardbrace and a great many riven rings of chainmail yielded beneath the force of the strike. The dark giant bellowed in untrammeled fury, the touch of Caylen's steel having sent a searing lance of pain through his great frame.

"So, the vermin has a bite after all," seethed Ebonfyre.

"There's more where that came from," growled Caylen.

Ebonfyre laughed, the sound baleful and devoid of mirth. "Let us see."

Ebonfyre's great notched blade then proceeded to weave a pitiless web of destruction, striking time and again like the venomous tongue of some colossal adamantine serpent. Before the fearful force of this ceaseless onslaught, Caylen was driven slowly and inexorably back. Gouts of blood began to escape from the score of furrows which the giant's blade was etching into his armour and flesh, and yet the Wolf-King steadfastly refused to falter before the malefic storm of preternatural steel. Barely parrying a tremendous lateral strike, Caylen desperately riposted with Wolf's Tooth, but the gleaming blade was easily knocked aside by the fiend's twisted sword. The clamour of the embattled blades was deafening, each strike, parry and riposte shrieking a resounding war-song of grinding pattern-welded disharmony. Roaring an ireful oath, Ebonfyre delivered another devastating blow and in a blazing corona of cerulean sparks, the glyph-scored blade of *Caled-draca* was shattered into a thousand silver shards, the thunderous impact breaking the bone of Caylen's forearm and driving him abruptly to his knees. With a hoary malediction upon his tongue, Ebonfyre swept his sword back to deliver a final merciless blow, but at that instant a slender throwing knife suddenly embedded itself between the joint of his blood-stained couter and rerebrace, sundering the chainmail beneath the argent plates. Ebonfyre bellowed in pain, grasping the knife and tearing it free. The Wolf-King smiled mirthlessly as he recognized one of Wulfric Oakenbrand's unerring blades. Seizing the opportunity, Caylen brandished Wolf's Tooth, driving all his rapidly fading strength behind a desperate, ruinous thrust. The sword pierced the giant's engraved steel fauld with a resounding crack, gelid ichor erupting forth to spatter the spell-forged blade. Ebonfyre shrieked in raw agony and fury, the terrifying sound chilling the blood of all who heard it upon the battlefield. Dragging his sword quickly clear of his foe and scrambling to his feet, Caylen followed the strike with another, but Ebonfyre's serrated blade parried the blow and a vicious kick sent the Wolf-King reeling, his weapon spinning from his grasp. Swiftly, Ebonfyre advanced on his dazed opponent, raising his jackal-blade for another dire attack.

"Now you die, savage!"

Suddenly, in a flash of silver and crimson, a huge axe blade arced from the gloom and wrought a great ragged cleft in the giant's breastplate. Ebonfyre reeled backwards several paces as Oughtred Bearsark loomed before him, his great battle-axe dripping with gore and brain-matter.

"Now you owe me a keg of ale, Wolf-King," Oughtred bellowed, bringing his axe down with thunderous force upon Ebonfyre's horned helm. The blow sheared off one of the helmet's gnarled ram's horn adornments and the ensuing strike clove neatly through the giant's right pauldron, scattering broken chainmail rings to the war-churned heather. Bright blood erupted from Ebonfyre's riven shoulder and Oughtred arced another strike toward his foe's armoured neck, seeking to hew the fiend's head from his body. But with a bestial growl, Ebonfyre's gauntlet lashed out and grasped the axe haft in a vice grip, stopping its arc and holding it fast.

"Gods curse your black sorcery!" spat Oughtred contemptuously.

Snarling, Ebonfyre swept his curved sword out in a wild blow which clove into Oughtred's cuirass and sent the red-bearded clansman crashing heavily to the blood-sodden earth. Dropping the ensanguined axe, Ebonfyre shrieked in primal rage and hefted his great jackal-sword to the moon-swathed sky. With blood bubbling in his throat, the ireful giant spun to face Caylen-Tor once more.

But now the Wolf-King stood before him, the shattered hilt of *Caled-draca* in his hand, his face a mask of ferine fury in the pale moonlight.

"It is over," Caylen growled. With pitiless force, he drove the broken blade of *Caled-draca* into Ebonfyre's chest, the razor-sharp shards punching cleanly through the ravaged plate armour. The broken tribal sword hewed through metal and bone, becoming embedded to its serpentine crossguard. Gasping for breath, Ebonfyre stumbled back three paces, his hand curling around the hilt jutting from his chest, his own curved blade wavering. Gathering up Oughtred's fallen axe, Caylen strode forward, and summoning all his faltering might he swept the imbrued weapon at his foe. The axe bit deep into Ebonfyre's cuirass, opening a gaping fissure from which blood and viscera spilled forth. Acrid smoke billowed from the terrible wound and with a sibilant curse, Talus Ebonfyre fell at last to his knees, his curved jackal sword falling from his grasp.

"This ends here," hissed Caylen, raising the reddened axe reverentially for the deathblow.

Ebonfyre uttered a cruel and mirthless laugh. "Zyrashana," he seethed. "Curse your ophidian soul!"

The dark giant bowed his head and let his horned helm fall to the heather. Slowly, he looked up at Caylen-Tor, his cruelly regal countenance unwavering, his eyes still aglow with a fathomless inner radiance. "Pitiful king of savages," he rasped gutturally. "You have won naught. Your rule is like mist upon the sea. Your mongrel people shall fade from memory. You shall be dethroned and your insignificant kingdom shall fall."

Caylen's grey eyes narrowed. "Mayhap," he growled. "But not this night." And with that, he swept the great axe at the head of Talus Ebonfyre. The blade clove through the neck of the dark giant, an iron prow rending a sea of bone and sinew. A heartbeat later, the head of Ebonfyre toppled from his body and fell to the earth, rolling to a stop at Caylen's feet. The kneeling corpse remained unmoving, a voluminous red tide of blood issuing forth from the cloven neck. Suddenly, a nebulous cloud rose from the seeping stump and swiftly coalesced into a pulsating mass of black mist. Two rutilant orbs of crimson fire were faintly visible within the depths of the writhing vapour and for a long moment the tenebrous eidolon seemed to stare balefully at Caylen, silently seething with a maleficent hatred. Then the wraith-cloud darted away into the stygian sky to be swallowed by the night.

Slowly, painfully, and with a great numbing weariness beginning to snake through his muscles like poison, Caylen-Tor dropped the bloodied axe and picked up the severed head of Talus Ebonfyre. Then he crouched to the giant's body and dragged free the hilt of *Caled-draca,* securing the ruined blade at his belt. Scant seconds later, he retrieved Wolf's Tooth from the red heather and rammed it home into its scabbard.

"Well fought, Wolf-King," came a faint voice from the gloom.

Caylen spun and staggered to the prone form of Oughtred Bearsark, kneeling to survey the clansman's wounds.

"I'll live," Oughtred rasped. "Go now. Finish it."

Caylen nodded and rose, moving to where one of the standards of the imperial army lay trampled upon the heather. Taking up the banner, he spied a lone imperial steed, its eyes white with fear, its ears flat against its skull. Calming the lathered beast, he secured the imperial banner in the saddle's cinch strap and vaulted to its broad back. The horse reared once, then yielded to Caylen's control. Grimacing with the pain which coursed through his broken arm, Caylen gripped the rawhide reins, and with his free hand lifted Ebonfyre's severed head high.

"It is done!" he bellowed. "The Witch-Queen's champion is dead!"

Caylen spurred the horse on to a gallop across the battlefield where sporadic skirmishes between Iron Jackal legionaries and clansmen were still raging. The surviving imperial troops gaped at the grisly trophy in Caylen's hand. The clansmen roared in triumph as their king proclaimed victory.

Dragging his shortsword clear of an imperial corpse, Wulfric called out to the surrounding tribesmen. "Victory! All hail Caylen-Tor!"

The chant was taken up by the clansmen as the depleted legionaries, their morale shattered, disengaged and wearily threw down their weapons.

Caylen's steed cantered to the centre of the battlefield and he dislodged the imperial banner from his saddle, hurling it to the blood-churned earth.

"My people!" thundered Caylen-Tor. "Wolves of the north, raise thine steel to the skies! Revel in the pride of your wounds! Let our victory-song ride the winds of this blood-gorged eve! For on this night of red swords, we have wrought a legend, forged in the fires of our rage, and tempered with the spilled blood of the slain!"

"By all the gods," whispered Wulfric. "We've actually done it!"

And the triumphant chants of the clansmen echoed the length and breadth of Blackhelm Vale.

* * *

The first light of dawn had begun to illumine the valley as Caylen and Wulfric traversed the corpse-mounds. Ravaged bodies littered the battlefield and already the crows and worms were feeding.

"Will Oughtred survive?" growled Caylen as he gazed forlornly at the cloven corpses of the many clansmen strewn about the heather.

"Most probably," Wulfric replied. "The wound is deep, but the surgeons say it will heal, as long as infection does not take hold. How is your arm?"

"I too will live," muttered Caylen, glancing at his myriad wounds. The blood of the fray still clung to him, now dark and crusted. "I want a count of the slain. The names of all our dead. We will leave none behind. But the foe may stay as they lay."

"It shall be so."

"And you, wolfshead?" asked Caylen. "What scars will you bear?"

Wulfric prodded his midriff and winced as the pain of two broken ribs lanced through him. "I've suffered worse. And you know, old Grimm suffered nary a scratch in the battle. I swear that hoary bugger's immortal!"

"Thank the gods," smirked Caylen. "That will spare me the lash of my wife's tongue, at least!"

A leaden silence ensued, punctuated only by the cries of the wounded as they were tended to by field surgeons and the harsh voices of crows as they hovered blackly about the slain.

"Was it worth it?" Wulfric asked suddenly.

Caylen fixed him with a baleful stare. "The foe has been driven back. I knew the price would be high. I was prepared to pay it."

"And pay it we did," breathed Wulfric.

A solemn expression crossed Caylen's face. "Grist for the mill of regal ambition," he whispered.

"What was that?"

"A truth I once learned," sighed Caylen. "Concerning the hubris of kings."

"Woeful is the burden of power," said Wulfric. "Yet it has not corrupted you, as it would a lesser man. You're no tyrant. You did what was required."

Caylen's brow furrowed as he stared at the ravaged body of an Iron Jackal legionary sprawled upon the heather. "My memory of the final clash is clouded."

Wulfric frowned, recalling the closing moments of the battle. "Our shield wall was breached and the Iron Jackal Legion had engaged our *ber-serkr* reavers. By the gods, I've never seen such sublime carnage as that! And you... you fought with the strength of twenty. Every one of your strokes was a killing stroke. You were pitiless... like a war-god from the sagas of old. You clove through the Iron Jackal like a scythe at harvest. Then, Ebonfyre found you in the fray."

Caylen sighed wearily. "That, I remember."

"It was over when you slew that vile devil," said Wulfric. "The legion broke, its spirit crushed. And yet, even at the end the foe still outnumbered us. Had they not disengaged, they could still have won."

"No," enounced Caylen grimly. "With their shamans slain, the Witch-Queen's host fought without the aid of black sorcery. In the end, it came down to a test of faith and steel. And in that test, we prevailed."

Wulfric nodded silently.

Suddenly, Drogha Tul emerged from the fading shadows to stand before Caylen-Tor. "The blade is broken," the aged man rasped.

"It will be reforged," gnarred Caylen, dragging the shattered remnants of *Caled-draca* from its scabbard.

"Yes, but it will never again be wielded by you, Caylen-Tor. Strange bedfellows do wolves and serpents make. Give me the hilt."

A sudden anger flared within Caylen's grey eyes and he held the jagged tip of the broken steel to Drogha Tul's throat. "No more cryptic words, old man. Speak plainly, for my patience is spent."

The old shaman did not move, and a crooked smile slowly creased his rugose features. "The Three Tongued Serpent shall be given up to the embrace of the waters. There, in the deeps of the sylvan pools shall it be reforged. Stronger, keener, more deadly shall the blade become. Destined for the hand of your progeny, this sword is. Now, give it to me."

Caylen eyed the ruined hilt for a moment before thrusting it into Tul's grasp with such force that the shaman was almost knocked from his feet. "I grow weary of your games, old one. You would do well to avoid me for a while."

Tul concealed the weapon within the folds of his darksome cloak and disappeared silently into the dawn mist.

Brodir Finn and two bloodied clansmen then moved before Caylen, flanking a captured imperial officer whose face was battered and swollen. One of the clansmen held the sundered imperial banner which Caylen had seized during the battle and the other carried a round bundle of sackcloth which was stained with dried blood.

"Hail, great Tor," said Brodir. "As you instructed, we have seized one of the imperial heralds."

The beaten man was thrust forward, and he gazed trembling at the towering figure of the Wolf-King looming before him.

"You speak the Northern dialects, I assume?" rumbled Caylen.

"I know your primitive tongue, and all the other tongues of the barbaricum," the herald sneered.

"Good," said Caylen. "That alone has saved your outlander hide this night. Now hearken to me, dog. I'm giving you a few things to take back home to your queen." At Caylen's signal, the clansman duly proffered the sundered banner to the herald. "This is one of them. The sigil of her army. Broken, routed, defeated."

The herald nervously accepted the tattered standard, his knuckles white as he clutched it tightly to his chest.

"And this," growled Caylen, taking the bloodied sackcloth from the second clansman. "She may recognize the object which rests within."

Caylen threw the stained bundle at the herald, who only barely caught it in his trembling hands.

"Also, relay unto her these words," hissed Caylen, leaning close to the man's ashen face. "If ever again she deigns to strike against my people, the slaughter this night will seem as naught compared to the havoc I shall visit upon her then."

The herald grudgingly nodded his understanding.

"Now, get the hell out of my realm!" thundered Caylen as the two clansmen dragged the man roughly away.

Brodir Finn smiled coldly. "You were right, Wolf-King. We were destined to know victory here."

"United, we are strong," said Caylen somberly.

"Ah, but unity is a fleeting thing, like mist at the break of dawn," said Brodir, moving away to where his tribesmen waited. "But mayhap the other chieftains will come to regret their refusal to fight with you. We shall yet see what the Web of Wyrd has in store for the Nine Clans."

Alone again, Caylen and Wulfric watched the sun slowly rise from behind the eastern slope of the valley. It was the colour of blood.

"The Battle of Blackhelm Vale," mused Wulfric. "A tale for the skalds to tell around the hearth-fires, I think."

"Aye," replied Caylen, turning grimly to the west. "The bards will sing of this battle. And for a time, the clans will remember the names of the honoured dead and give thanks for the freedom which was safeguarded by their noble sacrifice. But in a thousand years those names will be forgotten and all that history will recall is that here an empire fell before the resolve of greater men."

When news of the rout at Blackhelm Vale reached the Imperial capital of Mytos K'unn, Zyrashana's hold on power inexorably waned. Her many acolytes and courtiers, no longer held in thrall by the ever-present threat of the Imperial army, plotted against their empress, until ultimately Zyrashana was driven from the royal palace by the captains of her own personal guard, her throne duly seized by an ambitious vizier loyal to the former ruler King Ahaziah. Her spells of regal dominance broken, the dethroned empress Zyrashana fled to the eastern satrapies with a small entourage, including her three daughters and one son. At length, the conquered territories regained their sovereignty and the First Great Empire of Mytos K'unn was no more.

Following his victory, Caylen-Tor enjoyed a modicum of civil contentment within his kingdom. However, the grand tribal alliance remained at its heart a fragile and tenuous entity and exactly two years after the defence of Blackhelm Vale, following a disastrous harvest and a foiled assassination plot against the king, five of the nine tribes seceded from the union, declaring their independence once more. A period of bitter intertribal warfare ensued, and although Caylen-Tor ultimately gave up the mantle of Over-King, his adventures were far from over...

Book III: The King Beneath the Mountain of Fire

Following the dissolution of the tribal alliance, Caylen retained the chieftainship of the Wolf Clan and endured years of internecine conflict, prevailing in numerous tribal civil wars and firmly establishing the People of the Wolf as the mightiest of all the Old Clans. At length, a tenuous peace was brokered throughout the territories and the balance of power remained relatively stable. And yet, the old wanderlust still burned within the Wolf of the North's heart and the lure of adventure ultimately proved too great to resist. And so, Caylen gathered a crew of grim-eyed reavers from amongst the northern clans, and each spring they embarked upon a voyage of plunder and piracy, sailing the redoubtable dragonship *White Wolf* the length and breadth of their tribal homeland's mighty rivers and prowling the great ice-bound sea, then traversing the glacial waterways of the Snow Kingdoms to reach the perilous Bay of Serpents and the well-travelled route to the southern oceans in their pitiless hunt for treasure-laden prey. And no vessel that sailed the Nine Seas, not merchant sloop nor martial warship, was safe from the ravening blades of the Wolf-King's northern reavers…

Chapter I
The Isle of Black Sands

Caylen vaulted over the longship's gunwale and planted his feet firmly in the jet-black, basalt sand of the desolate beach. He was clad in a golden scale-mail hauberk, dark leather breeches and buckskin boots. Studded leather vambraces bound his forearms and a large wolfskin cloak was draped about his broad shoulders, secured by a single knotwork-encarved pauldron crafted from the hide of a bull tundra-mammoth. Scabbarded at his waist was his well-worn broadsword Wolf's Tooth, and in his calloused hand he bore a long-hafted battle-axe which sported an elaborate wolf's head motif engraved into the chalybeous steel of its great curved blade. Caylen's blond hair fell unfettered to his shoulders and a voluminous, grey-flecked beard adorned his scarred and weathered face.

"What a blighted isle this is," the clansman muttered sullenly, striding farther along the stygian shore to survey the terrain of the grim atoll to which his perilous voyage had borne him. The black sand stretched for some fifty yards before eventually yielding to an expanse of low hills strewn with jagged volcanic rocks, while in the distance loomed a range of colossal atramentous mountains, their peaks shrouded in cinereous mist. Turning his gaze skyward, Caylen scowled at the endless vault of brooding grey clouds which all but obscured the mid-morning sun. Scant seconds later, the first flakes of snow began to fall from the sombre heavens.

The sound of men wading ashore behind him abruptly summoned Caylen from his solemn ruminations. He turned slowly and cast an appraising glance at his great drakkar *White Wolf,* which was drawn up on the sloping black beach. The shallow-keeled ship was sixty-five feet long and boasted sixteen oar-ports on either side of its slender hull. The vessel was expertly crafted of ash and oak and an array of colourful shields adorned the rack along its top strake. The ship's vast, storm-battered sail was furled and the lofty mast and seal-skin ropes groaned faintly in the icy breeze. The prow was ornamented with an intricate figurehead carved of pinewood and fashioned in the form of a dire-wolf's toothsome, snarling head. As the fearsome effigy suggested, the great ship was a pitiless predator which had prowled the myriad seas for half a decade, preying upon the merchant sloops and military triremes of every kingdom of the antediluvian world which dared boast a naval presence upon the charted oceans. It was a grim fact known by every mariner, privateer and pirate from the jarldoms of the north to the satrapies of the south that to be hunted by the *White Wolf* upon the open seas was to face naught but death and red ruin.

A burly, grey-bearded man clad in a chainmail hauberk and a long woollen cloak moved laboriously up the beach to stand alongside Caylen. "Thank the gods we made it through that damned storm!"

Caylen frowned. "It was raw courage and well-honed skill that saw us through that tempest, Eirik. The work of men, not gods."

"And yet I'll wager you still court divine favour, great Tor."

"Do not call me that," Caylen growled. "The alliance is dead. I am king no longer."

Eirik smiled wearily. "To your tribal brothers, you will always be the Wolf-King."

Caylen sighed. "Stay with the ship, old friend. If I do not return by dawn two days hence, sail her back to Ulfheim. Make sure the skalds sing the tales of our deeds around the hearth-fires."

"We'll not set sail without you," grumbled Eirik.

"Heed my words," said Caylen, clasping the older man's shoulder firmly. "Be wary and guard the camp well, for we know not what manner of men or beasts haunt this cursed island."

Eirik nodded. "Good hunting, *Caylen-Tor*," he said as he trudged despondently back to the beached longship.

"Guthlac!" barked Caylen, turning to a group of warriors assembled by the shoreline. “Prepare the scouting party. We’re going inland.”

In response to Caylen’s command, a stocky, russet-bearded man armoured in a hardened leather cuirass signalled to three heavily armed reavers to follow him and strode briskly to Caylen’s side.

“What can we expect, Wolfclan?” asked Guthlac, donning an iron helmet with an intricately embossed eye-guard and securing his longsword in its leather scabbard.

“Dire peril and certain death, I should think,” replied Caylen, a gleam in his eye.

“The usual, then,” said Guthlac mordantly. “In truth, I still don’t like the notion of relying on that old mariner’s lotus-addled visions.”

Caylen nodded in agreement. “I scarcely trust Captain Aracus. But if there’s any truth to the legend of that jewelled city he’s been ranting about, I’m willing to risk the search.”

“Do you recall his tales of the southern continent? He claims he sailed for six weeks on a blood red sea and discovered an island of stone giants.”

Caylen produced a scrap of vellum parchment from a pouch at his belt and studied the crude map which had been etched into its yellowed surface. “And yet his charts have guided us here. To a mist-shrouded isle in the middle of a treacherous, ice-bound ocean.”

Guthlac scowled. “My guess is it’s all cryptic nonsense and mummery. The ravings of a madman.”

“Mayhap,” said Caylen, tucking the parchment back into his belt. “The old goat excels at that. He treats his wine cup like a scrying pool.”

“Well, I doubt this forlorn rock will offer up much of interest,” muttered Guthlac.

Caylen’s grey eyes narrowed. “We shall see.”

* * *

For an hour the party trekked in solemn silence, eventually cresting a low rise and emerging onto a great expanse of tundra which stretched for many hundreds of yards before them. The snow had begun to fall heavily and an icy wind swept in from the north, biting pitilessly through the men's clothing and armour. Shielding his eyes against the whirling flurries, Caylen peered out across the niveous plateau at the black mountain range which continued to loom ever closer with each onerous mile they traversed. Then he muttered an oath and pulled his wolfskin cloak closer about his heavily muscled frame.

"Wolfclan," came the low voice of Guthlac at his flank.

Caylen turned to see the swordsman staring intently off to the west, squinting through the amorphous veil of white which had all too swiftly engulfed the travellers on their journey.

"What is it?"

"That snow drift," rumbled Guthlac, a note of grave concern in his tone. "Why is it moving towards us?"

Caylen followed his companion's gaze, struggling to perceive a vague, dun-white shape which was all but obscured by the mounting blizzard. For several moments he stared fixedly at the nebulous apparition, his brow furrowing as it appeared to draw inexorably nearer. A heartbeat later, he hefted his frost-etched axe and bellowed furiously to his comrades. "Ice troll!"

The great beast barrelled into the armed men with a guttural howl of primal fury, its cruelly curved talons slashing murderously. The creature stood seven feet tall and was covered by a shaggy coat of matted white fur beneath which patches of pale blue skin were visible across its enormously muscled chest. Its slavering maw was studded with broad yellow fangs and its tiny eyes gleamed with feral rage. One of the reavers fell instantly beneath a pitiless blow from the troll's colossal hand, the man's blood spattering the virgin snow in a vivid blossom of crimson. Caylen barely evaded another sweep of the creature's reddened claws, diving desperately to the frozen earth as the beast lumbered past him.

"Surround the fiend!" thundered Caylen. "Teach it to fear your blades, wolves of the sea!"

Guthlac ducked lithely beneath a furious swipe of the troll's fist as the remaining reavers formed a wide ring around their savage foe, swords poised.

"Bring the devil down!" bellowed Caylen as he hefted his axe and charged into the fray. Instantly, the troll spun to face him, its teeth bared in a ferocious rictus grin. Raising its great sinewy limbs, the creature surged forward, intent on shattering Caylen's skull with merciless blows from its adamantine fists. But the Wolf-King's axe bit deep, opening a gaping red furrow in the beast's abdomen as it lurched forward. Uttering an ear-splitting howl of pain and rage, the troll lashed out with its curved talons, rending Caylen's scale-mail cuirass and scattering shards of burnished metal to the snow. Reeling backwards momentarily, Caylen raised his bloodied axe and smiled mirthlessly. "Never sweet, the kiss of cold steel," he hissed.

Instantly, the reavers vaulted forward to press the attack, their blades hacking into the wounded beast's alabastrine hide. The troll fell swiftly before the merciless onslaught of swords and axes, crumpling to the snow whereupon a final blow from Guthlac's longsword finally brought the desperate battle to a sanguineous close.

"It's been a while since I faced a troll," Caylen said, unbuckling his riven cuirass and casting it to the snow beside the fallen beast. "I had nearly forgotten the joy of such a clash!"

"Hrolf found no joy in it," Guthlac muttered, moving to the body of their fallen comrade.

"No, he did not," said Caylen grimly. "But he died in battle, and a warrior can ask for no more. Gather stones and we shall bury him as best we can in this frozen earth, so that his body is not defiled by such scavengers as may prowl this atoll."

Silently, the men set about their solemn task. The snow had ceased to fall and yet the faint orb of the sun still cast scant little light and warmth from behind the impenetrable veil of grey which enshrouded the hiemal sky.

Caylen silently adjusted his wolfskin cloak about his unadorned frame. His broad shoulders were scored with azure knotwork tattoos and his scarred and powerfully muscled chest heaved as he vigorously inhaled the icy air.

Guthlac moved to stand at his side. "Aren't you cold?"

"I am never cold," grinned Caylen. "I'm the Wolf of the North."

Guthlac smirked. "Of that I'm sure. Do we press on, or return to the ship?"

"Those black mountains yonder remain our destination. We'll decide our path when we stand in their shadow."

Guthlac nodded sombrely. "What if the captain's tale proves true? What if there is a dragon's hoard of gems beyond those peaks?

Caylen's grey eyes sparkled. "Then we sail home with enough loot to rival the golden princes of the east!"

"We're more likely to end up as troll-fodder," sighed Guthlac.

Caylen frowned and cast his gaze at the black peaks which loomed beyond the pearlescent expanse of unbroken snow. "Enough talk! We've precious few hours of sunlight left to us. We must not tarry here!"

And without a backward glance, the armed men resumed their solemn march towards the distant, shadowed mountains.

Chapter II
The Caverns of Ice and Shadow

At length, Caylen and the scouting party found themselves standing before the entrance to a colossal cave hewn into the jagged face of the bituminous mountain. Beyond the aperture gleamed a coruscant cavern of ice which ultimately yielded its glimmering radiance to a stygian void of deep and impenetrable shadow. The crude arch of the cave's mouth boasted a series of strange sigils which had been carved into the surface of the black rock, although the language represented by the eldritch glyphs was as much a mystery to the assembled men as the unfathomably ancient hands which had surely etched them.

"Who's going in first?" hissed Guthlac, his breath billowing from his lips in a dense cloud.

Caylen grinned. "The honour shall be mine." And with that, he strode boldly across the frozen threshold and into the lambent grotto.

"I'm at your back," muttered Guthlac.

"Keep watch for more of those shaggy brutes," Caylen called to the mariners as they followed him warily into cave's embrace.

Guthlac laughed mirthlessly. "What do you think I've been doing for the past hour?"

The cavern's icy ceiling was studded with an array of slender, gleaming stalactites which imparted to the men the disquieting sensation that they were entering the toothsome maw of some colossal beast from primeval myth. The walls appeared strangely smooth, akin to polished glass, and it seemed to Caylen that they were gently aglow with a faint azure luminescence. For many pensive moments the reavers traversed the lucent cave in taut silence, their weapons at the ready, until at length they stood before an asperous barrier of fissured stone which boasted the rough-hewn entrances to two shadowed tunnels.

"Which path do we take?" whispered Guthlac, peering into the tenebrous darkness beyond the twin passageways.

In response, Caylen stepped warily across the threshold of the left-hand tunnel. Instantly, the silence was shattered by a grinding, clamorous din as the rimy stone abruptly crumbled beneath his feet. For what seemed an interminably lengthy span of time, Caylen tumbled arduously down a pitch black, ice-encrusted shaft, the jagged edges of the channel riving a score of shallow lacerations into his flesh. Finally, he struck level ground with a bone-jarring impact and clambered furiously to his feet, his axe still clutched firmly in his bloodied hands. Uttering a litany of curses, Caylen swiftly surveyed the chamber into which he had so onerously emerged. The grotto appeared akin to the sections of the cavern he had thus far explored, illumined by an identical sapphirean glow and glazed with walls of smooth, scintillant ice. The only marked difference that he could discern was that the frigid, rocky floor of this subterrane was littered with an array of sundered bones and skulls of varying sizes; evidently the fragmentary skeletal remnants of creatures both animal and vaguely human in origin. With a shudder not wholly induced by his icy environs, Caylen instantly realized that he was standing amidst the jagged, charnel vestiges of some ravenous beast's savage repast.

"Gods curse my ill luck," the clansman hissed, his fingers brushing the hammer-shaped amulet which encircled his bull-neck. "It's the bloody larder!"

A low, ferine growl suddenly reverberated at his back and Caylen slowly turned to behold a hulking ice troll crouched not twelve feet from his position. With a grotesque leer, the sinewy, hirsute creature rose languorously to its full height, its eyes sparkling balefully in the grotto's wan light. In its great clawed hand, the troll grasped a rudimentary club fashioned from the cracked and hoary thigh bone of some massive, primordial animal. With a cold smile, Caylen unbuckled his wolfskin cloak and let it fall to the cave floor before reverentially hefting his glimmering axe.

"So be it, devil," he rumbled. "Let us test our mettle."

The troll uttered a blood-chilling howl and charged forward, its great osseous mace held high. Still smiling, Caylen stood his ground and raised his axe to parry the tremendous blow, the resultant clash splintering the bone club into a thousand jagged shards. Vaulting lithely from the beast's path, Caylen spun and brandished his rune-etched steel.

"Just like a troll," he spat. "Bringing a bone to an axe fight!"

Furiously and with a speed belying its great size, the beast surged forward, its yellow fangs bared. Instantly, Caylen's axe swept forth, opening a grievous furrow in the troll's scabrous hide. Dark blood erupted from the wound, spattering the cavern floor like a sanguineous mosaic. But before Caylen could deliver another blow, the creature was upon him, its feculent claws sinking deep into his thews and scoring his flesh. With a guttural roar, the troll then dragged Caylen forward and hurled him viciously against the frozen wall, the impact driving the wind painfully from the clansman's lungs and sending his axe spinning from his grasp. A heartbeat later, the beast's gnarled fingers encircled Caylen's throat, lifting him from his feet in a crushing, vice-like grip. Through a haze of pain, Caylen felt the troll's hot and noisome spittle splash against his face and found himself staring into the creature's malefic eyes, now glimmering mere inches from his own. Gasping for breath, he scrabbled in vain for the hilt of the broadsword at his belt as the troll's iron grasp tightened inexorably. In desperation, the clansman drew back his fist and drove his scarred and salt-coarsened knuckles hard into the bridge of the creature's rugous nose. There came a resounding crack and with a stertorous grunt the troll abruptly released its hold, staggering blindly backwards in a paroxysm of pain. Gratefully filling his lungs with a draught of icy air, Caylen leaped clear of the beast's shadow and swiftly dragged Wolf's Tooth from its leathern scabbard.

"Now, let us finish this," he hissed, facing his towering adversary once more.

Its face a troglodytic mask of sheer untrammelled hatred, the troll uttered a thunderous roar and lunged forward with renewed ferocity. The beast's huge hand swept forth in a savage arc which gouged a quintet of red furrows into Caylen's chest, but the clansman's glyph-scored steel was swift to answer the blow and the sword duly clove through sinew and bone to sever the troll's right arm cleanly below the elbow. A viscid torrent of blood spattered Caylen's face and torso as the beast's keening howl reverberated throughout the icy chamber. Dropping instantly to one knee, Caylen thrust Wolf's Tooth upward with all his might, piercing the troll's fibrous abdomen and embedding the blade to its hilt. With a final sepulchral growl, the hulking creature's legs buckled and Caylen dragged his crimson blade free as the great beast slumped lifeless to the rimy floor of the grotto. Regaining his feet, Caylen slowly wiped his befouled blade clean on the fallen troll's shaggy hide before returning it to its scabbard. Then, he recovered his axe and cloak from where they lay within the cavern and secured his wolfskin mantle once more about his bloodied shoulders.

A sudden commotion from the opposite side of the cavern caused Caylen to turn and with a sardonic smile he beheld Guthlac and the remaining mariners emerging hastily from a narrow, partially concealed passageway. Their weapons poised, the reavers glanced tensely about the chamber.

"You missed the battle," growled Caylen.

Guthlac scabbarded his blade and strode to Caylen's side, noting the bloodied body of the troll. "And you chose the wrong tunnel."

Caylen scowled. "No, I simply found a more direct route."

"What now, *Caylen Troll's Bane*?" asked Guthlac with a wry grin.

Caylen gestured to a large rough-hewn arch at the grotto's northern edge which appeared to lead to another section of the icy cave. "I'll wager that's the path out of this cursed place."

"Aye," said Guthlac. "But shall we not rest? The sun has surely set out there, and I've no wish to traverse this isle at night."

Caylen nodded, glancing thoughtfully about the pellucid cavern. The remnants of a huge, partially devoured aurochs lay upon the rocky floor amidst an array of cracked and heavily gnawed bones. Smiling, he called to a flaxen-haired mariner who stood by the passageway's threshold. "Aelfric! Ready your flint and tinder. That beast looks fresh, so let us find something in this damned cavern that burns and we'll make haste with a fire. And then by the gods, we'll fill our bellies like we're back at my long-hall in Ulfheim!"

* * *

Caylen stood upon a snow-kissed plateau beneath a glowering, horned moon. Tight in his grasp was the broken sword Caleddraca, *the mighty tribal blade that had shattered during the final stages of the cataclysmic clash at Blackhelm Vale some seven years past. All about him lay the desolate ruins of an ancient, cyclopean shrine, its cracked pillars and sundered walls strewn across the frosty plain like the forlorn bones of some hoary, time-lost colossus. With a start, Caylen realized that a massive white wolf was crouched at his side, its great silvern shoulders nigh on level with his own. The beast's azure eyes glimmered in the moonlight and its mighty muscles rippled beneath its eburnean fur. The huge wolf suddenly uttered a deep, ferine growl and Caylen followed its lupine gaze to see a towering figure stalking toward him from the depths of the icy shadows. The warrior was clad entirely in chitinous black armour and crowned with a fearsome full helm which sported two great downward curving horns. In its spiked gauntlets, the steel eidolon grasped a vast, cruelly curved greatsword etched with lambent arcane glyphs. Raising his ruined blade, Caylen swiftly adopted a fighting stance and readied himself for battle. The ar-*

moured figure closed to a scant ten paces distant and then abruptly halted, driving its sword deep into the frozen ground. As Caylen watched in rapt fascination, the black-clad giant slowly removed its helmet. The man's countenance was cruel, his youthful features chiselled and aquiline. His skin was pallid, his hair was the colour of alabaster and his eyes shone with a faint viridescent light. He fixed Caylen with a baleful gaze and spoke, his voice deep and sepulchral. "Look upon me Wolf-King, for I am the spawn of Zyrashana the Witch-Queen... I am the son of Talus Ebonfyre. Know that I have vowed vengeance upon you and your progeny. Beware, for you have incurred my wrath and I am the bane of men and the breaker of kings."

Caylen smiled coldly. "The son of Ebonfyre, are you? I encountered your father but once, lad. He lost his head over our meeting, if I recall."

The warrior's thin lips curled in an invidious sneer and he swiftly donned his helmet and took up his curved sword once more. "Mark me on this, king of savages. I shall bring woe and red ruin unto you and your line. Await my coming when the sun burns black and know that death follows in my wake."

The dire-wolf at Caylen's side bared its great ivory fangs and growled once more, its azure eyes narrowing malefically. High above, a ring of rutilant flame abruptly flared about the perimeter of the moon and the face of the lambent sphere swiftly became obscured by a shroud of bituminous black. Instantly, the niveous vista was engulfed by a mantle of deep, stygian shadow...

Caylen awoke with a jolt upon the rimy floor of the cavern and threw off his wolfskin cloak, a vexed expression on his face.

Guthlac swiftly approached from the opposite side of the guttering fire and proffered him a leather costrel filled with mead. "Wolfclan! It's your watch. By my reckoning, dawn breaks within the hour."

"That dream was passing strange," muttered Caylen as he slowly clambered to his feet and took a long draught from the costrel. "Mayhap the meat on that carcass was rotten after all."

"Either that or your wounds have brought on a fever," said Guthlac mordantly. "What did the dreamscape show you?"

Caylen sighed wearily. "A shadow from the past, or a vision of the future. The son of Zyrashana the Witch-Queen has evidently sworn vengeance against my progeny."

"Zyrashana!" exclaimed Guthlac. "I thought we'd heard the last of her after our victory at Blackhelm Vale!"

"As did I. Remind me to speak with Drogha Tul about it when next we return to my hearth."

"Ah, that old wizard's a wily one," said Guthlac. "I swear he'll outlive all of us, and he must have seen a hundred winters already!"

Caylen's brow furrowed. "Aye, that damned shaman haunts the halls of Ulfheim like a shadow, ceaselessly casting the runes of divination. He's convinced that my children are destined to fulfil some grand tribal prophecy. He swears that they were born to safeguard the clans against some nameless, cryptic evil yet to reveal itself."

"And do you believe that?" asked Guthlac with a wry smile.

Caylen shrugged and gathered up his axe. "I've heard stranger prophecies. Now, wake the others. We're pressing on, for I grow weary of this thrice-cursed icy tomb!"

Chapter III
Into the Savage Realm

Caylen and the men of the *White Wolf* emerged briskly from the cavern's jagged mouth and clambered forth onto a great promontory strewn with countless fragments of basaltic stone. The temperature had ascended steadily during their trek through the labyrinthine depths of the mountain, and the mantle of ice which had persistently veiled the shadowed tunnels had gradually receded until ultimately nothing but dry, unclad rock prevailed. As the reavers cleared the threshold of the grotto they were astonished to find that the brooding grey sky which had initially greeted them upon their landfall had at some point during their journey yielded to a cloudless vista of unbroken blue set with a dazzling golden sun which now glowered balefully down upon them like a great cyclopean eye. Moving guardedly to the edge of the broad cliff, Caylen and his companions collectively gaped in silent wonder at the enthralling spectacle now arrayed before them. Far below stretched the verdant expanse of a colossal jungle, which to the raven-keen eyes of the mariners seemed to resemble nothing less than the churning surface of a vast, viridescent sea. For countless miles the primeval morass spanned the atoll's hidden interior, reaching ceaselessly into the mist-shrouded distance until at last it met the great palisade of the black mountains which encircled the forest like the cloud-capped walls of a mighty, unassailable fortress. At the westernmost point of the jungle vista, a single blackened peak jutted imperiously from the teeming green depths, its cratered crown billowing great plumes of dense, white smoke.

"By the gods!" hissed Guthlac. "A frozen wasteland on one side of the mountains and a torrid wilderness on the other! This smacks of sorcery, without a doubt!"

Caylen nodded solemnly. "Captain Aracus did not speak of such a place, nor does his map mark anything beyond the caves. But if that forest hides a jewelled city, I'm fain to search its shadowed depths!"

"And just how deep shall we delve?" asked Guthlac guardedly.

"We'll scout a league, mayhap two," replied Caylen. "Then hasten back to the ship, to return with a full raiding party on the morrow."

"I concur," muttered Guthlac. "The more blades we bring on this expedition, the bolder I'll feel!"

Taking the vanguard, Caylen cautiously began to descend a narrow, scree-strewn trail which wound its way precariously down the eastern edge of the promontory, his companions close on his heels. The reavers had travelled no more than forty yards before a sudden thunderous din caused them to turn swiftly and gaze back upon their perilous path in mute consternation. With a cacophonous clangour, the upper reaches of the rock face which crowned the threshold of the cavern above them abruptly began to collapse, the black stone crumbling languorously downward to strike the plateau's surface with an earth-sundering crash. When the resultant cloud of dust had dissipated, the mariners grimly discerned that the entrance to the grotto had been wholly sealed by the rock slide, the narrow aperture now irrevocably barricaded by an unyielding wall of dense rubble and riven stone.

Caylen stared at the mass of shattered rock, his brow furrowed in disquietude. "Damn and blast! Our route back is lost to us!"

"This does not bode well," grumbled Guthlac.

Ashen-faced, Aelfric scrambled to Caylen's side. "I spied something upon the ridge! For a fleeting moment as the stone crumbled, I beheld a man, or something cast in the semblance of a man, for I swear he wore the raiment of a serpent's scaly hide!"

Caylen's eyes narrowed as he dourly pondered Aelfric's words. "This is vexing. We are not alone here. Something watches us, I'll warrant."

"What now?" growled Guthlac. "We've no hope of scaling those peaks!"

Caylen sighed wearily. "There must be another path through the mountains and back to the shore. We must find it, lest the carrion-crows of this accursed atoll pick clean our bones!"

And in sullen silence, the mariners warily continued their parlous journey down the escarpment to the distant periphery of the brooding jungle.

* * *

Deep within the jade labyrinth, Caylen and his shipmates hacked their way onerously through the sweltering verdure. All about them towered gnarled and colossal trees, their furrowed boles entwined by a capacious latticework of tangled vines. Golden rays of fragmented sunlight glimmered down from the lofty arborescent canopy and the strident cries of unseen birds and innominate fauna resounded ceaselessly from the seething maelstrom's trackless depths. Faintly audible beyond the insistent cacophony of the jungle, the mariners discerned the echo of distant drums, their ominous and rhythmic thrum reverberating insidiously from the veiled heart of the torrid hinterland.

For two gruelling hours the scouting party traversed the humid morass, doffing their cloaks as the temperature steadily rose to truly dolorous levels of calefaction. At length they found their path obstructed by a strange object which loomed partially hidden within the dank, vine-thronged undergrowth. As the mariners drew closer they discerned that it was an altar hewn from black stone, its blood-caked surface etched with an array of eldritch glyphs and sigils. Atop the darksome plinth squatted a vile, moss-encrusted statue carved to embody some foul and iniquitous union of man and serpent, its graven hide adorned with scales and its leering face akin to the toothsome countenance of a great snake.

Caylen smiled mirthlessly as he gazed at the black effigy, his eyes sparkling with the light of grim recognition.

"What unholy idol is this?" hissed Guthlac.

"Unholy indeed," growled Caylen. "I've seen its like before, in the catacombs deep beneath the desert fortress of Gul-Azlaan. Give the damned thing a wide berth, lest it begin to speak!"

Guthlac cast a puzzled glance at Caylen, but thought better of pressing him to elucidate.

"That carving fair resembles the thing I spied on the ridge," enounced Aelfric.

"I'll wager it does," said Caylen, wiping beads of sweat from his furrowed brow. "And I'm beginning to fathom just what may await us on this bedevilled isle. Onwards, lads! And keep your steel at the ready!"

The jungle slowly ceded another laborious mile to the unfaltering stride of the mariners, until at last the clawing green vault grudgingly yielded to the comparative paucity of a wide clearing blanketed by turgid, viridian grass. Keeping silently to the shadowed perimeter of the treeline, Caylen and his companions gazed incredulously into the centre of the verdant dell, their eyes wide in rapt astonishment. Kneeling upon the ground was a young woman whose delicately beauteous visage seemed oddly incongruous with the torrid and incult environs within which she dwelt. The girl's winsome features were bewitchingly elfin and her supple limbs were slender yet toned with muscle. Her skin bore the hue of sun-kissed bronze and her long, lustrous hair was blacker than sable. The nymph's lissome body was adorned with scant little clothing; a meagre doe-skin loincloth hanging from her narrow hips and several broad strips of soft leather binding her ample bosom. Unshod, she wore ornate wrist and ankle bracelets evidently fashioned from ruel-bone, and an ovoid, green crystal amulet hung from a rawhide thong about her neck. Oblivious to her enraptured watchers, the woman was digging assiduously into the soft earth with a crudely hewn stone knife and uprooting violaceous herbs which she then placed carefully into a small leather pouch at her side.

"By the gods, Caylen!" whispered Guthlac hoarsely. "Has this accursed heat addled my brain? Tell me you too can see that enchanting little sprite!"

"I see her," breathed Caylen. "Is she native to this isle, I wonder? And if so, where hides her tribe?"

Guthlac grinned. "Well, wherever they are, I hope all their wenches look like her!"

"They might know of a path through the mountains," growled Caylen. "Or mayhap even have information about the jewelled city we seek!"

"Aye… that was my reckoning too, of course," muttered Guthlac.

Caylen was pondering how best to approach the kneeling woman when there suddenly boomed from the far side of the clearing the resounding clamour of snapping vines and splintering boughs. The gnarled branches at the edge of the dell instantly began to sway violently as if assailed by a tumultuous tempest and the girl clambered hastily to her feet before the shuddering treeline. Abruptly, there emerged from the tangled forest a great saurian snout, thrice as broad as that of an aurochs and studded with a myriad jagged, bony protrusions. With a final clangourous crash, the entirety of the primeval beast then slowly lumbered forth from the jungle and bellowed an ear-splittingly horrisonant roar. The creature that had shambled from the trees was akin to a colossal reptile, its slavering maw packed with an array of dagger-like fangs and its armoured, long-tailed body bristling with thick, serried ridges of coarse scales. Astride the titan's spiky back perched a rider not unlike a man in shape and stature, but wholly inhuman in its mien and countenance. To Caylen's eyes, the mounted form was incontestably a member of the hoary race of serpent-men whose existence was whispered of in ancient legendry and the shunned scrolls of arcane lore. The rider's scaly green flesh was adorned with a cuirass of hardened leather and he bore a lengthy pike which terminated in a serrated three-pronged head forged of some strange, scintillant metal. As he commanded his lumbering steed to bear down upon the terrified sylphine woman before him, the crested serpent-knight's distended, ophidian face twisted into a cruel and toothsome leer.

Caylen spun instantly to the mariner crouched behind him. "Ruadh! Give me your spear!"

The burly, red-bearded man swiftly handed Caylen an ash-hafted spear tipped with a broad, leaf-shaped iron head. "May it fly true, Wolf-King!"

Surging from the undergrowth, Caylen drew back his mightily muscled arm and hurled the spear with all of his prodigious strength. The well-honed weapon sliced through the air like a divine thunderbolt, spanning the distance to the centre of the clearing in less than a heartbeat. The spear struck the serpent-man full in the chest with a juddering impact, pitching him from his mount and sending an arterial spray of viscid, green blood arcing high into the air. Before the rider had even struck the ground, Caylen was rushing headlong toward the fearsome squamate steed, his axe gleaming in the sunlight.

Seeing his captain's desperate charge, Guthlac immediately hefted his sword and loped from the clearing, shouting to the two remaining mariners. "Into the fray, lads!"

Caylen bellowed a thunderous war-cry as the direful beast surged toward him with its venomous jaws agape. Launching himself in a mighty salmon-leap, he twisted his body at apex of his martial bound and drove his axe furiously into the monster's great scaly head. The rune-etched steel clove through the creature's thick hide and bit deep into the skull beneath with a sickening, resonant crack. Instantly, the huge reptile's powerful legs buckled and it crashed heavily to the grassy jungle floor with a final protracted, sibilant hiss. Grimacing in revulsion, Caylen dragged his gore-flecked axe free of the monster's sundered skull and turned to face the girl just as Guthlac and the other reavers arrived breathlessly at his side.

"You are safe now, lass," growled Caylen as he gazed into the woman's sparkling, violet eyes.

Her delicate brow furrowing, the raven-haired tribeswoman offered no reply, instead merely appraising the assembled mariners guardedly and with evident trepidation.

"Mayhap she does not speak our tongue," ventured Ruadh.

Caylen nodded. "More than likely, I'll wager."

The girl's face swiftly adopted an expression akin to vexation and her gaze swept the treeline anxiously.

"Snakes that walk like men!" spat Aelfric in contempt, peering down at the lifeless, slit-pupiled eyes of the fallen serpent-rider. "Without a doubt, it was one of this wretch's brethren that I saw upon the ledge. Did it cause the rockslide that trapped us here, I wonder?"

"To what end?" scowled Ruadh, retrieving his spear from the scaly corpse. "If you're right, I cannot fathom the motives of these inhuman devils!"

"We must seek answers," grumbled Caylen. "And this woman may well provide them, if we can but converse with her."

"Wonderful," sighed Guthlac sardonically. "It seems we've found ourselves imprisoned in a domain of odious lizard-men! What madness is next?"

Suddenly, a guttural roar reverberated from the eastern edge of the clearing and the reavers turned to behold another reptilian behemoth thundering furiously forth from the jungle's depths. This saurian steed was near identical to the creature which Caylen's axe had dispatched scant moments ago, but the appearance of its rider differed starkly from the body of the serpent-man which lay sprawled upon the blood-spattered grass. The second beast's master was distinctly human in form, his muscular frame etched with strange tattoos and intricate patterns of deep scarification. The man wore a breech-cloth of coarse leather and his sinewy limbs were adorned with ivory armlets. He sported a shock of black, matted hair daubed with thick swathes of ochre pigment and his notched ears were transfixed by several tiny crescents of carved bone. Brandishing a slender spear of blackened wood with a cruelly barbed point, the tribesman abruptly released his rawhide reins and uttered an ululating war-cry, displaying his yellowed teeth which had evidently been chiselled down to fine points.

"Stand fast, sea-wolves!" roared Caylen, his axe whirling in his grasp. "Hack this foul thing to red ruin!"

With a strident hiss, the hulking creature charged, its great clawed feet striking the earth with bone-jarring force. And with their steel agleam, the doughty mariners of the *White Wolf* met the primeval titan's ravening onslaught with grim and steadfast resolve. Leaping from the brute's path, Caylen swept his axe forth in a pitiless arc which opened a deep furrow in its serried hide. Simultaneously, Guthlac thrust his longsword viciously between two segments of the beast's striated armour plating before immediately pulling the imbrued blade free and hacking a red cleft into its rider's unprotected thigh. Bellowing an oath, Ruadh drew back his powerful arm and hurled his ash-hafted spear unerringly at the scarred tribesman. The iron point lanced grievously into the savage's broad shoulder, eliciting a guttural scream and causing him to reel from his mount's spiny back. Rolling desperately to his feet, the wounded man clumsily loosed his own spear in retaliation, but the barbed head merely struck a glancing blow to Ruadh's bicep as it flew wide of its intended mark. Smiling cruelly, Ruadh drew his short-hafted hand-axe from his belt and advanced upon the tattooed primitive.

"You missed," the mariner growled. "I didn't."

Suddenly, the raven-tressed girl loomed like a tawny spectre at the tribesman's back, and with a graceful motion she drew her jagged flint dagger across his corded neck. Blood erupted from the gaping fissure wrought by her blade and the savage sank instantly to his knees, crimson froth bubbling from his lips. Witnessing this, Caylen grinned broadly and leaped to press the attack against the now riderless mount. But before he could close upon the beast, Aelfric vaulted to its scaly back and drove his sword-point furiously down into the scutes of its armoured neck. The blade sank deep and embedded itself to the hilt, the tip emerging slick and bloody from the creature's throat. Immediately, the great reptile's front legs buckled, causing Aelfric to tumble headlong from its back and land heavily before its spiked snout. Instinctively, the mortally wounded beast closed its massive jaws about the mariner's torso and held him in a slaughterous grip, its razor-edged teeth slicing and grinding through flesh, muscle and sinew. A heartbeat later, Caylen and Guthlac were at their shipmate's side, but in those scant seconds both beast and man had met their torturous demise. Grimly, Caylen prised the ravaged corpse of his companion from the creature's ensanguined maw and laid it upon the grass.

"Well fought, my friend," he said solemnly.

Guthlac slowly removed his helmet and ran his fingers through his sweat-matted hair. "I don't mind telling you that I've had my fill of this infernal island, Wolfclan."

The sudden sound of stertorous choking caused Caylen to turn fleetly and he stared aghast as Ruadh sank abruptly to his knees, his face pallid and bloodless. A moment later, the reaver collapsed to the earth, his fingers scrabbling desperately at his throat. Racing to their stricken cohort, Caylen and Guthlac watched in horror as the man began to convulse violently before rapidly falling silent and deathly still. Guthlac dolefully examined the shallow wound on Ruadh's bicep which the lizard-rider's spear had wrought. The narrow gash had emitted scant little blood, but its ragged edges were slick with a foul, viscid ichor.

"Poison!" hissed Guthlac. "That treacherous savage envenomed his spear!"

Caylen's face instantly became a mask of untrammelled rage. "Damn this accursed place!" he bellowed furiously to the heavens. "I have led three men to their deaths, in search of a treasure which may well exist only in a drunken pirate's wine-addled brain!"

Guthlac gripped Caylen's shoulder firmly. "Every man who strides the deck of the *White Wolf* is oath-sworn to follow you. These bold souls knew well the perils that our voyages entail. They died honourably, and given the choice, they would make that same vow again."

Caylen sighed wearily. "Gather wood from the forest. We shall build a pyre for our battle-brothers, and light a funeral fire the likes of which even the gods will envy!"

Like an amaranthine ghost, the woman suddenly appeared at Caylen's side, speaking quickly in an incognizable tongue and gesturing to the northern edge of the clearing.

"I cannot fathom your words," barked Caylen with a scowl. "Your prattling means naught to me, and I haven't the time to pay heed!"

Frowning, the woman swiftly removed the viridescent amulet from about her neck and made as if to press the jewel to Caylen's forehead. Instantly, the clansman's hand lashed out to grasp her wrist and hold it fast.

"Pray, let her do it," said Guthlac. "It may be her custom, and I am curious as to her intent."

Grudgingly, Caylen released his hold and allowed the woman to place the strange talisman against his brow. To his surprise, he felt a fleeting sensation of warmth from the green gem, and as he stared into the girl's alluring, almond-shaped eyes, he mused that they sparkled like twin amethysts. After several moments, she drew back the amulet and gazed at him expectantly.

"Delightful," muttered Caylen. "Your way of conveying thanks, I suppose. Well, there is no need. Now stand aside, for we have a grim task before us."

A wry smile then curled the woman's fulsome lips. "You're an ill-tempered one, outlander. But at least now we may converse."

Caylen's eyes widened in astonishment. "That jewel! Your words are no longer gibberish! What sorcery is this?"

The woman sighed exasperatedly and proceeded to place the amulet against Guthlac's furrowed brow.

"The crystal is enchanted," exclaimed Caylen. "By some spell, it makes her language clear to us!"

"Remarkable," grumbled Guthlac, donning his battered helmet once more. "Trolls, lizard-men and magic gems. Give me an honest sea-fight against an Atlantean trireme over this mad sigaldry any day!"

"Now hearken, strangers!" the woman said, casting a wary glance at the treeline. "Give your fallen friends to the fire if you must, but we must make haste to the settlement of my people. The emissaries of the Serpent King haunt this jungle, and they will surely see the smoke from your pyre."

"Who are you, wench?" snapped Caylen. "And is there a passage through these black mountains?"

"My name is Nalani," the woman said, her voice mellifluous yet edged with a tremulous note of fear. "Your questions will be answered when we are safely behind the walls of my tribe's stockade. Now cease your maundering and set about your grim task, for the Mountain of the Fire God awaits!"

Chapter IV
The Shaman's Prophecy

Caylen and Guthlac grimly surveyed the village to which Nalani had led them. The sizable settlement was encircled by a palisade of lofty timbers evidently hewn from the trunks and boughs of slender jungle trees. Each of the sturdy pales had been sharpened to a cruel point and a crudely reinforced gate flanked by several broader stakes was situated at the defensive wall's western edge. The dwellings within the primitive fortification were circular constructions fashioned from timber poles and interlaced with a latticework of smaller branches, clad with an exterior coating of hardened mud. The rooves of the huts were crowned by densely packed branches and further adorned with layers of grass and vines. At the settlement's southern perimeter was a rudimentary corral within which several long-horned hircine animals grazed, while a narrow, languidly flowing stream wound its way through the undergrowth where the village's abatis-ringed boundary met the dense verdure of the jungle.

"A war-hird could overrun this place in minutes," growled Caylen as he glanced about the encampment.

"And I wouldn't sleep well with that monster looming at my gate," muttered Guthlac, pointing to the colossal, black volcano which towered not six miles to the south of the village.

Nalani turned to address the mariners. "The God of the Fire Mountain has not awoken in many generations. His continued slumber is ensured by our oblations and offerings."

"No doubt," grumbled Caylen, gazing at the brooding peak and the dense clouds of cinereous smoke which billowed from its rutilant crown.

As Nalani ushered the men briskly through the settlement, its inhabitants stared silently at the strangers with varying degrees of curiosity and disdain. The tribe's cold-eyed warriors bearing their slender spears and curved clubs glared with ill-concealed hostility while the relatively few children merely gaped in rapt fascination. Caylen noted that the villagers were clad in a manner largely akin to the raven-haired woman; crude garments fashioned of animal hides and woven plant fibres with assorted adornments of ivory and stone.

"The dwelling of the shaman Akamai is yonder," said Nalani, motioning to a ramshackle hut which squatted within the shadow of a colossal, gnarled tree. The walls and door of the rough-hewn construction were adorned with an array of sun-bleached animal skulls and a tendril of grey smoke rose languidly from a wide aperture in its roof. "He will provide the answers which you seek. Follow."

Caylen and Guthlac duly accompanied Nalani into the shaman's abode. The interior walls of the hut were bedecked with numerous animal pelts and upon the earthen floor a small cookfire burned within a ring of broad, blackened stones. Atop the fire sat a stoneware pot from which writhed plumes of redolent vapour. Crouched before the fire was the shaman Akamai, his gaunt frame adorned with garments of tattered goatskin. The aged man's rugose face was etched with intricate tattoos and around his neck was a leather thong from which hung an array of serpents' teeth. The shaman's wispy hair was dun-white and his rheumy eyes were fixed firmly on the pungent concoction which bubbled within the stone vessel. Nalani briskly knelt beside the ancient tribesman and for many moments she whispered softly into his ear. Finally, she rose and motioned for the mariners to sit before the fire. Caylen and Guthlac obliged, staring expectantly at the wizened figure as Nalani seated herself beside them and inclined her head meditatively.

"Outlanders," rasped Akamai, his voice like the susurration of dry leaves. "For rescuing our daughter Nalani from the acolytes of the Great Snake, you have our gratitude. The shard of the Star-

Stone has allowed us to commune and the Fire God now hearkens to your words. Far have you travelled, and many questions burn within you. Ask them now, and we shall grant you the boon of enlightenment."

"Very well, old man. I am Caylen, master of the *White Wolf.* Who is this damned Serpent King? Does he indeed hold sway over this forsaken atoll?"

Akamai nodded grimly. "He is ancient and wicked. One of the last of his kind. How he came to the Island of the Fire God is knowledge long since lost to my people, but he has ruled here from his Black Pyramid for centuries beyond reckoning. We pay him tribute each blood moon; offerings of living flesh. He takes our chosen sons and daughters and in return we are spared the wrath of his serpent warriors."

"A tyrant, and an inhuman one at that," muttered Guthlac. "I might have guessed."

"You offer him your children?" seethed Caylen. "What does he do with these sacrifices, pray tell?"

"Some he devours, others he enslaves. The pitiless passage of time has wrought its toll upon his own kind and precious few of his hoary serpent-folk remain alive. So, he corrupts the tribes of this island and bends them to his vile will, compelling the people of the jungle to do his bidding by means of foul sorcery and the cruel lash of his acolyte's whips."

"The tribesman we slew in the clearing," pondered Caylen. "He was one of these slaves?"

Nalani nodded solemnly. "Yes. A hunter from the Sons of the Red River. The Serpent King's virulence has befouled many of the Old Tribes. The People of the Crystal Caverns, the Children of the Sky Tree, even many of our own folk of the Black Mountain now bend the knee in obeisance to him, their minds twisted by his accursed venom-rituals."

"Can you not rise up against this fiend?" spat Caylen. "Have you not sufficient warriors to resist his villainy?"

Akamai bowed his head forlornly. "Ten years past, our great chieftain Ikaika led a rebellion against the ophidian liege. It did not go well. Our beloved king was sacrificed upon the Altar of the Snake God and as punishment for his revolt, the tribute demanded of our tribe was increased twofold. Such was the price of insurrection."

"Since that black day, we have been without a king," said Nalani dolefully. "And woe has cloaked this tribe like a shadow."

"Yes, how very tragic," snapped Guthlac irately. "But heed me now. We entered this realm through the caverns which lie to the south of your encampment. That route is now closed to us. Is there another path through the mountains?"

Akamai sighed wearily. "The black peaks are impassable to men. None may scale those baneful heights. The old gates are forever shut and there is no other way to the sea."

"Damn and blast!" hissed Guthlac. "We are trapped here after all!"

"Perhaps," rasped Akamai. "And yet, it is said that the Serpent King guards a portal within his infernal shrine, a mystic gateway to the lands beyond the jungle. But it shall scarce avail thee, for no man enters the Black Pyramid and lives."

Caylen's eyes narrowed. "Indeed? I'm beginning to think a visit to this snake king's temple may well be in order."

"Madness!" exclaimed Nalani. "None may deign to seek an audience with that malign devil, and neither may one enter the serpent's nest unbidden!"

Akamai suddenly fixed Caylen with a feverous glare. "No ordinary man could hope to brave that perilous path, outlander. But in you, we sense great power. A mighty soul-fire burns within your war-scored breast and potent magicks entwine your heart! Our ancient prophecies speak of one whose voyages across the ice-bound sea shall bring him to our long-hidden shores... one who is destined to dash the serpents of the blackened earth beneath his feet. Mayhap you are the one whose coming was foretold."

"I suspect not," growled Caylen. "At any rate, I've never paid much heed to prophecies, for I hear too many of them. But there is one more thing I would ask. An old mariner's legend tells of a mist-shrouded isle upon which stands a great city hewn of precious jewels. Does such a place exist here? Speak the truth, old man!"

For a long moment, Akamai was silent. Then, he interlaced his bony fingers and nodded. "It is said that the Serpent King guards a great hoard of crystals; the remnants of a trove of sparkling gems which once encrusted the ancient temples of our distant ancestors. Those glimmering spires have been lost for countless aeons, since before the first cultists of the Fire God incurred the black mountain's searing wrath!"

Guthlac directed a quizzical glance at Caylen. "Perhaps there is some truth in the good captain's tall tale after all!"

"You cannot face the Serpent King!" snapped Nalani, her violet eyes suddenly agleam with fear. "Many before you have tried, and now their bones adorn the walls of his verminous fortress!"

"It is decided," enounced Caylen, heedless of the tribeswoman's concern. "We must find a way into this Black Pyramid!"

Akamai scowled. "You have spilled the blood of the devil's kin. That is something he will most assuredly not forgive. But if you are steadfast in your resolve to breach his temple, you will require our aid. The weapons of the foe are envenomed with the death-kiss of the snake lord. Ruin awaits all those who are touched by that malign blight. But, we can bestow upon thee a draught which is proof against his poison."

"An elixir to counter the serpent's venom?" exclaimed Caylen. "By all means, shaman! I have seen the doom wrought by that filth, and it is something I would most certainly not wish to suffer!"

Swiftly, Akamai took up from the earthen floor a small ovoid vessel carved of stained bone which he then proceeded to dip into the noisome substance bubbling atop the fire. Once the cup was full, he handed it reverentially to Guthlac. "Drink, and your blood will be fortified against the venom. But be warned, the infusion brings both pain and visions akin to the opiate embrace of the lotus!"

Guthlac grimaced in disgust as he raised the vessel to his lips. "I've supped fermented yak's milk in the rat-infested taverns of Bazalanin, old man! I'll wager this brew shall prove no worse!" Then, he boldly swallowed a measure of the mephitic potion before handing the bone cup to Caylen.

"Well?" grumbled Caylen, staring uneasily at the green liquid within the vessel. "Is it as vile as its stench suggests?"

"I was wrong, Wolfclan," wheezed Guthlac, his face suddenly ashen. "It's by far the foulest thing I've ever tasted!" And with that, the burly mariner promptly keeled over and lapsed into an insensate slumber.

Steeling himself, Caylen swiftly drank what remained of the malodorous draught. The viscid liquid struck the back of his throat like fire and instantly a wave of revulsion surged through his body. A shimmering panoply of scintillant colours then abruptly manifested before his eyes as a great sense of obtunded weariness engulfed him...

Alone and unarmed, Caylen stood before a monolithic wall of black stone etched with cryptic, viridescent glyphs. The ar-

cane sigils seemed to pulse with lucent energy and although the carvings represented a language wholly unknown to him, he nevertheless found that he could discern their meaning with absolute clarity. Compelled by an illimitable lucidity, his unerring gaze scrupulously swept the colossal edifice and the eldritch, cuneiform inscriptions slowly revealed their time-lost secrets…

"And lo, the ancient Serpent Kings who strode the cracked and cratered face of Pangaea like mighty ectothermic colossi did duly wage ceaseless war with the star-born First Ones, laying siege to the glorious Antarctic Megalopolis and the abyssal bastions of the Inner World during those immemorial epochs which are now lost beyond temporal reckoning and the meagre ken of Man. Know that those glorious Ophidian Lords did build upon the ravaged surface of the hoary earth their greatest aeon-cloaked and cyclopean shrines; the Nine Temples of the Serpent Kings, hewn from shimmering meteoric rock and the adamantine bones of the saurian titans who roamed the calescent globe before the First Cataclysm reshaped the very countenance of Creation. Know also that the star-forged Viridian Stones fell from the heavens countless aeons past, scarring the surface of the Tellurian Sphere as they plummeted to the earth wreathed in baleful flame. Only the most ancient mages of the Elder Races were privy to their true origin, and that knowledge has long since been lost to all but the most percipient sages of the world, for the stones were imbued with great sorcerous power which could be harnessed to grant illimitable wisdom or wreak immeasurable carnage! The crumbling, blood-etched pages of hoary grimoires such as The Tome of Shadows *and* The Chthonic Chronicles *are replete with nefarious spells and forbidden rites to shackle the sidereal mana of the stones and twist their empyreal energies to do the black bidding of witch and wizard alike. And thus did the servitors and cultists of the Chaosphere duly covet the mystic potency of the crystal; those vile acolytes of the Z'xulth who*

were empowered by the fanatical belief that it was sent to Earth from the abyssal reaches of the Utter Dark as a malign gift to assist their Black Order in preparing the world for the triumphant return of their vile gods, the infernal abominations who seethe eternally in the diabolical depths of their abhorrent ultra-stellar wombs! Cleanse and purify were thus the sacred watchwords of the Ophidian Hegemony, for it was well known that the snake-lords would not suffer a Z'xulth cultist to live, such was one of their most deeply revered tenets! And so, long did the Serpent Kings endure, fortified against the pitiless Ice Ages and the myriad climactic upheavals which grievously scarred the Tellurian Sphere, watching from their subterranean vaults and their mountains of power as the children of Man crawled to their prophesied ascendancy. And deep within their lava-kissed lairs the Serpent Kings plotted and schemed with ophidian malice and that supreme cold-blooded patience natural to their elder race, awaiting the day when they would surge forth from their basaltic fortresses like a vengeful and venomous wave of fanged fury and righteous rage to crush the cities of the ape-spawn beneath their scaled and star-shod feet, making the Earth theirs once again!"

Emerging abruptly from his trance, Caylen wiped a sheen of cold sweat from his brow and emitted a great, juddering sigh.

"What was revealed to thee, outlander?" whispered Akamai, his eyes gleaming fervidly.

"Lore all but forgotten by our people, it would seem," growled Caylen. "Long ago, in the catacombs beneath an ancient fortress, a black altar spoke cryptically to me concerning the race of snake-lords. The waking dream I just experienced has finally shed some light upon that vexing mystery. The Serpent Kings are the ancestral enemies of men. For eons they have drawn their diabolical plans against us. This is a dark truth indeed."

"Enlightenment can be a heavy burden," said Akamai. "And now, the veil has been lifted from before your eyes."

"Indeed," muttered Caylen. "I still set no store by your prophecy, but mayhap the gods did compel me to this isle after all… to end the tyranny of this Serpent King and free your people from his vile rule!"

Nalani cast an anxious glance at Akamai, but the shaman's stare remained fixated upon Caylen.

Suddenly, Guthlac awoke with a start and sat bolt upright, his gaze sweeping the hut in trepidation.

"Welcome back," gnarred Caylen with a wry grin.

"I dreamt of snakes!" gasped Guthlac, his breathing ragged. "And a sweet dream it was not!"

"And so, it is done," rasped Akamai. "The venom of the serpent-folk can no longer harm thee. Now, you must choose your path."

Caylen clambered briskly to his feet. "I shall seek out this villainous Serpent King," he rumbled adamantly. "Guthlac! What say you?"

Rising sullenly, Guthlac nodded. "Aye, why not? It's a damned foolish plan that will doubtless result in our deaths, but it seems our best hope for getting off this bloody isle!"

"Come the dawn, our hunters shall show you the route to the Black Pyramid," said Akamai. "The secret paths through the jungle are known only to our finest trackers. Not even the snake-men traverse the old, hidden trails."

A sneer suddenly curled Nalani's fulsome lips. "Dolts! Dullards! If you place such scant value on your lives, you are beyond help. Spend this night well, for it will most certainly be your last!"

"Gods, woman!" growled Caylen. "You've a sharp tongue! Do you harry all your guests so?"

"Guests?" laughed Nalani icily. "The last outlander who ventured here from beyond the mountains was much like you, seeking jewels and plunder. His vessel was dashed to ruin upon the rocks and only he and six of his companions were cast ashore. The white beasts of the caverns claimed most of them, and the jungle took the rest. Alone and on the verge of death, he chanced upon our settlement and told us his tale."

"Where is this man?" exclaimed Caylen. "I would speak with him!"

Nalani's delicate brow arched impassively. "After Akamai deemed him of no worth, we made a sacrifice of him, to appease the God of the Fire Mountain. So, outlander… perhaps you should be thankful that the lash of my sharp tongue is the worst thing you've suffered during your visit to our village."

Chapter V
In the Hall of the Serpent King

As the sun crested the eastern peaks of the black mountains, Caylen crouched in the jungle verdure flanked by Guthlac and two lean, hard-muscled tribesmen. Before them stretched a vast clearing devoid of vegetation and littered with an array of colossal, sun-bleached bones each broader than the keel of a longship. Towering imperiously above the skeletal remnants was a gigantic statue hewn from stygian, moss-encrusted stone. The great effigy stood some forty feet in height and was carved in the form of a hulking serpent-lord, its adamantine claws clutching a vast stave crowned with curved finials akin to the teeth of a titanic snake.

"There stands the monument to the vile one," spat the first tribesman contemptuously. "Carved in his infernal image."

Guthlac uttered a mirthless laugh. "This serpent king has a rather lofty opinion of himself, don't you think?"

Caylen nodded, gazing at the looming statue in scornful silence.

"Follow the path of bones," hissed the second tribesman. "Beyond the next ridge you will find the approach to the Black Pyramid. We will go no farther. Die well, outlanders."

And with that, the two hunters swiftly disappeared into the shadowed embrace of the jungle.

"They were a cheerful pair," muttered Guthlac mordantly.

"Aye," replied Caylen, gazing in awe at the gigantic, time-worn skeleton. "What manner of beasts once roamed this isle, I wonder?"

"Dragons, or mayhap something even more fearsome," mused Guthlac. "Bigger than that Kraken we encountered off the coast of Atlantis, judging by the size of those bones! At any rate, I'm thankful such titans seem to have long since perished."

"Indeed. Though the foes which await us may well prove no less deadly."

"It's a pity that feisty, whip-tongued wench didn't see us off this morning."

"She's a fey one," growled Caylen. "But there's some fire in her blood, to be sure. She fair reminds me of my wife."

Guthlac grinned. "Except Astrid Grimmsdottir isn't likely to cut your throat as you sleep!"

The trace of a smile touched Caylen's lips. "You don't know Astrid as well as I do."

The raucous cry of a great bird alighting upon the shoulder of the towering statue suddenly drew Caylen's attention. The long-taloned creature sported feathers of a myriad vivid hues and its broad beak was bristling with countless tiny, needle-sharp teeth. "This is a damned strange place. Like nowhere I've seen before, and my travels have taken me far and wide, make no mistake!"

"What are the chances of us getting off this blasted atoll?" gnarred Guthlac bitterly.

"Well, if Eirik paid any heed to my command, the *White Wolf* should have put to sea with the dawn."

"And do you think he gave the order to sail?"

"Of course not!" laughed Caylen. "Eirik's a stubborn old goat. He'll wait another day, at least!"

"So, are we to simply walk up to the serpent lord's front gate? Tell me you have a plan in mind, Wolfclan."

"Keep to the treeline. Be wary, and we'll see what warp and weft the loom of fate has in store for us."

"I thought as much," sighed Guthlac.

"Faith, reaver! You may yet have a fine tale to tell your chieftain, old Oughtred One-Eye, when you get back!"

"Come then," said Guthlac, donning his battle-scarred helmet. "Let us venture into that nest of vipers, and pray that the gods may take pity upon the mad!"

* * *

For half a mile, Caylen and Guthlac traversed the periphery of the sweltering jungle in tense silence, ever flanking the broad, bone-strewn trail. The matted morass of ferns and vines teemed with insects and snakes of varying hues and sizes, some of the serpents boasting such girth that they were nigh indistinguishable from the gnarled boughs around which their scaly bodies were encoiled. In the midst of the tangled green labyrinth the reavers suddenly caught sight of a great sabre-cat hunched over the bloodied carcass of some manner of large cervine animal. The massive beast raised its ensanguined head and fixed the mariners irefully with its gleaming amber eyes, uttering a resonant growl of warning as its muscles rippled beneath its golden fur. The two men froze momentarily before moving slowly away from the creature, breathing a sigh of heartfelt relief when it grudgingly returned its attention to its ravaged prey. For another five hundred yards they crept through the matted undergrowth with as much stealth as they could muster, ever vigilant lest the jungle disgorge some primal and deadly predator upon them. At length they crested a low rise and clambered from the dense verdure to gaze out incredulously upon a wide, craterous caldera wherein squatted the Black Pyramid of the Serpent King. The brooding ziggurat appeared to be constructed at least in some measure from caliginous obsidian, its vine-entwined edifice towering some ninety feet skywards. The great temple's wide base was cracked and riven with age and the vast slabs of black stone which formed a stairway to its upper reaches were fissured and crumbling. Standing silently before the hoary shrine, still as a graven effigy, was a lone serpent warrior. The ophidian sentry's sinewy, glaucous frame was encased in armour of fulgent scale-mail and in his taloned hands he clutched a wickedly serrated trident. Fixing the mariners balefully with his gleaming, yellow eyes, the creature's jaws abruptly parted and a forked, crimson tongue darted forth from between his acicular teeth.

"Come hither, humans!" the guardsman rasped, his voice deep and sibilant. "The High One has foreseen your arrival."

Caylen and Guthlac exchanged pensive glances and warily descended the asperous slope, approaching the hulking serpent with their weapons poised.

"We are expected, then?" said Guthlac, forcing a nervous smile.

The snake-man's leathery brow creased and his cranial ridge reddened in vexation as he motioned silently towards the cracked stairway.

"Come on, old horse," growled Caylen as he strode past the sentry and cautiously began to ascend the ancient steps.

"I have a very bad feeling about this," hissed Guthlac, squinting up at the black escalier with ill-concealed trepidation. "Only one guard, and he knew we were coming."

"Just keep your wits about you," whispered Caylen. "And make sure your steel is at the ready."

As they reached the lofty summit of the temple's steps, the mariners beheld a rough-hewn doorway beyond which writhed a bitumen void of deep shadow. Steeling themselves, they swiftly crossed the atramentous threshold and immediately found themselves in a narrow passageway studded with an array of lucent green crystals which illumined their path with a pulsating, viridescent light. Gazing at the glimmering gems, Caylen mused that they were not unlike the jewel which Nalani had worn about her slender neck, but more disquietingly, he recognized that they appeared to be composed of the same multifaceted crystallic substance as the eldritch altar-stone which he had shattered deep beneath the ancient fortress of Gul-Azlaan so many years ago. Tightening his grip upon his axe, Caylen supressed a shudder and strode grimly onward. The reavers traversed the lambent tunnel for several minutes before finally emerging into a cavernous, quadrate antechamber. The sanctum's obsidian walls were adorned with countless more scintillant crystals which served to bathe its tenebrous depths with a gently fulgurating glow. Halting in their tracks, Caylen and Guthlac stared in rapt and silent awe at the room's shadowed interior. Strewn about the chamber were many knurled and cracked leathery eggs each the size of an ale cask. An array of well-gnawed bones littered the floor around the sundered shells and a viscous, yellow ichor seeped noisomely from the empty vessels. And yet it was the awesome spectacle ensconced at the vestibule's centre that commanded the two mariners' absolute and unalloyed attention. Before them, reclining upon a pellucid throne evidently carved from a single colossal emerald, was the imposing figure of the darkly renowned Serpent King. The mighty saurian liege was heavily muscled and clad in gleaming lamellar armour which bore the hue of polished jade. Upon his ridged, ophidian brow he wore a circlet fashioned from lucid zircon and in his trenchant talons he gripped a sceptre of gnarled ebony crowned with the crystalline head of a hooded cobra. Atop a low plinth to the left of the lustrous throne stood a large triangular frame of limpid viridian crystal, its pointed apex towering some nine feet from the obsidian floor. Encased within the glimmering shell was a great slab of piceous glass, which although seemingly polished to relucent brilliance, nevertheless reflected nothing but abyssal shadow from its crepuscular surface.

Without exchanging a word, Caylen and Guthlac slowly and warily approached the emerald throne. As they closed to within ten feet of the crystal dais, the array of green gems encircling the chamber suddenly flared markedly brighter and a ghostly, sibilant voice echoed from the shadows to split the leaden silence.

"Welcome, manlings. Know now that you stand before His Ineffable Majesty the Great God-King Sauruuk, Sixth Serpent Liege of the Ophidian Hegemony, Supreme Commander of the Serpentem Vectem Legion, Immortal Overlord of the Glorious Order of Ningishzida, Herald of the Thirteenth Avatar of Apophis and Draco-Imperator of the Exalted Acolytes of Xiuhcoatl. Bask now in His divine radiance and be forever humbled by His malefic splendour."

For several moments, a deathly silence once more held sway within the obsidian sanctum. Then, Caylen levelled his steely gaze at the Serpent King and spoke, his voice deep and resonant. "I am Caylen, known to some as the Wolf of the North. Once a king, now but a storm-scored reaver. I am the Scourge of the Nine Seas and the Bane of the Witch-Queen. Hearken to me, snake-lord, for today I mean to liberate this realm from your capricious rule."

Guthlac cast a fraught glance at Caylen. "Liberate?" he whispered anxiously. "Since when did this expedition become a blasted crusade?"

A sonorous sound not unlike icy laughter abruptly welled in Sauruuk's throat. "Well met, human," he rasped, his tone harsh and guttural. "From a monarch to a lowly pirate, eh? A graceless fall indeed. At any rate, your arrival upon these hoary shores did not escape my notice. I have watched you, sirrah. You are not the first man to stand before me and boast of his mettle, and you shall most assuredly not be the last. Many have aspired to dethrone me over the centuries. I've picked clean the bones of every last one of them and worn their flayed skin as a mantle."

"I'm sure," grumbled Caylen.

"Ah, but you are no stranger to the lore of the Elder Races are you, fallen king? You have encountered the power of the Viridian Stone before, that much is clear."

"Aye," growled Caylen. "Beneath the fortress of Gul-Azlaan.

Those fiend-haunted catacombs were evidently hewn from that accursed green rock."

"A thousand plagues upon those traitorous infidels!" hissed Sauruuk furiously, his cranial crest flaring scarlet. "Long before your people raised their vaunted fortress upon that desolate site, the serpent-priests of our ill-fortuned temple forsook the Pax Ophidia and willingly embraced the black tenets of the Z'xulth! The deluded fools heedlessly defiled the sanctity of the sacred shrine and forever befouled it with the taint of the Outer Darkness! And yet the Shadow Sect paid a woeful price for such brazen blasphemy, for their vile sanctum was pitilessly purified and buried beneath the eternal sands. Now, their impure Order is forgotten and their thrice-cursed names are forever expunged from the hegemony's chronicles."

"I've blackened my steel with the blood of chaos-spawn before," muttered Caylen. "We at least share a measure of common ground in our contempt for those insidious devils. Be they abominations from the pit or demons in the thrall of a vile empress, my blade invariably makes short work of them."

"Empress?" hissed Sauruuk, his crimson tongue flickering fitfully between his translucent fangs. "Ah yes, the Witch-Queen of whom you spoke. She is known to us, as is her foul debasement of the elder serpent-rites. The duplicitous Zyrashana supped deep of the Envenomed Draught. She dabbled in neophyte ophidian magicks to serve her petty earthly ambitions. Such a pity that she wasted her arcane talents on debauched summoning rituals to conjure vulgar demons. In that regard she is not unlike her grandmother... another fey and ageless witch of my dubious acquaintance. The women of your race have a penchant for snakes, it would seem."

Guthlac turned to Caylen irately. "I've no qualms about admitting that all this cryptic prattle is quite beyond my ken, Wolfclan. So, let us ask about something entirely more earthly and tangible!

The remnants of the fabled jewelled city, mayhap?"

"Ha! How predictable and banal," rasped Sauruuk, his yellow eyes gleaming malevolently. "Although not overly surprising, I must confess. I have long observed that your ape-spawned race is incessantly enthralled by the scintillant glimmer of gems and the lustrous lure of gold. Well, know that there are jewels beyond measure hidden on this isle, human. Once, great spires hewn from rubies and emeralds glittered beneath the pitiless sun. Now they lie in ruins, to be trampled heedlessly beneath the hooves and paws of the beasts of the jungle. Moreover, the cavernous vaults beneath this temple are glutted with a plethora of gems! And yet, such a glorious surfeit of riches means naught to one such as I. Their gleam is hollow, and their value inconsequential."

Guthlac grinned broadly. "We would be more than willing to relieve you of such a wearisome burden, your highness."

Sauruuk's scaly snout abruptly contorted into a toothsome leer. "Those sparkling baubles would avail you nothing, manling. For you shall never leave this verdant atoll."

"Did your snake-thralls seal the entrance to the ice-caves?" asked Guthlac guardedly.

"Most certainly," replied Sauruuk. "It has been a very long time indeed since one of your kind escaped this enchanted isle. In my realm, humans either swear fealty to me or serve as fodder for the hatchlings. In your case, I strongly anticipate the latter."

"We shall see," growled Caylen. "It is not my intention to tarry here overlong."

"Ah, but you shall perish here, most assuredly," rumbled Sauruuk. "As will your shipmates." In response to a wave of the Serpent King's clawed hand, the nubilous glass within the great triangular frame suddenly flared with azure light and an image manifested upon its shimmering surface with crystal clarity. "Behold!"

Caylen and Guthlac abruptly found themselves gazing once more upon the barren beach of black sand and the familiar shape of the *White Wolf* drawn up on the desolate shore. So compellingly vivid was the lucid vista that the mariners could hear the breaking of the waves against the ship's keel and discern the briny scent of the frigid ocean.

"Ha!" bellowed Caylen joyously. "I knew Eirik would pay no heed to my command! My valorous sea-wolves await my return, bless their defiant souls!"

"Their forlorn vigil shall soon end," hissed Sauruuk. "Ere long I shall dispatch my serpent warriors through this mystic portal and slaughter your baseborn lackeys without mercy. I thought perhaps that such a revelation might amuse you during your sojourn here."

Caylen gripped Guthlac's shoulder and whispered gravely to him. "Don't wait for me, my friend. Sail the *White Wolf* home, and remember to warn Drogha Tul about that damned dream I had!"

"Eh? Why do you say this?" snapped Guthlac. "I don't..."

Before Guthlac could protest further, Caylen seized hold of the burly mariner and hurled him roughly through the glimmering portal. With a half-uttered curse upon his lips, Guthlac disappeared instantly across the lucent threshold, his sudden passage causing the eldritch witch-glass to ripple idly like the surface of a tranquil millpond in his wake. A heartbeat later, Caylen lunged at the trigonal frame and drove his axe furiously into the ornate structure. With a deafening crash and an explosion of viridian light, the portal shattered into a thousand crystal shards.

Turning to face Sauruuk's emerald throne once more, Caylen smiled coldly. "You'll not be sending any of your kinsmen through that gateway, snake-man!"

Sauruuk's ophidian eyes narrowed. "A useless gesture, human. There are other portals upon this isle, hidden deep within the labyrinthine caverns beneath the mountains."

"I shall search for them once I've dealt with thee, devil."

"I think not," whispered Sauruuk.

Caylen brandished his axe and took a single step towards the Serpent King. "Too long have you enslaved and slaughtered this island's people. I'm putting an end to your tyranny!"

Sauruuk's forked tongue darted forth from between his jaws in a cascade of viscid spittle. "A bold claim indeed. And how, pray tell, do you intend to liberate those lowly savages?"

"By cutting the head off the snake," growled Caylen, his knuckles whitening about the wolf-axe's notched haft.

Sauruuk rose from the scintillant throne and hefted his gnarled sceptre, the sharp ridges upon his great echinate head suddenly flaring a deep shade of crimson. "Deluded primitive. Did you actually think I would have allowed you to enter this sanctum bearing your crude weapons if I thought you posed even the remotest threat to me?"

"Come then!" thundered Caylen, surging resolutely toward the towering figure. "Test your strength against me!"

With a blinding fulmination of light, a jagged tendril of viridescent energy suddenly lanced forth from the crystal cobra atop Sauruuk's staff. The sorcerous bolt struck Caylen full in the chest, hurling him backwards and grievously searing his flesh. Momentarily stunned by the assault, Caylen shook his head in an attempt to clear his vision and raised his axe once more. Instantly, another blistering thunderbolt screamed forth from the cobra's mouth and etched a sulphurous furrow into his thews. A wave of sublime agony tore through Caylen's body and his limbs began to burn with a torturous pain akin to the touch of white-hot flame. Gritting his teeth, he brandished his axe defiantly and stepped forward once again. A third stroke of ruinous, eldritch lightning smote Caylen, scoring a great incandescent lesion into his abdomen. Drawing breath in ragged gasps and struggling against the overwhelming pain wrought by the arcane attack, Caylen hefted his axe and took another faltering step forward, his eyes ablaze with baleful fury. Another sinuous tendril of refulgent sorcery then lashed Caylen like a conflagrant whip, charring his flesh and causing his knees to buckle. With a feral roar of pure rage, Caylen collapsed heavily to the black stone tiles. Defying the call of unconsciousness which alone could offer blessed respite from the withering bombardment of searing sorcerous might, the clansman strove once more to lift his axe as he gazed up at the hulking form of the Serpent King which loomed imperiously before him.

"Coward!" rasped Caylen through gritted teeth. "Face me without your foul magicks, if you dare!"

"Pitiful human," Sauruuk rumbled. "Know that I was commanding glorious legions of serpent-knights when your apish forebears were still huddling in caves! Did you truly aspire to stand against me? Now you will pay the price for your sublime arrogance!"

Then, a final pitiless bolt of coruscant energy shrieked forth from the crystalline cobra's mouth and Caylen was engulfed by a suffocating sea of black oblivion.

Chapter VI
A Sacrifice in the Shadow of the Snake God

Caylen slowly regained consciousness to find that his wrists and ankles were shackled by broad chains of blackened iron. His ravaged body still burned with searing pain and as he glanced about at his surroundings, he discerned that he was fettered upright upon a great altar of obsidian which had been fashioned after the grotesque form of a huge, coiled cobra. The foul effigy's fanged mouth gaped wide and as he tested his unyielding bonds, he realized that they were implacably fused to the adamantine black scales of the vast, carven snake. Caylen's eyes narrowed in contempt as he realized that a seething throng of serpent warriors and human tribesmen ringed the altar, all of them gazing upon him in rapt and silent anticipation. The minacious gathering stood within a wide clearing surrounded by the tangled verdure of the jungle, and in the distance Caylen descried the lofty pinnacle of the Serpent King's black ziggurat towering above the jagged treeline. The baleful sun glowered from his zenith in the azure sky and Caylen reasoned that several hours had evidently elapsed since his ill-fated confrontation within Sauruuk's malefic sanctum. Straining in vain once more against the eldritch chains, he noticed that his axe and sword had been strewn heedlessly upon the black plinth before him, their chalybeous blades glimmering in the pitiless sunlight. With a shudder of revulsion, Caylen suddenly realized that the cracked base of the elapine altar appeared to be heavily stained with disquietingly portentous patterns of dried blood and other nameless ichors.

"So, they mean to sacrifice me, do they?" whispered Caylen furiously. "Well, by all the gods of my ancestors, I'll not make a willing supplicant!"

Suddenly, from the trees at the northern edge of the clearing rode Sauruuk the Serpent King, mounted ostentatiously upon a bipedal reptilian steed. The creature's scaly hide was striped akin to the pelt of a tiger and its great slime-flecked jaws snapped and gnashed with unfettered ferocity. The gathering of serpents and tribesmen parted swiftly, permitting their liege-lord and his hulking mount to approach the black altar. The saurian steed's vast clawed feet scored the ground deeply as it stalked forward and its long, sinewy tail thrashed in feral agitation. Sauruuk reined in the heavily muscled beast some twelve feet from Caylen, appraising his shackled captive malevolently.

"See how easily the wolf is leashed," hissed the Serpent King, his red tongue flickering exultantly.

"Unchain me, wormcast," growled Caylen. "And we'll have our reckoning."

"You are in no position to be issuing challenges, human. Your meagre strength proved no match for my divine power."

"You fear me," rumbled Caylen, pulling his snake-forged bonds taut. "You dare not face me in fair combat. You are a craven thing fit only to slither upon its belly like all your foul kind!"

Sauruuk's elliptical pupils abruptly narrowed as his yellow eyes glimmered with rage. "Your blood shall anoint this sacred altar to honour the glorious god of my elder race!" With that, he wheeled his ravenous mount and addressed the leering, expectant throng. "Make of this man an offering to the great Sidereal Serpent!"

The gathered servitors howled rapturously, hefting their spears and clubs in savage jubilation. In response, Sauruuk's mount opened its toothsome maw and gave vent to a great, ear-splitting roar. Immediately, a cowled figure strode forth from the massed horde bearing a serrated blade of viridian crystal. As the cloaked individual reverentially approached the altar, Caylen discerned that it was an ancient, raw-boned serpent-man who inhabited the tattered and feculent robes. The ophidian shaman slowly ascended the blood-stained dais, his eyes glimmering balefully. Emitting a susurrant hiss, he raised the jagged dagger in obeisance before the great black cobra.

Caylen's lip curled in a defiant sneer. "I'll ram that dirk up your scaly arse, you diseased old bastard!"

"We hereby venerate the divine celestial snake," the eidolic figure rasped, his blackened tongue protruding from his muculent jaws. "He who slithers serenely through the cosmos, anointing the abyssal void with his sacred seed."

Snarling with rage, Caylen strained furiously against the darkling chains, his iron muscles rippling and bulging beneath his scarred flesh.

"An offering of flesh and blood," the shaman hissed, raising the blade higher in his ankylosed claws. "A sacrifice to ensure the rebirth of the Pax Ophidia and the ultimate resurgence of the great saurian imperium!"

Caylen's corded thews surged and swelled mightily as he continued to pit his unrelenting strength against his impliable bonds. Suddenly, from the base of the altar came the sound of rending metal and cracking stone.

The shaman's voice rose to an ululant crescendo and the sacrificial blade whirled in his taloned hands. "All hail the Exalted One! Praise the ineffable god of gods! Blood! Blood for the divine serpent! *Sssakuul, ka'anduruk, kandara-ka, sathulmarakuk, ka'aldaka!*"

Then, the gnarled dagger slowly began to descend towards Caylen's heart and a breathless silence enshrouded the throng which had gathered before the black altar.

To Caylen's astonishment, he suddenly felt a great searing heat emanating from the centre of his heaving chest. The potent sensation of warmth grew steadily until it began to spread from his torso and course through his limbs, enveloping his thews in a mantle of calidity. Abruptly, arcane tendrils of writhing blue flame leapt from the clansman's flesh, entwining his muscular frame and dancing across the chiselled contours of his scarred body. The undulating azure flames swiftly coalesced until they had entirely cocooned Caylen's form in a coruscant chrysalis of scintillant energy, the sorcerous shell crackling and sizzling like a thunderstorm in microcosm. With a start, Caylen realized that his senses had instantaneously become more acute; his ears discerned the rustle of the breeze in the distant trees, his lungs swelled with the scent of the verdure and the beasts therein, his eyes descried even the tenebrous aura of heat surrounding the men and serpents within his field of vision. Then, in a dazzling blaze of sapphirean witch-fire, the Wolf-King became as one with his mystic totem. All eyes within the clearing widened in stark amazement as they bore witness to the startling transformation. The aura of energy surrounding Caylen's body abruptly assumed the form of a great lucent wolf, its eyes ablaze with an icy, azure radiance. Howling with lupine rage, Caylen ferociously heaved at the iron chains which bound him, the blackened links at once yielding to be instantly rendered no more than twisted detritus. A ferine snarl welling in his throat, Caylen then wrenched the manacles from his wrists and ankles and drove his lambent, claw-sheathed fist into the scaly heart of the onyx altar. With a deafening cacophony, the great snake effigy immediately shattered into ten times a thousand darkling shards, its ophidian countenance exploding into charred and riven ruin.

Turning his radiant gaze next upon the bewildered serpent-shaman who now stood terror-stricken before him, Caylen swiftly grasped the ancient figure by his scaly throat and hauled him pitilessly from his feet. Dropping the gnarled sacrificial dagger, the shaman scrabbled in vain at the great searing hand which clasped him agonizingly aloft. Abruptly and with a sickening crack, the shaman's flailing ceased and Caylen hurled the broken corpse to the earth.

Stepping down from the cracked dais, Caylen scanned the throng for Sauruuk's whereabouts and then growled with disdain as he spied the Serpent King wheeling his mount and fleeing briskly into the labyrinthine aegis of the jungle. Moving to give chase to his foe, Caylen's advance was halted by a sudden volley of slender shafts and blowgun darts emanating from the seething horde of tribesmen and serpent warriors. Feeling the hot bite of the myriad envenomed projectiles, Caylen was instantly thankful that he had recently supped deep of Akamai's noisome antivenin draught. Levelling his gaze at the assembly of savage adversaries, Caylen bared his teeth and prepared to surge into the fray to meet their spears and blades with the naked might of his ensorcelled fists. Suddenly, from the shadows of the surrounding trees there came a storm of arrows and barbed javelins. The missiles rained down upon the thralls of the Serpent King like a merciless storm, swiftly felling a score of the painted tribesmen with withering efficacy. Turning to survey the periphery of the jungle, Caylen beheld Nalani and a party of her warrior kinsmen poised at the tangled treeline, already preparing another volley of shafts and spears.

With a grin, Caylen spun to the ruined altar and gathered up his axe and sword, realizing that the powerful sensation of invigorating warmth which permeated his body was dissipating steadily and the arcane glow suffusing his frame had suddenly begun to wane. Never before had he experienced such a surge of sorcerous energy, not even when the most fearsome of battle-spells had been woven about him in the fray, and although he was loath to now be dispossessed of the mystic might which had empowered him, he nevertheless felt a surge of comfort to be hefting his familiar weapons of steel once again. Turning once more to the jungle's boundary,

Caylen beheld Nalani beckoning him desperately to her side as her tribesmen loosed another volley of shafts from their palm-wood bows before proceeding to disperse rapidly into the depths of the jade vault. Weighing his options in a heartbeat, Caylen decided to join the beauteous savage in her flight, reasoning that the servitors of Sauruuk would yet prove ample grist for his bloody mill of cold steel another day. And so, with the last vestiges of azure energy flickering upon his scored flesh, Caylen-Tor surged headlong into the torrid embrace of the verdant jungle.

* * *

In the tranquil seclusion of a benighted glade, Nalani's slender fingers gently traced the contours of Caylen's chest as she applied a viscid, herbal balm to his many wounds. The redolent puce unguent swiftly set to work easing the pain of the numerous furrows and gashes which had been scored into the reaver's flesh, soothing the baneful crimson welts wrought by the Serpent King's harrowing sorcerous assault. High above the surrounding tree tops, a veil of cloud slowly cleared the face of the gibbous moon and the two figures became bathed in a lambent, eldritch light. Clenching his jaw, Caylen once more found himself enraptured by the woman's sparkling eyes, marvelling at the bewitching intensity of her amethyst gaze.

"I thought you dead," Nalani whispered, her hands sliding languorously down to the blistered skin of Caylen's abdomen.

"It will take more than a snake's treachery to slay me," growled Caylen. "You witnessed my capture?"

Nalani nodded. "I followed you to the devil's pyramid. You did not detect me, for I am silent as a ghost in the jungle. I saw you enter the temple and I lingered until I beheld your body being borne from that place by the serpent's thralls."

"My meeting with that scaly fiend did not go as I had planned," grumbled Caylen.

"Where is your friend? Did he perish?"

"No," replied Caylen. "I sent him home. Through the portal of which Akamai spoke. Then I destroyed it, to ensure the unhindered escape of my crew."

"A selfless deed."

"Mayhap. Why did you come to my aid?"

"When I saw that the serpents intended to make a sacrifice of you, I gathered a scouting party with Akamai's blessing. You were willing to risk your life to free my people. We could do no less in return."

Caylen scowled. "I have unfinished business with the Serpent King."

"You summoned the wolf-spirit!" exclaimed Nalani. "Akamai said he sensed great power within you! But even with such might, I doubt you will be able to defy the foul one and his horde."

"I know not how I invoked such arcane might," muttered Caylen. "And I have no inkling as to whether I could wield such sorcery again."

"And now, he will come for us," whispered Nalani. "He will wreak vengeance upon my tribe for daring to thwart his foul blood-rite."

Caylen's eyes narrowed. "I shall stand against the Serpent King and his army in defence of your people. Though it may well be my final act, it is all that remains to me now."

With a shuddering sigh, Nalani slowly pressed her fulsome lips to Caylen's in a passionate yet forlorn kiss. His heart racing, Caylen embraced the woman lustfully, returning her ardour tenfold.

Suddenly, the surrounding verdure noisily disgorged the gaunt figure of Akamai the shaman, his rheumy eyes burning with an almost delirious light. "No time for that!" he cackled, brandishing a gnarled staff of banyan wood. "We have foreseen the future! The devil stirs in its lair!"

"The outlander will fight beside us," blushed Nalani as she leaped briskly to her feet. "We shall all die together!"

"Perhaps not," rasped Akamai. "The prophecy shall be heeded! Our people shall be led into battle by one who hails from across the icy sea!"

"Aye," snapped Caylen, rising irately. "I'll indulge you and your damned prophecy, old man. I shall lead you."

"You'll do more than lead us, outlander," grinned the haggard shaman, leaning heavily upon his crooked staff. "Come the dawn, you'll be anointed our blessed king!"

Chapter VII
Enthroned Beneath the Mountain of Fire

As the dawn painted the eastern sky with rutilant hues, the tribal procession made its way swiftly through the jungle towards the base of the great volcano. Men, women and children marched resolutely through the foliage, many bearing torches fashioned of pitch and palm fronds or carrying broad drums of seasoned wood with stretched goatskin heads. Almost the entirety of the settlement had embarked upon the ceremonial trek, with the full complement of the tribe's warriors present and armed for battle. At the head of the column strode Caylen with Nalani at his side, assisting the wizened figure of Akamai through the tangled verdure. At length, the dense jungle gave way to a colossal clearing blanketed by a layer of coarse, cinereous ash. Caylen emerged warily from the trees to behold a vast, rock-strewn plateau riven by a score of jagged fumaroles which ceaselessly disgorged noisome clouds of acrid vapour. Grimly surveying the chasmed, piceous expanse, the clansman noted that the fissured terrain was ringed by a deep circular trench from which rose a shimmering, nebulous heat-haze. The crumbling, sulphur-encrusted remnants of ancient stone statuary lay strewn upon the asperous ground and Caylen cautiously clambered over the sundered fragments of a carven, sun-bleached effigy to peer into the gaping depths of the abyssal furrow. Far below, he discerned the searing glow of an undulating river of rutilant lava, its crimson surface roiling and bubbling like an angry, incandescent serpent. The sensation of baleful heat and foul effluvia was palpable and Caylen solemnly turned his gaze toward the vast Mountain of Fire which brooded half a mile distant. The ominous black peak's summit was ringed by a corona of molten rock and a gargantuan pillar of white smoke billowed ceaselessly from its cracked and jagged crown.

"You stand now upon the sacred Circle of Flame," rasped Akamai as he shambled breathlessly to Caylen's side. "An ancient and hallowed site, sanctified by the elder tribes who first venerated the great Fire God. Long ago, mighty temples stood defiantly here in the mountain's shadow, proclaiming their grandeur pridefully to the heavens. Now, the pitiless ravages of time have rendered this place naught but a ruin; a desolate tomb haunted by the restless ghosts of the hoary priests who once offered their oblations to the cruel deity of ash and flame."

"Delightful," muttered Caylen mordantly.

"Bah! Time enough for prattle later!" barked Akamai, hobbling off towards the looming mountain. "The snake lord is on the move! Make haste!"

Nalani turned to Caylen and fixed him with a sardonic gaze. "To think, an outlander pirate who came here in search of plunder shall soon be proclaimed our king."

"I have assented to this ritual only to honour your tribal traditions," growled Caylen. "I was a king once before, and although my tenure as monarch of my clans ultimately served a greater purpose, I am less than eager to take up the burden of a crown again."

"And yet Akamai's prophecy may well be fulfilled by your enthronement here."

"Bah!" fleered Caylen. "Such tales are fine for telling around the hearth-fires on dark nights, but I place scant little faith in the cryptic auguries of seers and soothsayers. Although having said that, I do believe that I was guided here by my gods to face the Serpent King."

Nalani emitted a sullen sigh. "Why would your gods guide you here simply to die?"

"We shall see, lass," grumbled Caylen. "I've carved my own bloody path through life thus far. I can but hope that my journey has not yet reached its end."

"If we survive, you realize that the king must take a consort?" offered Nalani with a coy smile. "It is our tradition that he has a woman to share his bed."

Caylen's brow arched. "I'm sure it is. Although I'm not sure how my wife would feel about that."

"Your wife is not here," scowled Nalani. "She will not know."

"Oh, she'll know," muttered Caylen with a mirthless grin. "She has the witch-sight for such things!"

* * *

Caylen gazed tensely about the great, lithic cavern to which Akamai and the tribal procession had led him. Hewn into the very heart of the vast black mountain, the sweltering cave was illuminated by a myriad rivulets of searing magma which oozed and seeped sluggishly from the vesicular walls, imbuing the spacious grotto with a disquieting, rutilant radiance. At the centre of the cavern, raised upon a broad, cracked dais, squatted a spicate throne carved of darkling obsidian. Only Akamai, Nalani and two tribal elders had accompanied Caylen into the torrid, sulphurous depths of the sanctum, the remainder of the villagers waiting at the foot of the rocky slope which led to the mountain's hidden vault.

"Here have we anointed our kings for more generations than can be easily reckoned," proclaimed Akamai as he moved reverentially into the chamber. "The mantle of power awaits thee. Proceed."

Caylen warily approached the eldritch throne, watching the writhing shadows which skittered across the blackened surface of the cavern's jagged walls. Grudgingly and with some trepidation, he slowly assumed his seat. Immediately, he descried a series of elaborate glyphs which had been etched into the atramentous stone above the cavern's narrow entrance. The strange sigils appeared to be inscribed in the same cuneiform language as those which he had beheld after imbibing Akamai's malodorous potion. To his surprise, Caylen found that he could presently discern the meaning of the odd pictograms just as easily as he had during his feverous, venom-induced trance. Casting his gaze over the inscriptions, he studied them in grim and ruminative silence…

"K*now, O seeker of forbidden truth, ye who deigns to claim sovereignty within the caverns of the Fire God, that inscribed in the Antediluvian Scrolls was* the Sixth Chronicle of Chaos, *an ancient and malign tome first committed to crumbling parchment during the final days of the ruinous War of the Lexicon. That baleful and curse-bound grimoire did tell of the nefarious Lord Angsaar, Bane of the Atlantean Kings, Scourge of Lemuria, Arch-foe of the Immortals of Ultima Thule, and how the benighted Chaos Liege engaged his Immortal Nemesis within the sorcerous walls of the monolithic Seventh Temple of the Serpent Kings, a slime-flecked ziggurat now long since given over to the ravening embrace of ice and shadow. Know also that those death-clad titans did wage righteous red war over not only the arcane lore and occult artefacts enshrined within the primeval pyramid, but also over the fate of the perfidious sylphine enchantress who had appointed herself the fell guardian of that most vril-steeped and star-wrought of sites. Queen Tanit Vyperia! The divine Adelinda Coaxoch Ophidia, seventh wife of Amaalphagus, Beguiler of Zurra, Bane of the Grand Arbiter of Temporal Jurisprudence, Sorceress Supreme of Lyonesse, Majestrix of the Praesidium of Ys, former paramour of the Lemurian Emperor, Scourge of Atland and Immortal Consort of the Demon Lord Maalech Xul! Bitter was their struggle and harrowing was their clash, for when the witch-fires of dark sigaldry at last guttered and died about that thrice-riven tomb, the aegis of ty-*

rannic evil had triumphantly cast its maleficent shadow upon the doom-fraught kingdoms of the world..."

"The fell words of this sanctum were carved by those who first excavated this hoary chamber," rasped Akamai as he moved to Caylen's side. "It is said that the lore revealed by the glyphs is ever changing, unique to each king who reclines upon this darksome throne. What did they disclose to you, outlander?"

"A load of cryptic nonsense," snapped Caylen. "Let's get this damned ceremony over with."

"As you wish."

In response to a gesture from Akamai, an elderly, white-haired tribeswoman approached the throne bearing a crude staff fashioned from human bones and adorned with the mottled feathers of a sacred hawk. Silently, the woman passed the grisly sceptre over Caylen's head three times in a formalized, ritual motion before beckoning the remaining elder to her side. The wizened, heavily tattooed man nodded and duly ascended the dais in a venerational manner. In his gnarled hands he carried an ornate headdress crafted from a sabre-cat's skull, decorated with an array of broad and vivid plumes. Murmuring an almost inaudible ceremonial blessing, the man carefully placed the elaborate crown upon Caylen's head. The elders then turned and strode briskly from the chamber.

"Is that it?" asked Caylen, nonplussed.

Akamai nodded. "Our ceremonies are brief, outlander. We have scant need for ostentation and the elaborate rituals of the progenitor tribes."

Rising from the throne, Caylen sighed ruefully. "So, I am once more *Caylen-Tor*, it would seem. As strange as this new kingdom appears to me, mayhap it is not as starkly different as I first surmised. At any rate, I fear that my reign may be a fleeting one."

A crooked smile suddenly creased Akamai's rugose face. "If that is what the Fire God has decreed, then best make it a memorable tenure, yes?"

Stepping down from the dais, Caylen removed his osseous crown and thrust it into Nalani's arms, noting the nervous smile which the gesture elicited from the beauteous woman. "My thoughts exactly, old man."

"When you have gathered your thoughts, the People of the Black Mountain have assembled to pay tribute," breathed Akamai, motioning to the cavern's entrance. "Your glorious destiny awaits, great king."

"Oh, I don't doubt it," muttered Caylen. "Once again I stand ready to lead men to their deaths against an implacable foe. The burden of kingship evidently does not change, and past deeds cast long shadows. And yet perhaps it is in the very flaws unique to kings that a solution to this dilemma may be found."

Suddenly, a tribal warrior rushed desperately into the cavern, his expression grave. "The army of the Serpent King has gathered at the Circle of Flame!"

Nalani gasped, her eyes wide with fear. "So swiftly has the devil followed us to defile the sanctity of this sacred site! What shall we do?"

Akamai nodded solemnly, leaning upon his gnarled staff. "As it was foretold, the day of reckoning is at hand. Our people await your command, *Caylen-Tor!*"

"We cannot prevail in a pitched battle," said Caylen grimly. "But I have a plan in mind."

"What plan?" asked Nalani, her elfin nose wrinkling in puzzlement. "How will you avoid this clash of tribes?"

"By communing once more with the snake lord."

"Folly! What could you possibly say to him that would serve to avert this impending massacre?"

Caylen smiled coldly. "I shall appeal to his hubris, for that is a quality which all kings possess in abundance."

Chapter VIII
The Wolf and the Serpent (The Clash of the Kings)

Sauruuk's forces had assembled upon the rocky plateau in the shadow of the black mountain, taking position at the western perimeter of the Circle of Flame. The Serpent King sat astride his striped, bipedal steed, flanked by his ophidian generals who were perched atop their hulking, reptilian mounts. Well over two hundred serpent warriors and human tribesmen had marched with their fearsome liege-lord and they now waited silently in serried ranks, their martial array of weapons poised for battle.

Caylen-Tor stood defiantly at the centre of his own tribal army, the mountain of fire at their backs. His tribesmen were armed with long, barbed spears, curved wooden clubs inlaid with the teeth of vanquished beasts, flint daggers, corded slings and slender bows. Many also bore broad oval shields of woven cane covered with animal hides upon which had been emblazoned vivid totemic pictograms. The elder, veteran warriors of the exiguous army were clad in wicker helmets adorned with great crests of vibrant feathers and cloaks woven of multicoloured plumes. Caylen's lupine gaze remained fixed upon the imperious figure of Sauruuk some two hundred yards distant.

"Your weapon, my king," intoned a young tribesman as he proffered the great blade Wolf's Tooth to his newly crowned monarch.

Caylen smiled grimly and accepted the ornate sword, admiring its gleaming, rune-etched steel and the engraved knotwork bands which adorned its stout crossguard. "My thanks, lad. This blade has saved my life more times than I can count. Mayhap it will do so again today." With that, he buckled the belt and scabbard about his waist. "And my axe," growled Caylen, turning to another retainer who waited anxiously in the ranks. The tribesman duly presented to Caylen the great wolf-axe, its curved blade glinting balefully in the morning sunlight. An exultant grin spread across the clansman's face as he hefted the fearsome, long-hafted weapon. "Now, I am ready to address the Serpent King."

Nalani appeared suddenly at Caylen's side bearing a black palm-wood bow strung with a braided cord of plant fibre. Across her shoulder she carried a rawhide quiver of arrows, all of which sported cruelly barbed wooden points. "Words will not avail us this day," she hissed. "It is a waste of time."

Caylen brushed a lock of raven hair from the woman's eyes. "Just be ready, lass. And if I fail, make sure your aim is true with that bow."

Nalani frowned, her violet gaze downcast.

Grim of visage, Caylen turned to the assembled tribesmen. "Today, I am proud to stand with you, warriors of the Black Mountain. I hereby vow that I shall strive to avert bloodshed. But if it comes to a clash, begin with volleys of arrows and then spears. When the devils are close enough that you can see the hatred in their eyes, meet them with blade and club. And above all, die with honour." And without another word, he turned on his heel and strode towards the waiting horde of Sauruuk.

"You are a fool, Caylen-Tor," whispered Nalani forlornly.

Caylen vaulted over the great rutilant trench and halted at the very centre of the rocky, circular arena. Slowly, he surveyed the direful war-hird ranged against him before levelling his unflinching gaze at the Serpent King and smiling icily.

"We meet again, human," rasped Sauruuk, his forked tongue flickering in vexation. "You escaped my clutches once. You will not do so again."

Caylen's grey eyes narrowed malevolently. "Escape is not my plan. I mean to end you this day."

"Ha!" roared Sauruuk, his echinate skull-crest brightening with ire. "Do you aspire to pit this tribal rabble against my horde? I shall butcher every last one of these mewling primitives!"

Ignoring Sauruuk's threat, Caylen addressed the human tribesmen in the enemy ranks directly, his voice deep and resonant. "Men of the old tribes! I am Caylen-Tor, the Wolf of the North! Hearken to me, sons of the Black Mountain, the Red River, the Crystal Caverns and the Sky Tree! Today I offer you freedom! Today I offer to liberate you from the tyranny of your cruel serpent masters!"

Low murmurs arose amongst the warriors within Sauruuk's ranks, although no man present made so much as a move.

"Cast off the shackles of the Serpent King's venom magicks!" thundered Caylen. "You need not bend the knee in obeisance to this monster who preys upon your children and corrupts them with his virulence! Today, your servitude ends!"

Many of the tribesmen began to cast furtive and wary glances at the serpent warriors with whom they shared the ranks.

Sauruuk shook his scaly head scornfully, the cranial ridges which adorned his skull abruptly flaring crimson. "Such an entreaty will avail you naught," he rumbled. "It is not only the sacred Rite of Venom which enthralls these savages. You have no idea what a simple task it was to exploit the ancestral enmities of these disparate tribes."

"Oh, I have some experience of warring clans," said Caylen with a wry grin. "Believe me."

Sauruuk's ophidian eyes gleamed balefully and he brandished his crystalline staff. "Enough talk! I grow weary of this preamble. If it is an insurrection you seek to incite, you shall fail. Now, prepare to perish with your pitiful warband."

"I see the fear in your eyes," growled Caylen, loud enough that

Sauruuk's assembled warriors could clearly hear his words. "I saw it when we battled within your sanctum, and I see it magnified tenfold now."

A resonant clacking sound suddenly issued from Sauruuk's throat as he strove to calm his agitated steed. "I fear nothing! Least of all a weak and flaccid manling!"

"Words are just air, lizard-man. Let deeds be the measure of truth."

Sauruuk's hulking mount abruptly uttered a staccato roar, its great foam-flecked jaws snapping ferociously.

"Keep a tight rein on that damned palfrey," rumbled Caylen. "Or I'll carve my next pair of boots out of its scaly hide!"

"Be wary, human," spat Sauruuk. "And choose your next witticism with care, for it shall most assuredly be your last."

Caylen's cold smile grew wider. "I challenge thee, Sauruuk. Single combat. No sorcery, no tricks. Just steel on steel."

Something akin to a crooked sneer slowly creased Sauruuk's coriaceous snout. "And why, pray tell, should I agree to this vulgar pageantry? I have the overwhelming advantage upon this desolate battlefield."

"Perhaps just to prove that you are not afraid after all. Or simply to affirm that the race of the serpent is indeed superior to the race of man."

"Bah!" gnarred Sauruuk tersely. "Such an axiom requires no validation! I need not fight you to prove that!"

Caylen eyed the assembly of warriors surrounding Sauruuk. "See, my brothers? He does fear me after all! The great and glorious Serpent King, vaunted master of this atoll, trembles before the sword-arm of a lowly human! Perhaps cowardice is a trait common to all snakes!"

The murmurous prate amongst the gathering yielded abruptly to shouts and tersely barked oaths as voices both human and ophidian rose in burgeoning unrest.

"I would crush you!" roared Sauruuk irefully, his talons curling around the hilt of the great, curved sword which was scabbarded at his side. "You are not my equal by any reckoning!"

"Then prove it," growled Caylen. "If you best me, the day is yours. But should I prevail, you must swear before your kinfolk that my tribesmen will be allowed to go free, and that no retribution shall be visited upon them."

Sauruuk's scaly lip curled in contempt. "Such insipid and pathetic stipulations. How very like a human."

"This is a covenant made before our gods," said Caylen. "It cannot be broken."

Sauruuk's great armoured chest swelled pridefully. "So be it!"

A chorus of gasps and exclamations arose from the assembled warriors as Sauruuk swiftly dismounted his steed and stalked to meet Caylen-Tor, leaping across the span of the calescent trench with contemptuous ease. Caylen stood well over six feet tall, but as the two kings faced one another within that grim, ash-wreathed arena, it was apparent to all who witnessed the confrontation that the ophidian fiend towered over his human foe by at least ten inches.

"Mark me, no sorcery," said Caylen, hefting his axe.

Sauruuk nodded. "Agreed. I shall dispense with the Envenomed Sceptre which laid you low. And in turn, you vow not to invoke your wolf spirit."

"Aye," assented Caylen. "Such are the terms of this duel."

Sauruuk casually tossed his gnarled cobra-staff to one of his mounted generals before dragging his sword from its scabbard. The great curved blade was forged from some manner of scintillant blackened metal and its razor-sharp edge bore cruel serrations akin to the teeth of a colossal shark. "Why did you not summon your wolf totem when you stood before my throne, human? It would have made our encounter marginally more entertaining."

"I underestimated you," replied Caylen drolly, aware that the statement was not entirely a lie. "I shall not repeat that error."

"It matters not!" growled Sauruuk, brandishing his fearsome denticulate sword. "I need no sorcery to put you down!"

"Then let our steel exchange words of war," whispered Caylen, his eyes agleam with the rapturous joy of battle.

With a fearsome hiss, Sauruuk immediately arced a mighty blow at Caylen's neck, but the Wolf-King's axe met the ferocious assault defiantly with a resonant clang and a shower of rutilant sparks. Thrice more the Serpent King attacked his foe, and each strike was parried by Caylen's great, lupine axe-blade. Pressing his attack, Sauruuk lunged savagely, aiming his jagged sword at Caylen's heart. The clansman barely knocked the blow aside, the cruel edge of the black-toothed blade opening a crooked and crimson furrow in his chest.

"I claim first blood," hissed Sauruuk, brandishing his weapon and circling his foe like a ravenous ferine predator. "This shall be a day long remembered by the savages of this isle... the day they witnessed the harrowing of the Wolf-King!"

Caylen instantly directed a thunderous blow at his adversary's scaly skull, but Sauruuk parried the strike contemptuously and riposted with blinding speed. The counterattack scored a broad gash in Caylen's bicep and blood began to course freely down his heavily muscled arm.

"You are overmatched," the Serpent King growled exultantly.

"We shall see," replied Caylen.

Roaring an oath, Caylen loosed a flurry of mighty strokes against Sauruuk, his silvern steel blazing like a bolt of storm-born lightning. Each strike was met disdainfully by the serpent's serrated sword and the two warriors locked blades, their weapons grinding and keening in a primeval test of raw, martial might.

"Why do you risk your life for these savages, human?" slavered Sauruuk. "They mean nothing to you."

"They are my kinsmen, regardless of their tribe," rasped Caylen through gritted teeth. "And I shall not suffer them to die beneath the cruel yoke of an inhuman tyrant!"

"How valiant of you," gnarred the Serpent King, his forked tongue darting forth from between his grooved fangs. "And how foolish."

With preternatural strength, Sauruuk then proceeded to push his foe back, raining a series of pitiless blows upon the beleaguered clansman. Caylen met each strike desperately, his bones shaking from the naked force of the juddering impacts. Slowly, the Wolf-King was driven towards the edge of the calescent trench, his axe weaving an instinctive and fulgent web of defence against the unyielding onslaught of blackened steel. Finally, Caylen stood teetering upon the gaping precipice, scarcely one step from a headlong plunge into fiery oblivion. Hammering a final withering blow against his enemy's resolute guard, Sauruuk hooked his sword's jagged quillons behind Caylen's axe haft and wrenched the weapon furiously from the clansman's grasp. The mighty wolf-axe tumbled from Caylen's hands, spiralling gracefully down into the incandescent chasm until it struck the roiling lava with a strident hiss where it was swiftly reduced to little more than scintillant slag.

"Damn your ophidian eyes!" seethed Caylen. "I liked that axe!"

"Join it then," Sauruuk sneered, drawing back his serrated blade for another blow. "Allow me to grant you the solace of death, as I smite your ruin in the black mountain's fiery blood!"

Dropping instantly to one knee, Caylen dragged his sword desperately from its scabbard and rolled clear of the trench's parlous edge, clambering swiftly to his feet once more in the centre of the grim arena.

Sauruuk slowly turned to face his foe, his yellow eyes narrowing malevolently. "I have toyed with thee long enough. Prepare to die, manling."

Vaulting forward with startling speed, the Serpent King directed a devastating strike at Caylen's head, but the clansman lithely ducked beneath the black sword's cruel arc and drove the searing edge of Wolf's Tooth against Sauruuk's lamellar cuirass, sundering the eldritch armour and opening a grievous wound in the snake-lord's scaly flesh.

A discordant wave of shocked gasps and fully voiced oaths surged through the assembled ranks of the watching armies and a ragged cheer abruptly arose from the tribesmen of the Black Mountain.

His ophidian eyes wide in surprise, Sauruuk glanced down at his abdomen to see a great gout of viscid green blood erupt from the dire wound. "Deftly done, human."

"I'm just getting warmed up," smiled Caylen, wiping sweat from his furrowed brow. "Your thralls have just learned that you're not a god after all."

"Bah!" roared Sauruuk, hefting his sword and advancing once again upon his foe. "This paltry rabble I now command is as nothing compared to the glorious legions of elite serpent warriors who once marched beneath my banner! I was marshalling invincible armies in battle when your puling ancestors were still foraging from the branches of trees!"

"I'm sure," smiled Caylen coldly.

Sauruuk bared his gleaming fangs. "I find your surfeit of faithlessness disheartening."

Once again, the two blood-clad monarchs traded pitiless blows, their spell-forged steel ringing with the timeless clarion of struggle and slaughter. Sauruuk's envenomed sword found its mark once more and another red testament of war became etched into Caylen's corded thews. In return, the Wolf-King's blade bit deep into the serried hide of his ancient nemesis and the snake-lord's flesh grudgingly yielded its viridian ichor.

"I cannot be bested, manling," rumbled the Serpent King. "All for which you now strive shall be in vain, this I promise you."

"Your hubris will be your undoing, Sauruuk."

"Is it hubris to seek to ensure the survival of one's own people?" snarled Sauruuk. "My race fades inexorably from the face of creation. The handful of surviving brood-queens are diseased, afflicted by some nameless, insidious malady. Each spawning season, fewer and fewer of the royal eggs hatch successfully. While your cursed kind breeds in abundance, infesting every corner of the globe, spreading like a simian plague!"

Caylen's brow arched. "Perhaps you must simply accept the fact that the time of the serpent has passed and the age of man has dawned."

The fires of a righteous rage flared suddenly within the Serpent King's eyes. "Never! This world was beautiful once... a terrifying and primal paradise. Now it is nothing but a filthy charnel-pit of chittering apes!"

Sauruuk suddenly charged at Caylen with renewed vigour, his black blade awhirl. A fearful flurry of blows pelted pitilessly down upon the Wolf-King as the two titans waged their dire struggle in the brooding shadow of the Black Mountain. Neither warrior sought quarter in the harrowing exchange of strikes, nor gave it. The strident clash of steel echoed throughout the clearing and the surrounding verdure as the trenchant swords of serpent and man met time and time again in a resonant thunder-song of rage and unshakable resolve. Fulgent showers of sparks blossomed from the dire discourse of the blades as the iron-thewed champions of their peoples wheeled and leaped in that martial dance of death and bloodlust.

Slowly, the withering toll wrought by the jungle's torrid clime and the ineffable might of the enraged Serpent King began to weaken Caylen's defence. Each juddering blow sent a lance-sharp surge of pain coursing through the clansman's rippling muscles as his hulking adversary tirelessly pressed his unwavering attack. The serrulate blade of the war-frenzied Serpent King inexorably continued to exact its sanguineous price from Caylen's thews as the reaver's guard increasingly yielded to the insistent onslaught, and a litany of vivid crimson furrows became etched into his storm-coarsened flesh. Finally, a bone-shaking, calamitous strike dashed Caylen to his knees and the Serpent King loomed over his faltering nemesis, his ophidian eyes bright with fury. Half a heartbeat later, the great saurian liege exultantly drew back his great notched blade to deliver the deathblow. But in that fleeting instant, Caylen struck, driving his northern steel mercilessly into Sauruuk's armoured abdomen. The wolf-blade bit deep, cleaving through the lamellar scutes, rending flesh and muscle to sink a full ten inches into the Serpent King's mighty, squamate frame. Bellowing with primal rage and shock, Sauruuk stumbled backwards as Caylen dragged his sword free amidst a fountain of bright green blood.

Rising to his feet, the Wolf-King vaulted towards his wounded foe just as Sauruuk surged forth in a final desperate, pain-maddened attack, his jagged blade poised to deliver a cataclysmic blow. The rune-etched steel of Wolf's Tooth parried the devastating strike with a stentorian din more deafening than any tempestuous peal of thunder and Caylen instantly spun the sword with a deftness honed by innumerable duels to hack into Sauruuk's scaly forearm.

In a scintillant flash of pattern-welded fury, the broad blade sheared through sinew and bone to cleanly sever the fibrous limb of the Serpent King. The taloned hand and the serrated blade it held tumbled to the earth as viscid, viridian blood pulsed freely from Sauruuk's riven stump. A deathly silence abruptly enshrouded the ashen arena, nary a sound fleeing the gaping mouths of the rapt and enthralled watchers as they found themselves compelled to solemn wordlessness, humbly aware that they were mute witnesses to a confrontation the likes of which no living being had beheld for nigh on two millennia.

"This ends now," rasped Caylen, painfully brandishing his dripping blade. "You are finished. The day of your dethronement has dawned!"

Drawing breath in short, ragged gasps, Sauruuk slowly fell to one knee, his crimson tongue lolling from his maw. "Never, human!" The bulging, scaly folds of the Serpent King's throat abruptly swelled outward and from Sauruuk's jaws erupted a viscid cascade of hot, yellow venom. The scalding ichor spattered Caylen's face and neck, its blistering touch bringing with it a rush of searing pain. The clansman stumbled backwards, desperately striving to wipe the foul and caustic discharge from his eyes and lips. Seizing his opportunity, Sauruuk cast his gaze suddenly toward the assembled ranks of serpent warriors, swiftly extended his remaining hand. Instantly, the mounted snake-man who held the Serpent King's cobra-staff hurled the gnarled sceptre aloft. The sorcerous stave spiralled gracefully through the air, but before it could reach Sauruuk's waiting grasp, the blade of Wolf's Tooth flashed in the sunlight, intercepting the weapon at the height of its arc and shearing the black haft asunder. With a viridescent explosion of arcane energy, the crystalline head of the ensorcelled staff abruptly shattered into countless, miniscule shards. Cold, guttural laughter suddenly welled in Sauruuk's throat. "Well played, sirrah."

Caylen strode slowly toward his fallen adversary, still clearing the vile and acrid poison from his mouth. "That was a sly and devious trick, Sauruuk. I am fortunate indeed to have been rendered immune to your foul venom."

"More than you shall ever know," rumbled Sauruuk, an ever-widening pool of his own viridian blood gathering beneath him.

"Now you present me with a quandary," growled Caylen, lifting his sword. "Your defeat has been witnessed by every man and serpent present here, and they all heard you swear your oath to me."

"Cease your prattling and slay me, if that is your intent," hissed the Serpent King, clutching the dire wound in his abdomen.

Caylen smiled mirthlessly. "Do I deliver this final blow in mercy or in vengeance? Or shall I spare your life? Is living out the remainder of your days burdened with the knowledge that you were bested by a mere human penance enough?"

Sauruuk's lip curled and his cranial ridges flared a deep shade of scarlet. "My life is not for any man to give or take!" he snarled furiously.

With astonishing speed, the Serpent King suddenly lunged forward, embracing Caylen in an iron grip and barrelling him brutally from his feet. The two warriors crashed to the earth and scudded towards the edge of the wide trench, the Wolf-King's sword spinning from his grasp. Sauruuk's curved talons raked Caylen's chest as they tumbled as one over the rim of the lethal precipice. Instinctively, Caylen grasped the side of the jagged furrow, his fingers digging painfully into the rocky surface to which he then clung in grim desperation, flailing perilously above the mortiferous chasm. But Sauruuk was not so fortunate, for the Serpent King's momentum carried his great bulk over the edge of the pit and he tumbled headlong into the fiery abyss to ultimately meet the sea of rutilant lava which seethed and roiled pitilessly in the searing depths below.

Caylen slowly dragged his battered body from the rim of the trench, blood coursing freely from the myriad grievous wounds which he had suffered. He then climbed arduously to his feet and recovered his sword. Bone weary, he turned to face the waiting horde of the Serpent King. "Thralls of Sauruuk, now you must choose whether or not you shall honour your fallen master's oath. Your king is vanquished! He fell before my steel in fair combat!"

The assembled serpent warriors exchanged pensive glances, murmuring amongst themselves in hushed and sibilant tones. The human tribesmen within their ranks now appeared to wear dazed and bewildered expressions, gazing anxiously at their comrades as if they had suddenly awoken from a fever-dream.

Caylen's voice rang out resonantly as he addressed the gathering once more. "Men of this isle… return to your tribes, for your servitude is at an end. There shall be no more sacrifices to the snake god! Kinfolk of the serpent, you may flee unharried to your lairs within the jungle. I shall visit no retribution upon you, this I vow. But if ever you deign to move against the tribes of man, know that you will face my wrath, and be assured that the ire of the Wolf-King is a terrible thing indeed! Heed me when I say that the people of this island are henceforth under my protection. The protection of Caylen-Tor!"

A thunderous and exultant cheer arose from the tribe of the Black Mountain as the army of Sauruuk promptly began to disperse. The serpent-riders grudgingly wheeled their hulking mounts and rode away into the dense verdure, gradually followed by the grim-visaged reptilian foot soldiers. Those of Sauruuk's human warriors who hailed from the tribe of Akamai slowly began to cross the clearing towards their kinsmen, while the men of the island's other tribes melted slowly away into the adumbral expanse of the jungle.

Nalani and a group of tribal warriors leaped the span of the chasm and rushed joyously to Caylen's side, their eyes bright with renewed hope and heartfelt gratitude.

"You look like you've been mauled by a sabre-cat," breathed Nalani as she firmly gripped Caylen's arm and surveyed the innumerable wounds which were etched upon his ravaged flesh.

"I feel even worse," growled Caylen, wincing as the pain of his injuries surged through his body. "I'd give anything for a good horn of northern ale!"

At length, Akamai appeared before Caylen and inclined his head in reverence. "And so, outlander, the prophecy is fulfilled. The dominion of the Serpent King is ended."

"Has Sauruuk's black sorcery perished with him?" asked Caylen with a scowl.

Akamai nodded. "The venom-magick will fade and the spell's power will weaken. In time, the minds of the tribesmen he enthralled will be free of his vile influence."

"And will the Serpent King's warriors truly go in peace, old man?"

Akamai sighed wearily. "Perhaps. For now, they will crawl back to their nests. There will they seethe and brood, reflecting upon their lord's defeat and perpetuating their age-old enmity against us. For a time, they will remain silent and unseen, but the day may come when they will once more gather their forces and seek revenge."

Nalani's violet eyes sparkled, her hands tracing the contours of Caylen's bloodied chest. "And on that day, Caylen-Tor will be there to meet them!"

"Mayhap, lass," said Caylen. "But it is still my intention to return to my clan across the sea. The Serpent King spoke of other mystic portals hidden beneath the mountains. I mean to find those sorcerous gateways and make my way home."

Caylen watched as a frown crossed Nalani's elfin face, her delicate brow furrowing in despondency.

"The caverns beneath this island are vast and fraught with peril," mused Akamai. "The ancient carvings of the elders speak of hidden passageways which lead to the world below... the legendary realm of the undying sun!"

"Then I shall delve into those caverns," enounced Caylen. "Once my wounds have healed, of course. Mayhap I'll raid Sauruuk's vault first and take with me some of the jewels he was boasting about."

"But that is a journey for another day," said Nalani. "For now, we must return to our village, and celebrate the victory of our king!"

Caylen sighed, the trace of a wry smile touching his lips. "Very well. I shall tarry here a while, and honour the traditions of your people. The folk of this tribe are brave and noble souls, without a doubt. So, by the gods, I'll damn well show them how a clansman carouses!"

Smiling radiantly, Nalani took Caylen's hand and led him swiftly from the shadow of the great black mountain.

And so, Caylen-Tor remained with the tribe of Nalani for a time, presiding over the noble savages of the Black Mountain as he recovered from his grievous wounds and ruminated upon his destiny. At length, he bade farewell to the tribesmen of the verdant jungle and ventured deep into the labyrinthine caverns which brooded beneath the ensorcelled atoll, there seeking the mystic gateways which might bear him home to the grim and distant lands of his northern clan. His journey to the interior world of the Undying Sun was indeed fraught with ineffable peril and matchless wonder, but what the Wolf-King discovered within that hoary and fiend-haunted domain is a tale for another time...

Appendices

CHRONICLES OF THE ANTEDILUVIAN WARS, Volume IX: Histories of the Kings and Queens of the Ancient World Before the Second Great Cataclysm

Part VI: Caylen-Tor and the Empress Zyrashana (The Rise and Fall of the Witch-Queen's Dominion)

Military historians have conducted extensive research into the early life of the northlander king known as Caylen-Tor, although admittedly much of the lore gathered by their investigations has been derived from obscure clan legendry and the myriad sagas recounted by tribal skalds and bards. Born into the Clan of the Wolf in the wind-whipped, hardscrabble territories south of the Snow Jarldoms, Caylen was the son of the renowned tribal warrior Culain-Ulvur and the grandson of the infamous reaver Black Vargr, the Iron Butcher of the Tundra. His mother was reputed to have been a mysterious shamaness who held court in the shadowed depths of the eldritch Forest of Darkenhold. (The significance of Caylen's ancestral connection to Darkenhold and the legendary Forest King of tribal myth is explored in a subsequent volume of *the Chronicles of the Antediluvian Wars.*) It is unclear whether Caylen's far-famed epithet "The Wolf of the North" was acquired before or after his acquisition of the tribal crown, but the moniker was certainly already being widely applied to him during the period concurrent with his victory at Blackhelm Vale. As for the Wolf-King's exploits prior to his tenure as king, it is known that Caylen ventured south during his early adulthood to seek adventure, swiftly learning the common trade-tongue spoken by most of the civilized nations west of the satrapies. Embarking on many perilous expeditions and quests in the exotic lands beyond his tribal borders, Caylen soon earned considerable renown as a sell-sword, most notably enlisting in the mercenary ranks of the Vyrgothian Alliance and seeing action at the siege of Gul-Azlaan against the Koord Imperium. Some years after the siege, Caylen returned to his rugged homeland and set about uniting his people under the aegis of a single tribal king. Initially being appointed chieftain of his own Wolf Clan after winning the tribal combat rite of *holmganga*, Caylen's path to securing the unified throne was similarly fraught with copious amounts of bloodshed and battle. It is clear that his tumultuous rule of the newly united realm as the "Uth-Tor" (the One King) was ceaselessly harried by secessionist murmurings and the threat of outright revolt. There were many within the upper echelons of the disparate tribal governments who viewed the rule of an overking as a direct threat to their own clan sovereignty and as a debasement of cultural and ancestral traditions.

Some historians have conjectured that Caylen's handfasting to Astrid Grimmsdottir was merely a union of convenience to strengthen relations between the Wolf Clan and the Tribe of the Long Spears, but it is clear that the king harboured a deep respect and affection for his wife, particularly during the years following the dissolution of the tribal alliance when he would charge the shieldmaiden with the task of governing Ulfheim while he embarked upon his piratical sea voyages. Also, extant clan records confirm that it was Caylen's firstborn son with Astrid who alone received the tribal honorific "Ar-Tor" (Son of the King), a title he would bear proudly for the entirety of his life. (The exploits of Caylen-Tor's children following the Ar-Tor's wedding to the Kymrii princess Gwynna Fairhair are recounted in a subsequent volume of *the Chronicles of the Antediluvian Wars*, as are the circumstances of Caylen's mysterious disappearance during one of his many voyages as master of his renowned dragon-ship the *White Wolf*.)

As for the tribal army of Caylen-Tor which so memorably prevailed against the legions of Mytos K'unn, scholars from the Collegium of War are now convinced that the preparations undertaken by the Wolf-King's forces before the Battle of Blackhelm Vale were extensive and thorough, suggesting an impressive level of strategic acumen. Clearly, the Imperial army was utterly unable to maximize the effectiveness of its numerically superior force during the final clash, and was ultimately forced to engage Caylen-Tor's army almost wholly on the clansmen's terms.

The fact that Zyrashana proclaimed her relatively limited dominion as "The First Great Empire of Mytos K'unn" can arguably be viewed as an exercise in self-aggrandizement rather than an attempt to apply any manner of accurate political epithet. The comparatively few territories conquered during her brief reign were not governed by any effective Imperial mandate, and the states of Numadai, Panashaia and Bazalanin continually seethed with unrest and rebellion. Additionally, the unruly Eastern Satrapies staged a partially successful revolt while the bulk of Zyrashana's forces were deployed against the King of Delania's army, leaving the imperial garrisons with insufficient manpower to quell the insurrection. Following the occupation of the Delanian capital, the legions of the Witch-Queen immediately assailed the borders of Zulantia and Turanan, sacking frontier villages and overrunning a series of scantly defended military outposts. It is likely that the Imperial army did not at that juncture possess adequate might to stage a full-scale invasion of those kingdoms, and the raids were evidently solely focused on capturing conscripts and seizing plunder to fund the continuing campaign. Zyrashana's single-minded desire to press westward and seize control of the primary trade routes to the coast was an overly ambitious gambit at best, and any hope she may have harboured of maintaining both her eastern possessions and capturing the western fiefdoms was perhaps an unrealistic one.

The precise circumstances surrounding Zyrashana's initial plot to dethrone Mytos K'unn's rightful ruler King Ahaziah have been recounted in a previous volume of *the Chronicles of the Antedilu-*

vian Wars, but the true aspirations of the Witch-Queen and her long-term goals remain a matter for debate. Did she truly desire to create a lasting empire, or was her swift and merciless campaign merely a bid to seize as much glory as possible before the inevitable collapse of her fragile dominion? It is widely believed by docents and historians that the Empress Zyrashana's own inexorable journey to dethronement began the moment her army crossed the border into the sovereign lands of Delania, for although she won a resounding victory against King Gustanhav's host, the action placed her army on a direct path into the tribal territories of Caylen-Tor, where she would ultimately face her cataclysmic defeat. At any rate, the rapid fall of the Delanian capital has proved to be a subject of great debate amongst many of the Collegium of War's veteran generals and military scholars.

Traveling without the burden of ballistae and siege engines, the imperial expeditionary army was much more suited to pitched battle than it was to the art of siege-craft. Scaling ladders and makeshift battering rams had been the Empire's primary tools against the walled city, and casualties claimed by the defenders' torrents of flaming quicklime and saltpetre were far fewer than had been anticipated. The fact that the Delanian army had been thoroughly bested and its king slain doubtless had a deleterious effect on the morale of the city's defenders, and the surprisingly swift capitulation of the Delanian forces attests to this.

Prior to the Imperial invasion of the Delanian Commonwealth, it is known that Gustanhav's realm had been teetering on the brink of civil war for several months, as the Parliamentary Council deliberated upon a petition to transfer executive power from the Royal House to an elected senate. The Delanian royalists deemed the petition a treasonous mandate, condemning it as a plot concocted by heretics who denied the royal family's divine right of succession. The fact that King Gustanhav personally rode to meet the Imperial legions can in hindsight be regarded as a gesture intended to win support within the Council rather than as a well-reasoned and strategically sound choice of tactics. At any rate, the Imperial occupation of the Delanian First City has since become legendary for the sheer scale of its brutality. Imperial losses against the Delanian host were relatively minimal, but historians have noted that leaving an administrative garrison within the walls of the Delanian capital had significantly depleted the ranks of the Expeditionary Army by the time the legions arrived at Blackhelm Vale. Constantly bolstering the Imperial forces with conscripted troops from the dominions in the east assured that Zyrashana's forces withstood a strategically acceptable level of attrition, but the decision to march west into the tribal lands before such reinforcements had been deployed has subsequently been noted by military inquisitors as a dire tactical misjudgement.

Reliable information as to the true nature of Talus Ebonfyre's relationship with Queen Zyrashana is scarce at best. Similarly, research has not yet yielded any firm evidence concerning the diabolism and necromantic rituals in which the pair were alleged to indulge. The progeny of the Witch-Queen were reputedly a fey and sullen brood, her three daughters already well versed in the arcane arts imparted to them by their mother, and her son by all accounts a cruel and cold-eyed child despite having seen scarcely ten winters by the time of the clash at Blackhelm Vale. The sires of Zyrashana's witch-daughters were believed to have been three nefarious thaumaturgists, but the identity of the sole boy's father was not such common knowledge. There were those who whispered that the child was the son of Zyrashana's fallen champion and paramour Talus Ebonfyre, although no one but the Witch-Queen could attest to the truth of the matter. What is known is that Ebonfyre was one of only a handful of survivors of the Darkening of Kor-Avul-Thaa, although what effect such a harrowing experience may have had upon his mind can be nothing more than a matter of conjecture at best.

Part VII: The Great Wars of the Koord Imperium

The ascendance of the Imperium has been exhaustively debated by military scholars for many decades. Originally an alliance of minor principalities tenuously united under the rule of an ineffective central administration, the true genesis of the imperial mandate can be traced to a succession of invasions of the union's southernmost frontiers by the war-bands of the barbaric tribal Sand Nomads. Demanding to be safeguarded against such attacks, the ministers of the principalities voted for the implementation of a temporary act of government bestowing immediate executive power upon the Military Council until such time as the threat of invasion subsided. The Military Council itself was headed by the ambitious and cunning General Kanaan Khan who easily repulsed the forces of the Sand Nomads and then promptly proceeded to implement a well-orchestrated coup during which his fanatically loyal army seized control of the Citadel of the Central Congress. The administrative independence of the disenchanted suzerainties was swiftly abolished and General Khan formally announced the birth of the Imperium, declaring himself Emperor and threatening any uncooperative territories with swift and pitiless military reprisal.

The Imperium grew steadily over the subsequent decades, annexing many neighbouring realms and assimilating numerous rival states. A senatorial body existed to assist the Military Council in matters of civil government, but in reality the senators were easily bribed and browbeaten into compliance by the overbearing agents of the military machine. Traditionally, all rulers of the Imperium were selected by the Military Council from the highest echelons of the army based on martial acumen and not birthright or lineage. This tradition of warrior-emperors was an effective method of maintaining the military as the executive core of the governmental entity, eschewing the ineffectuality of civilian chancellors or the tenuous claims of succession of any potential royal families.

Historically, it was during the period of the Imperium's initial territorial expansion that the enmity with the Vyrgothian kingdoms began. Minor border disputes swiftly escalated into a series of large-scale conflicts which subsequently became known as the Great Wars. The wars raged sporadically for decades, until the shrewd and ruthless Emperor Koord ascended the throne of the Imperium and vowed to abandon any tenets of diplomacy and destroy the Vyrgothians once and for all. Koord was a dour and pitilessly practical man who detested debauchery, intemperance and appeasement in all forms. He viewed the senatorial circle of the Imperium as a den of corruption populated by sybarites and degenerates, and secretly planned to abolish the senate once the war against Vyrgothia was won. The Emperor duly appointed the renowned warlord Baalthus Vane to lead the resurgent Imperial war machine and it was under his exemplary leadership that the Imperium's forces, spearheaded by the fearsome Legion of the Ebon Tiger, won their most memorable victories, including the Rout of the Southern Host, the Battle of Turonium, the Pacification of the Vraii, and the Capitulation of the Horde. Year by year, the beleaguered Great Houses of Vyrgothia, ruled by the elected Over-King, were hammered by a series of military defeats which included the Breach of the Wall of Lithios and the fall of the ancient Vyrgothian fortresses Gul-Nomedes, Gul-Azlaan and Gul-Tryarch. Ultimately, the infamous Rout of the Fields of Kai-Vorg placed the Imperial forces within striking distance of the Vyrgothian Alliance's mightiest and most renowned bastion, the legendary Gul-Kothoth. The Siege of Gul-Kothoth and the Vyrgothian Over-King's discovery and subsequent manipulation of the ancient arcane artefact known as the Obsidian Crown (one of three sorcerous weapons which along with the Shadow Sword and the Black Sceptre comprised the fabled Trinity of Might) is recounted in a subsequent volume of *the*

Chronicles of the Antediluvian Wars.

(For an account of the closing stages of the Battle of the Plains of Kai-Vorg, read the short story "Chronicles of the Obsidian Crown" published in the fantasy anthology Barbarian Crowns. *And for the first two instalments of the cataclysmic Siege of Gul-Kothoth, refer to the lyrics to the Bal-Sagoth songs "And Lo, When the Imperium Marches Against Gul-Kothoth, Then Dark Sorceries Shall Enshroud the Citadel of the Obsidian Crown" and "The Obsidian Crown Unbound".)*

THE ARCANA ANTEDILUVIA (OCCULT TREATISES OF THE ANCIENT WORLD)

Part XVII: Serpent Lore and the Sorcery of the Ophidian Hegemony

Occult scholars from the Esoteric Academy of New Atlantis are well versed in the history and arcane lore of the ancient Serpent Kings. After centuries of study, the Quorum of Hierophants discovered much concerning the terrible wars waged by the Ophidian Hegemony against the human progenitor race known as the First Ones. The hoary snake men battled their steadfast foes over many hundreds of years, laying siege to the mighty Antarctic Megalopolis on several occasions. Warlike and proud, the Serpent race had vowed to drive the First Ones from the face of the cratered globe, but ecological upheaval and severe climactic shifts continually hampered their efforts to annihilate their ancestral enemy. Utilizing the power of the star-born Viridian Stones, the fearsome anthropomorphic saurians built a series of huge cyclopean shrines to celebrate their supremacy and safeguard their eldritch artefacts and occult lore. When the First Cataclysm befell the primeval world, the Serpent Kings retreated to their mountainous caverns and lava-wreathed fortresses to await the time of their re-emergence. At length, the proliferation of mankind upon the Earth coincided with the inexorable decline of the serpent folk, and they grudgingly fortified themselves within their secret sanctums, still harbouring their undying enmity for the descendants of their hated nemeses and the newly emerging tribes of Man. As for the First Ones, many withdrew to the fathomless splendour of the cities of the Abyssal Plain, while others embarked upon the colonization of the vast subterranean expanses of the Interior World, there to be sustained by their mighty and inexhaustible Vril Suns. And so, the ascendancy of Man continued.

Many of the myths and legends of the early human civilizations reflected the tribal memories of the elder serpent race, incorporating them as primary facets in their scriptures and teachings. The sacred texts of many antediluvian peoples acknowledged the peerless power of the serpents, while numerous hominid cultures over the aeons have worshipped the mysterious snake-men as gods. It is believed by the inner circle of the Esoteric Academy that sages and magi have over the centuries received knowledge of the early epochs and the Ancient Sea-Wars of Panthalassa through clandestine contact with the Emissaries of the First Ones. Furthermore, the Quorum of Hierophants is now convinced that the battle prowess of the Serpent Kings was matched only by their sorcerous potency. Masters of the arcane arts, the lords of the Ophidian Hegemony commanded magicks undreamed of by the majority of human wizards. Studying the fearsome secrets of Serpent Sorcery was a perilous and terrifying undertaking for a human mage, and only the most ambitious and gifted practitioners of sigaldry could hope to successfully harness the dread energies of the sinister venom magicks. The witch Zyrashana reportedly dabbled in such ophidian diabolism, but archival sources indicate that her grandmother, Queen Tanit Vyperia, attained a level of proficiency in that dark art unmatched by any sorceress before or since.

(Read more of the nefarious exploits of Queen Vyperia and her plot to ensnare the Elizabethan privateer Captain Caleb Blackthorne in the stories "Into the Dawn of Storms", "A Voyage on Benighted Seas" and "The Scion at the Gate of Eternity", published in the "Swords of Steel" paperback trilogy from DMR Books.)

Part XVIII: The Forbidden Chronicles of the Z'xulth

The vile genesis of the Z'xulth is shrouded in unfathomable mystery, unknown to even the elder races of the cosmos. All that can be safely ascertained is that the Z'xulth were amongst the first sentient creatures to exist in the universe, roaming the trackless void when the galaxies were naught but errant clouds of sidereal dust. Sustained by a sinistrous and terrifying quasi-sentient energy source, the Z'xulth's infernal dominion grew as they pitilessly presided over their sovereign chaosphere. Ineffably supreme, the darkling lords duly decreed that they should rule the entirety of the empyrean and force all life to submit to their malefic will. At some point in distant galactic prehistory, a coalition of the universe's other elder races engaged the Z'xulth in a tremendous war which shattered the stars and left the face of the cosmos grievously scarred. The Z'xulth were ultimately driven back, their dominion inexorably whittled away, until they were forced into a dark limbo which resided in between dimensions, a blighted place which came to be known as the Black Galaxy. For millennia the Z'xulth festered and plotted within the Black Galaxy, exerting insidious control over other beings in an eternal attempt to liberate themselves from the infernal void.

Since time immemorial, there have been those who have revered, worshipped and deified They-Who-Lurk-And-Breed-In-Limbo, hailing them as gods and ever striving to restore their dark masters to their rightful thrones. Clandestine cults such as The Brotherhood of Dark Elucidation ceaselessly toil to extract forbidden knowledge and glean enlightenment from the black mana of the elder fiends, delving deeply into legendary grimoires of infernal spells and malefic rites in attempts to open portals to the dreaded Black Galaxy. Shunned and nefarious texts such as *the Tome of Shadows, the Scrolls of the Third Circle, the Chthonic Chronicles, the Lexicon of Antediluvian Blasphemies, the Ancient Book of the Six Keys, the Black Bible of Kor-Avul-Thaa, the Diabolist's Manuscript, the Cursed Codex of the Unliving Cultists* and *the Thirteen Cryptical Prophecies of Mu* are inscribed with a plethora of sinister rituals and invocations to summon and commune with the ageless devils, although the dread toll exacted by such foul endeavours is invariably ruinous.

Know also that descended from the avatars of the Z'xulth are such terrifying creatures as The Dwellers In Eternal Shadow; tireless agents of evil who ceaselessly devote themselves to the restoration of their sinister progenitors. In addition, many pitiless malefactors have no qualms about tapping into the darksome power of the arch-fiends to further their own sinister agendas; perhaps the most well-known and dangerous being such perfidious revenants as Lord Angsaar the Dark Liege of Chaos, the ancient vampyric demi-god Amaalphagus, the demon-warrior Maalech Xul and the terrifying hybrid fiend Zurra, within whose ersatz veins runs the genetically manipulated black blood of a Z'xulth Deathbringer. Such prime examples of pangalactic villainy aside, be assured that those who adulate the Z'xulth shall ceaselessly plot to ensure their aberrant masters regain their ancient dominion, grimly confident in the vile belief that at some point in the far future, their ultimate liberation shall finally come to pass, and the ravening lords of Chaos shall once more rule the galaxy.

(Read of the sinister exploits of Lord Angsaar and Zurra in the lyrics of the Bal-Sagoth Hexalogy, learn of the power of Maalech Xul in the Caleb Blackthorne trilogy from DMR Books and discover

more about the vampyre king Amaalphagus in the Saga of Joachim Blokk, a trilogy of short stories comprising the tales "Darkfall: Return of the Vampyre Hunter", "Blood Sanctum: Revenge of the Vampyre Hunter" and "Crimson Frost: Redemption of the Vampyre Hunter".)

About the Author

Byron Roberts is the vocalist, lyricist and founder of the UK extreme metal band Bal-Sagoth. An English Literature graduate, Roberts conceived Bal-Sagoth as a symphonic black metal project built upon an elaborate fantasy and sci-fi oriented lyrical concept, inspired by the novels, short stories, comics and movies he grew up with, particularly the classic pulp stories of Robert E. Howard and H.P. Lovecraft. The lyrical mythos of his Bal-Sagoth universe goes far beyond the band's six album discography, encompassing novellas, short stories, and even graphic novels. Byron's character Caylen-Tor first appeared in the lyrics of the second Bal-Sagoth album *Starfire Burning Upon The Ice-Veiled Throne Of Ultima Thule*, which was released in 1996. In addition to his musical and literary pursuits, Byron has long been involved in historical battle reenactment societies and is proficient with a variety of medieval and Dark Age weapons. For more information on Byron's work, visit www.bal-sagoth.net and www.byron-a-roberts.co.uk.

Printed in Great Britain
by Amazon

69530632R00135